the
6pm
slot

Naomi Datta

RANDOM HOUSE INDIA

Published by Random House India in 2011
2

Copyright © Naomi Datta 2011

Random House Publishers India Private Limited
Windsor IT Park, 7th Floor, Tower-B,
A-1, Sector-125, Noida-201301, UP

Random House Group Limited
20 Vauxhall Bridge Road
London SW1V 2SA, UK

978-81-8400-170-9

Typeset in Berling LT Std by Jojy Philip

Printed and bound in India by Replika Press

For
My Parents

Contents

Acknowledgements

First my dear friend Anita—if she hadn't coaxed and cajoled me, this would have been three incomplete chapters. Thank you for assuring me that if nothing else, you would browbeat your parents into buying the book.

My husband Adrian for being very supportive, if not entirely approving, of a wife who seemingly spent all her time on Facebook after chucking up a career in television. Thank you for the patience. (Just for the record, I didn't spend all my time on FB. Only about 90 percent of it.)

My editor Milee for carefully nurturing and guiding the book from its first draft to its final published version, and for always being prompt, tactful yet honest!

My first boss Anuradha for drilling in the lesson that there could be sense and sensibility in television.

My sister Gopa for her unconditional support, even though she has reservations about a novel which is not about a girl trying to get married! Rubina Jacob—for no particular reason, but if I don't she will never forgive me!

Television—for all the wonder and blunder years and all the stories.

And last, all my FB friends, thank you for all the enthusiasm about the status updates. Now you are stuck with a book. Buy it!

No cataclysmic event in real life ever starts with menacing background music prepping you for it, like it does in the movies. No warning drum beats. No heartbeat, audibly and obtrusively beating away to an alarming crescendo. In real life, calamities have a touch of the matter of fact, and drama just sort of slips in.

And in corporate life, they almost always begin with a power point presentation—the gospel of the white-collared, and their bane too.

It was often said about Rahul that if ever he were in a situation where his life flashed past him, it would be in the form of a PPT. It wouldn't be a clichéd montage of sepia tinted moments. Instead it would be the key highlights of his life, in snappily written bullet points, in a succession of slides. And most of the defining moments of his life would have to do with the crafting and presenting of assorted PPTS—each a work of art in itself.

But the latest PPT on his laptop, though beautifully crafted, with punctuation in place, made him frown.

A delicate crease, but a cause of worry for those who knew him well.

No one actually knew him better than the podgy middle-aged man sitting across the table. Harish was Rahul's shadow—he anticipated his needs and articulated his wants. He was Rahul's deputy and second in command. The Mr Hyde to Rahul's Dr Jekyll. His antithesis and his alter ego rolled into an unseemly tub of lard. The two men were roughly of the same height and age. But in terms of physicality and persona, they were quite different. Rahul was fair. And Harish, swarthy. Rahul, in spite of touching forty, was lean, toned, and fit—three days a week of cardio, weights twice a week, and squash on the weekends ensured that. And Harish, well, carefully and proudly nurtured his ever-expanding pot belly.

If Rahul was charming affability at all times, Harish was deliberately coarse and earthy. He frequently spoke in a smattering of bilingual expletives. Rahul was the tactful diplomat, Harish, the man who always spoke his mind. Except that there wasn't a single thought that he could call his own. It was always what Rahul led him to think, and Rahul had led him to think that he was, in fact, a man capable of independent thought. It would not be entirely correct to say that the two men were joined at the hip because, in fact, it was their souls that were conjoined. In this cordial synergy of souls, Harish and Rahul had flourished for the seven years they had known each other.

Rahul referred to the seven years as their 'meteoric rise'. Rahul had lucked out when he found himself the head of an entertainment channel, Youth TV, better known as YTV. He was the Managing Director of the channel and Harish, the Associate Managing Director. All this had happened just a year ago.

Since then, Rahul's primary effort had been to hold on to that luck. In this he was abetted by a succession of pimped and polished PPTs that went to the Managing Board every week—bar graphs, histograms, pie charts with hyperbolic text, each proclaiming a growing channel share, new markets that had been conquered, and ratings which showed no sign of decline.

However, the PPT that opened up in front of Rahul on this muggy Mumbai afternoon had a different story to tell. The channel's average was steadily dropping with the exception of one show—the oldest show on the channel—a stand-up comedy challenge. In its fifth season, Rahul could take little credit for its continued success. Meanwhile, the competition's new reality show, which had people eating roaches and kissing rats, had captured the imagination of the youth and topped the ratings. Fewer people were watching YTV, and YTV's Board was watching every move that Rahul made.

Rahul said to Harish uneasily, 'Bro, Stetson is on the warpath. He called before leaving for Cannes, saying he doesn't care how we do it. The numbers have to improve.'

Harish nodded and then repeated with a touch of envy, 'He is in Cannes?'

'Yup, he is shopping for television formats. You know the Board is looking at launching a pure lifestyle channel in the next quarter, and he is doing the groundwork for that. We have a breather but we have to do something... anything,' Rahul said with a hint of desperation.

For Rahul, the Board began and ended with one person—Stetson Ganesh. In an earlier incarnation, Stetson was the academically brilliant IIM alumnus, S.V. Ganesh. After fifteen years of successfully selling soap for his previous company, S.V. made a surprise move to YTV as its CEO. The transformation was complete—not YTV's unfortunately, which went from being a middling success to a middling failure, but S.V. Ganesh's. His latent adolescence, suppressed under years of regimentation, got a fresh lease of life. Sartorially, S.V. was now a changed man. From safari suits, he went to wearing frayed denims, floral shirts, and, the crowning glory, a bright red Stetson. Thus the name—Stetson Ganesh.

Stetson dressed like a dysfunctional cowboy and ran YTV like a despotic military general. And in Rahul, whose defining personality trait was a lack of personality, he found a perfect foil. So YTV went from format to format, and from failure to failure, dictated by Stetson's bungling notions of television. It was a heady mix—Stetson's authoritarian cluelessness and Rahul's genial spinelessness.

But his new diktat, for once, put the ball completely in Rahul's court. Rahul knew it wasn't an indication of trust as much as it was an indication of impatience. Stetson was looking for a good enough reason to shunt him out.

Harish dabbed his forehead, and looked at Rahul expectantly. Rahul knew that posture well and also knew that whatever he said next would be met with Harish's whole hearted endorsement. Not straight off but eventually. He also wondered why Harish perspired so much even in air-conditioned environs. In fact, he had always wondered about it, in all the years they had known each other. But since at that point of time, it was a lesser, albeit long term, concern, Rahul let the thought go.

'Let's take it one step at a time,' said Rahul.

Harish looked at him with quizzical intent. Whatever his limitations, Harish was a practised sycophant. And no true practitioner of the art bobs his head enthusiastically at the first utterance. There must be a semblance of a questioning attitude to begin with. No one wants indiscriminate bottom licking.

Rahul stood up and said firmly, 'Let's take the weakest slot—the 6 pm slot—and turn it around. Let's change the fucking rules! The mother fucking competition has nothing worthwhile on at that time. Instead of primetime beginning at 8 pm, we bring it forward and give the Board something to ram up their asses!'

Harish nodded eagerly and noted, with a tinge of pride, that Rahul was getting better at the fine art of enunciating expletives. However, a seasoned practitioner like Harish knew there was still a long way to go before Rahul cracked it completely.

Expletives never came naturally to Rahul—the complete mamma's boy. In fact, they privately made him wince. But whenever Rahul was in the mood to be masterful, he resorted to carefully practised, well enunciated swear words. The truth was that he was slightly intimidated by his creative team—a motley crew of unkempt, pony-tailed, chain smoking, foul mouthed men and women. And the only way he could mask his discomfort in interactions with them was by spraying his conversation with expletives.

However, Rahul's efforts made this rather degenerate team wince too. No matter how hard he tried, to his team, the expletives always sounded like a Victorian girl gasping at the pricking of her finger while embroidering her doiley. It was tragic but the creative team would perhaps have respected him more if he had just stuck to saying 'gosh' or maybe 'damn' at best when he was really worked up.

Harish shifted his attention from the explicit additions to Rahul's vocabulary and desperately prayed for a brainwave that could make the 6 pm slot the most viewed in the history of television. But even God finds some miracles difficult to pull off, and the miracles that Harish prayed for and which related to his non-functional brain, almost always fell into that realm of difficulty.

Harish, resigned to a non responsive divine force, quickly resorted to his most used weapon—bluster. He was quite sure he didn't want his rather fulsome posterior on the line with whatever strategy Rahul had dreamed up, so he leaned forward and said, 'We should get in the strategy team on this one. It is an audacious move, sir, but you know what limp dicks they are. Behenchod, gaand phaad denge with this one.'

'We don't have the time for those fuckers to be sitting on their asses and then telling us it can't be done because "inventory is over-committed" or whatever crap they come up with,' said Rahul with a challenging look at Harish.

Harish's sweat glands, unlike his brain, were working overtime. 'Should I then get the creative team in and have a brainstorming session?'

'No, I think I have the solution…sex. We need to sex it up,' said Rahul.

Harish nodded slowly and ingratiatingly.

'Here's the thing. We get a hot woman, like a shit hot babe. We put her in nothing. Put her in her panties. Have a show around her. We'll have all the horny bastards wanking off at the sight of her. That's what we want. It's television's all-time score. Sex sells and this time, we'll be selling it.'

Harish relaxed visibly. It wasn't such a bad scheme after all. There was a multitude of randy, repressed men in this country. It may not displace people eating roaches from the ratings, but it couldn't do too badly.

Struck by a sudden pleasant notion, Harish said eagerly, 'I will personally supervise all the auditions. Daal denge saaliyon ko bikinis aur G-strings mein, sir!'

Rahul laughed. 'I am touched by your commitment to the cause, but you don't need to sacrifice so much of your time. I think I've found the girl for it.'

Harish tried not to look peeved. He failed. Rahul tried not to notice. He succeeded. 'You know her too.' He said, 'Vrushali Salve. Shit hot.'

Vrushali Salve, the Maharashtrian mulgi, was a fairy tale success story in the world of fashion. Vrushali's sea green eyes and impossibly long legs had once made her everyone's favourite clothes horse. But her time had ticked away. At twenty-eight, in spite of one item song, it was clear that the bus to Bollywood had gone past Vrushali's stop.

Desperate to regain losing clout, Harish thought frantically of something smart to say that would endorse the boss's stance yet re-affirm his independent thinking. He cleared his throat and said slowly, 'Hot to hain, sir. Very good choice. But don't you think ki uski jaanghein thodi moti hain?'

Rahul surveyed him coolly. Somehow the convent-educated boy in him was never taken aback by his deputy's crudity.

Harish repeated, this time in English, 'Thighs, sir, she has big thighs. Didn't thunder thighs go out of fashion in the eighties?'

8

Rahul smiled at Harish knowingly and pronounced, 'Indian men like thunder thighs.'

That weighty generalization effectively settled the matter.

Creative Masturbation
Makes Headway

Starlet Rakshanda's secretary trilled at the other end of the phone, 'I'm sorry, Tania. But he can't make it for the show. Poor Googu. It's the heat. He hates it.'

Blasted cat, thought Tania as she hung up the phone. She turned to her screen and wrote out a terse email (cc-ed to all the bosses) informing the head of celebrity management, Aditya Menon, about the cancellation of Rakshanda's cat for the show. She asked pointedly if Rebecca or Chewbecca could be roped in instead. Though she knew that there was no way in hell Shahrukh Khan's dogs could be so summarily summoned, but in a mail going out to all the bosses, she had to cover all her tracks. After the mail was sent, Tania looked across impatiently to where Aditya sat, two places away from her desk, trying to tell from his profile if her mail would send him scampering to conjure some other four-legged celebrity.

Aditya was busy on his phone and showed no sign of having noticed her email. Tania sighed. She would have been surprised if Aditya had gotten into a flap trying to procure her elusive pet because nothing ever got him into a flap. He was always so irritatingly calm, thought Tania resentfully.

She turned away and logged on to her Facebook profile and typed out her status update, 'If only it would really rain cats and dogs!'

———

Aditya got off the phone laughing to himself. The perks of celebrity management. He had just managed to fob off Charlie Angel—India's most infamous drag queen. Charlie made a living by living off reality show appearances and often made news for his many aborted suicide bids. Charlie was wooing Aditya relentlessly, personally as well as through his equally persistent manager, to get him to host a show on YTV's Bollywood band. 'Think of it,' he said in his carefully constructed, husky voice, 'we can call it *Chai with Charlie*.'

Aditya had pretended to consider it most seriously and had finally extricated himself from the conversation by assuring Charlie that he would push his case with the powers that be. 'They are unimaginative guys, Charlie. It may take them some time to see the potential in this show,' he had said glibly before finally hanging up.

He scoured his inbox. There was a mail from Tania with the subject 'URGENT'. Aditya considered the mail and smiled crookedly to himself. Tania, the chronic

11

sender of emails, was at it again. Is there anything the girl doesn't put on email, he wondered. He resisted the urge to say something cutting and decided to do what he did best—bluff his way out. That was Aditya's special talent—he could talk his way out of anything. He was a good natured hustler. Nothing ever fazed him and certainly not the whims of television production.

The other spectacular talent he had was that he always left work at 6 pm sharp. He clattered out his reply to Tania's mail (cc-ed to all the bosses).

wassup tania

sorry about googu. raks had warned me that the heat makes him irritable. SRK should be very excited about chewbecca and rebecca, although I think one of them is dead, but with the kolkata knight riders doing so badly, he might be reluctant to let any member of his family be exposed to the public eye. it would be insensitive of us to bring it up. it may also come in the way of future movie tie-ups with him.

but the entire celeb team is on the phone right now to get you a replacement. tiger may be willing. he is koel chatterjee's dog. am gonna try my best to swing this for you. ko owes me one.

aditya

To further convince Tania of his total empathy with her crisis, Aditya also made sure to 'like' her new status update on Facebook, after which he duly went back to his online chat with his best friend in Dehradun.

Meanwhile, Tania, reassured by the fact that Tiger was a minor celebrity pet, waited. A mongrel, Tiger had been adopted by the publicity hungry item queen Koel Chatterjee. Or at least that is what *Bombay Times* had said in its front page story. Tania was hopeful that Tiger would be able to bear the heat with more fortitude than the faint-hearted Persian Googly. Maybe it wouldn't even need a make-up van like Googly did. The thought of saving production costs lifted Tania's mood as she waited for the canine confirmation.

Two hours and five emails later, when there was still no sign of any celebrity canine, Tania went over to Aditya's work station. Since Aditya sat two places away, she didn't burn too many calories but managed to get him slightly irritated. 'Now I have to network with the kutta billis of these fuckers,' he barked. 'What is life coming to yaar?'

Tania flushed uncomfortably. Aditya was one of the few people in office she enjoyed talking to. His lazy, good natured charm, and sharp wit made for easy company. And he rarely ever snapped at anyone. He had just made an exception for her—that was all she needed to cap a really lousy day.

Aditya saw her face fall and felt rather sorry about his outburst. He liked Tania too, even though she could be a little like a school teacher at times. So he smiled and said,

'You know what would be a coup for your show? If we could locate Sunshine.'

Tania asked gloomily, 'Who is Sunshine?'

Aditya laughed. 'How do you not know the finer details, Tani? He is the puppy that Vivek Oberoi gave Aishwarya Rai. Now that she is Mrs Junior B, where do you think he is? Sunshine, not Vivek!'

'You have totally missed your calling, Aditya! You should have been running *Bombay Mirror*. I can't believe they missed out on such a great story!' Tania laughed.

'A great story? You heartless girl…what about that poor puppy? You know, I don't think you have the sensitivity to be doing a pet show. Googu must have sensed that vibe and cancelled,' observed Aditya.

Tania glowered. 'I don't pretend to love animals. But even if I did, that Googu was completely unloveable. All he did was sit in one place and yawn in my face when I went for the first pre shoot meeting; stupid thing, and he looked absolutely contemptuous when I mewed at him.'

Aditya interjected incredulously, 'Come again? You mewed? You said "Miaow"?'

Tania said irritably, 'No, I said "bow wow"! Of course I "miaowed", what else was I supposed…what is so funny, Aditya?'

Aditya was doubled over his laptop laughing. The vision of prim Tania, proper down to her perfect pedicure, mewing at a disdainful Persian cat was something that should have been witnessed in person.

Tania smiled reluctantly and said, 'Okay, it was a bit stupid. But I thought I would make the daft creature more comfortable. More than him, I wanted to assure that bimbo secretary that Googu was going to be in the right hands.'

Aditya stopped laughing and said seriously, 'Tani, you don't just say "Miaow" to a Persian. Did you do any homework at all? Ordinary cats say "Miaow" and break it into two syllables – "mi" and "aow". A Persian breaks it into three syllables: "mi" and "a" and "ow", with special emphasis on the "a". Of course he wouldn't respond to you, you sounded totally downmarket! No wonder they cancelled.'

Tania said quickly, 'Really?' and then catching the flash of humour on Aditya's face, exclaimed, 'You moron... you just made that all up! You...and I almost believed it!'

Aditya was in a great mood by now. 'Tania, stop being such a sour puss. Oops, sorry, that wasn't meant to be a pun. I wasn't trying to be catty!'

Tania gave in and joined in the laughter. Aditya and she then spent a good half hour ruminating on various celebrity pets. She soon forgot about Googly and Tiger almost completely, only deciding to head back to her desk when Aditya gave her a few more details on Tiger. He said, 'He won't be unfriendly like Googly. In fact, from what I hear, he is a little too friendly. He is very randy and that idiot Koel is not getting him a mate, so he

15

makes do with the legs of unsuspecting guests. He is just your regular friendly masturbating dog'.

Tania waved Aditya away in mock disgust and returned to her desk, still smiling. But as she sat down, she was morose again as thoughts of Googly returned to haunt her.

At that point, Tania would have loved to swap places with Googu or anyone for that matter. She was weary with what she was doing. In a channel that celebrated the temperamental, the twisted, and the left of centre, Tania had made the mistake of acquiring the reputation of being a disciplined, unimaginative worker. To make matters worse, she had made the even more fundamental mistake of looking like one. No pierced navel or chin, no rumpled three-day-old pyjamas and, worst of all, Tania wouldn't be caught dead in fluorescent rubber slippers at work.

Given all of these damning factors, it was no surprise that Tania was not part of the core creative team—the temperamental talented. The team that worked on all flagship properties of the channel, be it the stand-up comedy challenge or the soon to be launched reality life swap show. The team headed by the mercurial Biswajeet Bose.

Bose's deal with the channel was that he dealt only with Rahul. And his team dealt only with him. So while technically and hierarchically Harish was senior to Bose, he had no say in anything that Bose or his team did.

Instead Rahul picked and chose the shows that Harish could oversee, as well as the people who would work with him. What came Harish's way, then, were the fillers and the second rung shows. Actually make that third rung shows. But Rahul had blithely assured Harish that his core function was to be the brand custodian—to ensure that the brand values of YTV remained sacrosanct and consistent through all its programming. Which is why Harish was included in Rahul's meetings with Bose to maintain brand consistency. But besides a few lewd jokes, Harish was not expected to contribute much, and he obediently didn't. Harish didn't mind too much—he had no illusions about his creative genius.

Tania, too, was resigned to her lot at YTV even though she knew that working on a second string filler show, like celebrity pets, was not going to further her career. In the age of the pink slip, she was feeling vulnerable and dispensable. She opened her tiffin. Maybe the chicken sandwich would lift her spirits.

Right then Harish, who had just come out of Rahul's room, hollered, 'Oi Tania kidhar hai?'

Much against Rahul's strict sense of corporate decorum, Harish never used the intercom. He firmly believed in a direct correlation between decibel and productivity levels. To be noisy was to be working.

Tania, who was busy tucking into her grilled chicken sandwich, cringed. Carefully keeping the irritation out of her voice, she jabbed Harish's extension and said,

'Eating the last bit of my sandwich. Be there in five minutes.'

'Yaar, always stuffing your face and then going on detox diets. Chal, eat…Indian men like thunder thighs,' Harish remarked good naturedly.

Tania chewed on that bit of information and her last bit of bread simultaneously. She wondered what scheme she was going to be co-opted in now.

She found out in the next ten minutes. Tania was going to be the woman responsible for young India going into multiple orgasms. All of this would climax in the 6 pm slot—the new primetime—like never before. It was a launch pregnant with possibilities. Harish had already begun work on the PPT and was feeling quite chuffed with his word play in the slides.

Tania Shah, the inoffensive, not-very-gifted supervising producer had just been handed the assignment of her career. If it worked, she would join the ranks of the temperamental talented. Even piercing her navel wouldn't have elevated her as much as this would. But since she received the news of the change in her fortunes so passively, Harish would have never suspected the thoughts that busily sprinted through her head. Tania took on her new responsibility with a singular lack of expression and some amount of relief. She saw her career rise from the depths of fur, paws, and tails, and shake its prime coat.

'So,' said Tania, 'the show is basically about this hottie who will cross and uncross her legs. But what else will she do? We need to have some sort of rationale for her existence.'

'She'll talk dirty,' was Harish's pithy response.

Tania raised one eyebrow and asked, 'At 6 pm?'

Harish looked at Tania with some unease. Why was the girl suddenly asking questions? Tania never questioned. She always took what came her way, and managed a half decent job. The temperamental talented, on the other hand, spent too much time in what Rahul in a mix of resentment and awe called, 'creative masturbation'. And this time around, Rahul was a man in a hurry. He needed someone who could get the job done fast, and Tania was the girl for it.

Harish snapped, 'Yes. 6 pm. We are extending prime-time. Based on that, we take it into 7 pm. We'll do this in a phased way till the 6 to 9 time band belongs to us. Get it?'

Tania smiled patiently. 'I get that. But we cannot have adult content on an early evening slot, especially on a channel with a demographic tilt towards the youth. The I & B Ministry is watching, and this is inviting a show cause notice.'

Harish had always suspected that Rahul had a certain fondness for Tania. Now he knew exactly why. Any reasonably okay-looking female who could use words such as 'demographic tilt' in normal conversation would be to Rahul's taste. But Harish recognized the value in Tania's words and didn't know what to do. Tania suggested they talk to Rahul, who could perhaps give them a road map.

Harish was unhappy at not having made that suggestion himself but made the most of his situation by cracking a feeble joke on upward delegation. Tania smiled politely and they walked into Rahul's cabin.

As they entered Tania smiled at Rahul warmly, and Rahul returned the warmth with a rather endearing crooked grin. Harish suddenly felt like an ill used wife. All the snarling and frowns for me, he thought resentfully, and the minute he sees a pretty girl, he turns into Mr Congeniality.

Harish said peevishly, 'We can't have some hottie talking about sex at 6 pm. Horny I & B bastards will watch and yank us off air. I recommend we do a late night show like the hottie's hotline or something.'

Rahul looked at him impatiently. Tania interjected, noticing that Harish had omitted to mention that it was she who had had that momentous realization.

She said effusively, 'When Harish and I were discussing the concept, the thought suddenly struck me and we thought it best to come to you. I am very excited about the new launch…and we wouldn't want any bottlenecks.'

Harish gaped at her with a mix of admiration and bemusement. First 'demographic tilt', now 'bottleneck'—the girl was on a roll. Just the kind of boardroom speak that Rahul approved of. He stared at Rahul, who was smiling his head off at Tania.

20

'Yes. Very valid concern. But I never suggested that the hottie should be conducting some soft porn show,' said Rahul ruefully.

To this Harish said volubly, 'It would be na, if she is wearing only her chaddis.'

Rahul clucked at him and said, 'No fucker. Of course she will be wearing...erm...chaddis. She'll be sexy, really sexy. But this will be like a hotline for love. If you have a love problem, call us. Hottie will resolve it and while she's at it, she will titillate the pants off you.'

'We are looking at a clear male skew for this one then,' said Tania.

Harish laughed at this typical Tania-stating-the-obvious statement and said, 'No sweetie. We want hardcore lesbians to watch. That is one market that we haven't made any inroads into.'

Tania laughed uncomfortably, feeling as she was meant to—slightly stupid.

Rahul threw his head back and laughed, and slapped Harish's back approvingly.

Harish's pudgy face glowed. The centre of his universe had just slapped him on the back.

The Protein Shake Syndrome

The next few days were a test for Tania's fast fraying nerves as Bhosle, the head of production at YTV, cut every corner he could find on the show's budget.

Bhosle prophesized, 'Model na? Will want those whey protein shakes. Make sure you tell your anchor right in the beginning that getting protein shakes for her is not part of the budget. Tell her right away to bring her own shakes. I am not putting it in Food Incidentals. Too expensive.'

Tania felt Bhosle was missing the larger purpose for a mere protein shake but Bhosle knew better. In his experience, the larger purpose often became the protein shake.

After all he had the fable of Zain Bakshi and the genesis of 'Food Incidentals' to back him up. It was YTV's production legend.

Zain Bakshi—the channel's biggest face—had refused to do a shoot unless he got a Subway sandwich without cheese or mayonnaise. The shoot had got stalled for two hours after production refused to comply and tried to get Zain a regular chutney sandwich. Zain had locked himself up in his make-up van. Rahul was called in and tried to explain to Zain that recessionary pressures meant that the purchase of Subway sandwiches would be questioned by the Board. 'Moreover, it comes under fringe benefits,' Rahul had said earnestly. 'And these days, there is fringe benefit tax.'

Zain had just laughed humourlessly and plugged in his iPod. Then Harish suggested cracking a discounted deal with Subway, since they would save on cheese and mayonnaise. No one paid him any attention. But since no one ever did anyway, Harish went back to surveying his pot belly, and thought of the role that cheese and mayo may have played in its cultivation. Zain refused to budge. His appetite was gone, but it had become a matter of principle by then. The stand-off between Zain and production lasted four hours, till Aditya, who had known Zain since college, intervened by buying him a Subway sandwich. He convinced him to swallow it along with his hurt pride.

Zain allowed himself to be brought back to the shoot floor. Aditya promptly put the cost of the sandwich in his travel and expense account. This meant that finally YTV *had* incurred the costs, but at least it was not out of the stipulated production budget. That sort of thing mattered a lot in Rahul's notions of correct corporate conduct.

After that, Rahul had convened a meeting with Bhosle and Harish. It was decided that a special provision would be made for Food Incidentals in future show budgets. But Bhosle was told to use this provision only under exceptional circumstances. The definition of these 'exceptional circumstances' was left to Bhosle's discretion. And he was quite sure that protein shakes were not in its purview.

'We'll be saving on food costs if she has only protein shakes. Adjust it!' Tania had had enough, and told him to just get on with the rest of the shoot budget.

The meeting went on in a strained manner. Tania had no patience for Bhosle's martyred air—she had too much to deal with in any case. She was uneasy about the new on-air talent to be—Vrushali. She had not been replying to Tania's texts and calls but the minute Rahul had intervened, Vrushali had become all gushing professionalism and charm, with very plausible excuses for not being available earlier. It was quite clear that Vrushali was making sure that her one point contact person was the head of the channel.

Good for him, thought Tania sourly, another one to add to his harem of divas. Tania thought Rahul was a bit too soft with the on-air talent of the channel, with the result that most of them thought nothing of involving him in the most trivial of issues. He had once taken a call from a particularly ditsy host at 1 am. She had bitterly complained about the colour of her shoes at a shoot. Not only did Rahul hear her out, he also saw it stemming from great passion towards her work. Tania was sure that he would soon witness many displays of similar commitment and passion from Vrushali Salve. She braced herself for her next combat, because Carol Pinto, head stylist and a toughie, was purposefully striding up to her.

First, Tania received the inevitable style debrief in Carol's raspy voice, 'Dahling, Tan, what are you wearing? Tunics are so last season and kitten heels, ugh, burn them.'

Then came the griping on the budget. 'I can't clothe a mouse on this shoestring budget. What do you want me to do?'

Tania was prepared for this and said, 'The good news is that for this particular show, we can actually make the anchor wear only shoestrings or rather G-strings.'

Carol puffed at her cigarette, and rolled her kohl-lined eyes. 'Ah skin show again. Who is the girl for the show? Not Natasha, I hope. She has neither a butt nor boobs. She is a school girl—perfect for those rubbish feedback shows—but you want to make her a sex symbol. Get some silicon, dahling. And while you are at it maybe a brain too.'

Tania responded drily, 'Like you need a brain to turn on the men!'

Carol cackled, 'You don't need anything that resembles a brain to do anything on television, babe. A brain can be a liability. You think your gifted boss Harry would have made it so far had he any such burden?'

Tania laughed. No one could ever call Carol politically correct. 'Carol, it's a new girl. Vrushali Salve.'

Carol looked even more bored. 'Sweetie, that Vrushali chick is past her prime. She was hot at some point but now I am not so sure. Big thighs, if I remember correctly?'

'Indian men like thunder thighs,' said Tania blandly.

Carol mock shuddered. 'Rahul and that joker Harish don't stand for all Indian men, Tania, and thank the lord for that!'

Tania smiled but felt that she had every reason to feel as worried as she had been feeling the last couple of days. 'She is coming in today and she is all yours, Carol. Make her the hottie of young India's wet dreams.'

Carol rolled her eyes and drawled, 'I can hardly wait.'

Just then the thunder thighs in question walked into the YTV office. They were attached to a slender upper half and a striking face. Not pretty, but definitely striking. The best feature was a pair of sea green, almond-shaped eyes set in a milky white face. The nose was nondescript, but the mouth, large and prominent.

Too gummy, thought Tania as she approached her.

Pear shaped, Carol noted mentally as she stubbed out her cigarette.

Harish ogled unashamedly.

Rahul had thoughts of a rather private nature; thoughts which would have scandalized his mamma if she knew.

26

'Hello peoples,' said Vrushali airily.

Tania winced at the extra 's'. Rahul, usually a stickler for the proper usage of the plural, didn't notice. Harish smiled benignly. Vrushali chattered about the traffic, with her focus completely on the men.

Tania didn't hear a word of what Vrushali was saying. Her entire attention was on the siren's accent. It was remarkable; the accent was a cross between a municipal school in Ghatkopar and a call centre in Powai. Rahul had not felt the need for a screen test but Tania suddenly wished she had gone with her instincts and insisted on one.

She interrupted the chatter and said, 'We have to shoot a pilot in the next week.'

'Pilot?' asked Vrushali, turning very cold eyes on her.

Tania noticed the girlish giggle and the waving of hands, which had held Rahul's attention, disappear the minute Vrushali turned to her supervising producer.

Tania explained, 'A pilot is like a test show. It doesn't go on air, but we plan and shoot it like the real thing. That way we can figure out the format and iron out issues, and of course get your look in place. The sooner we do this, the better it is for us because we have to launch the show in less than a month.'

Vrushali turned to look at Rahul eagerly. 'Yes. I do want to get started yeah. You know anything that I do it, I do it with passions buddy. Money I am getting lots walking on ramp. This is chance to do different and exciting stuff yeah. Anything and everything I do with passions from the time I was fifteen yeah. I was working since then you know. I want peoples who are working with me to be equal in my passions. You know buddy like full on buddies.'

Vrushali's passionate little speech had totally different effects on the four individuals in the room.

Tania was suddenly and passionately missing Googly and Tiger. Carol was dispassionately looking at Vrushali's bosom or rather the lack of one. The speech had caused that particular part of her anatomy to heave, and Carol's expert eye had immediately noticed the shortfall.

Tania also realized that the hottie had an unfortunate tendency to either drop words or use them where they were not needed. Vrushali completed most sentences with a 'yeah' or a 'buddy' and added an extra 's' to things. But at the same time, because of the confidence and ease she spoke with, she managed to create an illusion of coherence and even fluency. It was an odd combination. She sounded like a middle class Maharashtrian housewife who had picked up all her English by watching American daytime soaps.

Harish noticed the odd accent too but didn't know how to react. But then, Harish would have been surprised if he had known how to react, so he looked at Rahul.

Rahul was beaming at everyone in the room. 'Sure,' he said, 'we are all passionate about work here. And we are going to take everyone's pants off with your show, Vrushali.'

Harish laughed loudly, 'We will start by taking off yours.' Once he realized no one else was joining in, he hastily added, 'On the show only of course.'

Vrushali giggled without any humour, further adding to the momentary awkwardness.

Rahul stepped in smoothly and said, 'Tania, you need to be joined at the hip with Vrushali. Both of you work together to give us one helluva…I mean…a *motherfucking* kick ass show. You guys need to meet, talk, and brainstorm. In fact, give us a heads up on everything that you have planned, Tania.'

Vrushali looked at Tania coldly but smiled for Rahul's benefit. Everyone looked at Tania expectantly.

Tania wondered why 'motherfucking' sounded almost like an endearment when Rahul said it. She had also made two important decisions. The first was that her hip would exist independently of Vrushali's. The second one was even more crucial.

She stared steadily at Vrushali. 'First things first, there won't be any protein shakes on this shoot floor. There is no provision for it in the budget, and we won't be making any exceptions.'

29

Back in his cabin, Rahul had a self congratulatory air about him. Harish was sure that the show stopping PPT on the 6 pm slot revamp must have floored Stetson completely. Harish felt obliged to feel equally gung ho. 'Sir, complete item hai. Very YTV. Very hot. Matlab I thought seriously dirty thoughts when Vrushali was here. Matlab hardcore locker room.'

Rahul smiled at him with all the affection that one feels for a leery but harmless uncle.

'But sir,' continued Harish tentatively, 'her speech is a bit accented na? A little too desi for Brand YTV?'

Rahul looked unconcerned. 'Harish, now you're talking like one of those public school educated dickheads. Put a teleprompter. Make it more Hinglish. Anyway, we haven't hired her to yap. If we wanted a yap show, we would've had Natasha. I want this to be sexy stuff.'

Harish didn't say more. He didn't point out that in most books, 'public school educated dickhead' would be an apt description for Rahul. He knew that Rahul secretly yearned to cut a more dashing figure of romance. If only he had been a maverick college dropout instead of a B-school topper. That sort of thing had a lot of stock in YTV.

Harish, instead, commended Rahul for using purple as the colour of the slides for the 6 pm slot PPT. 'Very subtle,' he said approvingly. 'Less imaginative guys would have used red because that is the colour of love and sex, but that would be so clichéd.'

———

Harish found Tania waiting for him when he walked out of Rahul's office later. She brought up the issue of Vrushali's confused grammar. 'It's a disaster. The girl can't talk right!'

To which Harish had a ready answer. 'Make her speak more Hindi. And I want to be in on the styling meeting. I want boobs on this show. Don't give me that subtle sexuality crap. We want Delhi and Punjab hooked. Make them hang in there.'

He smiled happily at the double meaning that he had managed to inject so effortlessly in the last part of his instructions.

Two years ago, prudish Tania would have been taken aback at this piece of communication. But the Tania who desperately sought acceptance among the temperamental talented smiled appreciatively at Harish's innuendo.

That was the cool thing about YTV. Everything was

cool. Men dissected women's bodies in the presence of other women. Meetings were replete with sexual references about wanking off, hard ons, shagging, and blow jobs. So much so that an enthusiastic female newbie had even said in a meeting, 'It wasn't like I was wanking off you know. There was a real fuck up.'

At which point, Biswajeet Bose, the head of the temperamental talented, had interjected, 'Of course you weren't wanking off, lady. Unless you have something in your pants that we don't know about, and in that case, I shouldn't be calling you lady in the first place.'

Laughing gleefully, Harish continued, 'I am making a clean breast of what we want on this show, Tania. Don't say you weren't warned; this show cannot go BUST.'

Tania wondered whether she should tell Harish about her exchange with Vrushali. Tania had suggested to the siren that she speak more in Hindi. At which point, Vrushali had coldly said, 'My comforts levels is with English yeah. My Hindi is okay okay only.'

She decided to hold on to that piece of information. In his current frame of mind, he'd probably ask her to run close shots of Vrushali's cleavage with subtitles on it. And he wouldn't mean it as a joke. She whisked out her planner instead and said briskly, 'Five days from now we shoot the pilot. That is the fifth of July. We do that on a working set to test the format. That gives us only ten days to tweak things around but I guess it will have to do. We shoot again for the final show on the twenty-fifth on the final set. And we launch on the first of August. It is very tight, but we will scramble through. I need you to approve the set first.'

Tania then proceeded to spell out her plan to Harish. 'The idea is to have a set which looks like a studio apartment. Remember Satine's boudoir in *Moulin Rouge*? No? Never mind...I'll send you web links for it. Point is that we'll do a desi rendition of it for our show. It'll all be kitschy, with red heart-shaped cushions, sequinned throws, sheer curtains, and sexy lights. In the den, she'll solve people's heartaches, casually lounging on her settee or pouring herself a drink perched on a bar stool, or in her bubble bath.'

Harish said excitedly, 'It can't be an alcoholic drink. Not allowed. Maybe we can place a cola or something. Make money of it.' He resisted the impulse to rush to Rahul and tell him about his ability to think on his feet. He said then, 'Go on. Sounding good.'

'This would also mean costume changes within the show. So she could kick off her shoes and prop up her legs on the coffee table as she goes through mails on her laptop. We'll make sure that she is wearing something really short when she does that, so we have the best view of her legs.'

Harish interrupted. 'Maybe a flash of panty also. Just a hint. Blink and you miss it. Otherwise we'll get into trouble with the government.'

She continued unperturbed, 'She could also do a sort

of striptease before she gets into the bubble bath. She'll strip as she takes a call on the speaker phone, till she's just in her bare essentials. Then she'll go behind the shower screen, and you'll only see a silhouette which is ostensibly without clothes. Next shot we have of her will be in the bath tub.'

Harish's attention was fully captured by the mention of the bath tub. 'Make sure she splashes around a bit. Sticks out her legs, rubbing soap on them as she talks on the phone. Otherwise if three-fourths of her body is in foam, you are leaving too much to the imagination. Indian fuckers don't have that much of imagination. They haven't seen that many naked women and that's why they are such horny bastards.'

This conversation had an eavesdropper. Aditya who sat only two places away from Tania's desk asked in a tone of deep interest, 'In all that splashing maybe there is an angle we can work out that will show maximum leg and thigh? An underwater camera perhaps?'

Harish glared at Aditya, unsure of what to make of his suggestion. The underwater camera appealed to him though, so he turned to Tania who told him firmly that a grown woman flouncing around in a bubble bath would look a little dim witted.

Aditya countered poker faced, 'Maybe you can pass it off as orgasmic writhing?'

Harish writhed in delight at the suggestion and beamed at Tania.

Tania shot Aditya a sharp quelling look. He smiled back, unaffected. She turned back to Harish and said patiently, 'Why would she be in the throes of an orgasm if some guy in Patiala wants to know how to ask a girl out? This is not a sex show. It is a *love* show. And she has to be set up as a love diva—mysterious and all knowing. Splashing water like a duck won't help.'

Harish ducked the question and said authoritatively, 'Ducks don't splash water, saali.'

Tania gave him a perfunctory smile and then told him that she meant to shoot this with handheld cameras. 'It will look real and more intimate,' she said.

Harish didn't have an opinion on that, but decided to make-up for the lack of it by coming up with what he thought was a stroke of genius. 'The last shot,' he said excitedly, 'must always be in the bathroom; a steamy bathroom where she'll be holding on to her towel. She'll write the number of her hotline on the fogged up mirror, and then look into the camera and say 'call me' in this really sexy way.'

Aditya interjected again, 'You will need to talk to Bhosle about getting a geyser for the hot bath scenes. I think they don't allow appliances on the shoot floor. Also, steam will fog our lenses.'

'Fuck off,' said Harish, convinced now that Aditya was ridiculing things as usual.

'He's right,' said Tania. 'We'll need to think this through.'

Harish didn't even want to think of the possibility of thinking, so he quickly moved the meeting to Rahul's office. 'We have some shit hot plans, sir,' he began, but then couldn't remember anything of what Tania had told him except for the steamy bathroom, the foggy mirror, and the number written on it. So, much to Tania's exasperation, he told Rahul just that.

Rahul said bemusedly, 'The whole set is just a bath tub?'

Tania quickly stepped in and explained the entire concept.

Rahul nodded appreciatively throughout but at the end of it, shook his head slowly and said, 'It's a great idea but it won't do.'

Tania was disappointed but managed to ask politely, 'Why? Is there any specific reason why we can't do this?'

Harish in a bid to anticipate what his mentor must necessarily be thinking said knowingly, 'Too cheesy. You know, I thought as much.'

'No, not cheesy.' Rahul said. 'Except for that foggy mirror part, which was stupidly corny. Just that...' and he trailed off thoughtfully.

Tania tried not to look at Harish who was looking hard at his watch and enquired, 'Just what?'

'It's too much of a production. This show doesn't have a sponsor yet. The Board has given it the green light with the specific understanding that we keep costs to a minimum. Vrushali has already cost us some amount of money. We don't have that much leeway to splurge on an expensive set.'

'Oh,' was all that Tania said. She now knew why this show had come her way. None of the temperamental talented would have allowed budgetary cuts on their creative vision. But since Tania was not temperamental and not too talented either, she said as she always did, 'So now?'

Harish said, 'We keep it simple.' So simple that he didn't deign to elaborate further.

Rahul was looking at Tania sympathetically, 'It was a great idea, but I am sure we will have great content. It won't matter how we shoot it. Get a bean bag, prop it up somewhere, and plonk her on it in hot pants. And put a phone beside her. Done. No sweat.'

Tania said nothing.

Rahul squeezed her arm, and said, 'I know how you feel. But that is the mandate—keep production costs down. Keep it basic. I told Bose too.' He continued, 'It is tough for creative people to pare down their vision of what a product should be. But sometimes we have to. Let's not make a *Mughal-e-Azam* out of everything. Let the idea drive it. I find that difficult too, I must confess, but I'm doing it. I'm consciously pulling back on the time I used to spend on PPTs. I don't try and change fonts in every line. I just go with Garamond now when earlier I would have a sleepless night deciding between Calibri and Lucida Console.'

37

Harish interrupted wistfully, 'Remember the time when we thought Arial Narrow was the most hip font. We used it on every fucking PPT.'

Rahul smiled at him almost sadly, and then turned back to Tania to say, 'Not just fonts. Everything is scaled down now. I don't try and think of kick ass openings or movie lines and clips that I can put on every slide. I don't agonize over the best end—the progression, the anticipation before the big bang climax slide,' Rahul was talking slightly faster now and his words were passionately spoken.

'Just yesterday I actually finished one in an hour—used a cut and paste format in Times New Roman,' he shuddered slightly. 'It was like killing my soul. I never thought I'd ever do that. But you know what, it got the job done just fine. It didn't need to be a fucking production,' he said with a tinge of bitterness.

Tania said and understood nothing. Rahul seemed to have drifted into some private hell of his own. He was hoping that his leading by example, his supreme restraint and sacrifice would inspire Tania to similar feats of emulation. She nodded blankly, knowing that she was being given the rough end of the stick.

Harish understood why a succession of slides could drive a grown man to such depths of despair and frustration. He felt the turmoil, the moral dilemma that Rahul must have felt when he opted for a cut and paste format. The two men's eyes met in a look of deep understanding.

At that moment, they felt almost a cosmic bond of brotherhood.

Tania felt she had intruded on an extremely private moment and cleared her throat uncomfortably.

Rahul recovered and told her cheerily, 'Forget the set, Tania. Get a kick ass design for the phone. It should be an iconic instrument of love—burned into our viewer's brain for life.'

Tania had a brief, cheerful vision of Rahul and Harish in front of a firing squad. All she had to say was the golden word, 'Fire!'

Rahul, noticing her distraction, asked impatiently, 'You with me, Tania?'

Tania cooed, 'Yes. Yes. I was just thinking of the iconic instrument of love. It is a super idea. Let me get cracking immediately.'

It was a conspiracy. Back at her desk, Tania sat moodily glaring at her desktop—an ancient, boxy, lumbering machine. The internet was slow and the keyboard constantly got jammed. But each time the jerk from IT came to fix it, it perversely worked just fine. Tania felt the whole affair was a plot between her computer and the IT department to demonstrate her ineptitude at just about everything. She wished she could unleash a deluge of sinister malignant viruses on the entire system.

She looked up to find Aditya smiling down at her. He

had come by for a morning chat. Although Tania had a lamentable tendency to mope, he enjoyed her company. She was unpretentious and well intentioned and when she wasn't being uptight, she had a dry sense of humour that needed to be encouraged. But even he couldn't lift her spirits today. She asked him petulantly, 'How come your net never acts up? You let those IT guys bum cigarettes off you and they just make sure nothing comes in the way of your many online chats.'

Aditya asked her sympathetically. 'Did you come riding to office on your menstrual cycle today?'

Tania glowered. 'What a typical male thing to say. Everything doesn't boil down to the time of the month. You are stupid and shallow and full of yourself like all the other men here.'

'What happened, Tani?' he asked her gently.

Tania calmed down and sighed. 'I don't know. It's this stupid show. Rahul wants a basic set. He fed me some crap about the fact that he was keeping his PPTs simple too. He made it sound like he had made some supreme sacrifice for some larger cause.'

Aditya countered. 'You don't get it, do you? It *is* a supreme sacrifice. PPTs give him orgasms.'

Tania laughed and then said glumly, 'And then my host, Vrushali, has a very desi accent. She opens her mouth and there ends all mystique.'

Aditya smiled. 'If she was one of those NRI chicks with their lower middle class London accents, you would not have had a problem. So why complain? A lot of our core audience may be speaking the same way she does. Do you really think intelligent, well-read people watch YTV or any TV for that matter?' Aditya continued seriously, 'Tani, you have to learn detachment. Learn not to get bogged down. Work smart. Television is not about great creativity—it is about common sense. The people you work with, unfortunately, don't have too much sense. So execute their brief—because you have to—but make sure it doesn't end up being passed off as your idea.'

Tania sighed. 'Easier said than done, Aditya,' and then she added half jokingly, 'you are quite sensible when you want to be no?'

Aditya laughed, 'Promise you won't tell anyone? Appraisals are due and I won't get a hike if they find out I have any sort of sense!'

Tania asked, 'Will that help me find an iconic phone? That's Rahul's latest instruction, just by the way!'

'Hmm…An iconic phone?'

'Yes,' said Tania sullenly. 'He says the phone should stand out. That should be the first thing that viewers notice on the show. The design should be breakthrough and cutting edge—an iconic instrument of love.'

Aditya said blandly, 'I thought he already had one—an iconic instrument of love that is.'

'Really? Why didn't he just give it to me then?'

Aditya laughed. 'Do you really want it? It comes attached to him unfortunately, you silly school girl.'

Tania's eyes widened and she laughed in spite of herself. 'You are a very vulgar man, Aditya Menon. Please go back to your desk and waste the rest of your day while I start my quest for the "iconic phone".'

'The dirt is in your mind, darling. It was his heart that I was referring to,' he chuckled as he made his way to his desk.

As luck would have it, it was Rahul who was finally instrumental in finding the iconic instrument of love. He ambled across to Tania's desk looking smugly triumphant. Harish waddled behind, tripping over in his boss' self importance.

At that point, Tania was nursing a headache as she had spent a good part of her day scouring the internet for an intriguing phone design to no avail. As she sat there looking at the multiple options thrown up by the worldwide web, her head spun slightly. She looked up to find Rahul smiling at her.

'Great news. We have a sponsor on board. Sales presented the PPT we sent across and the deal is almost through,' said Rahul gregariously.

Tania made sure to look suitably excited and asked, 'Who are they? From the existing pool?'

Rahul explained, 'No, it's the first time we are getting these guys on board. So we have to build this relationship. Tania, *you* have to. It's Dyson India.'

Dyson India was the second largest mobile communications company in India. Simply put, it made handsets. And Dyson India was weeks away from launching a new variant—the Dyson X30.

Rahul continued animatedly, 'The entire launch campaign is naughty and raunchy. Being positioned as a phone for young adults on the move and adults who multi-task everywhere—at work, at play, in their love lives, and in their sex lives—Dyson X30 becomes the instrument that helps them juggle their many multiple roles. Even their tagline is oddly appropriate for our show. *Dyson X30 Love Calls—Are you hot enough?*'

Enlightenment dawned on Tania. 'The Dyson X30 is our "iconic instrument of love" then? What does it look like?'

'Like any other phone. It's a regular handset; sleek but not exceptional. How does it matter to us?' said Rahul indifferently.

Tania had another vision of the firing squad with Rahul in front of it. She asked passively, 'It won't stand out then, will it? It won't be the first thing viewers notice about the show?'

Harish laughed. 'Dyson's behenchod brand managers certainly think that. But it is a regular piece of shit yaar. Just make sure Vrushali refers to most of its functions when she takes calls on it, on the show. Don't do it in that fucking home shopping kind of way. Make sure it is done in a YTV way.'

44

Tania repeated, 'Just a regular kind of phone then.' In her head, Harish had just been gagged and joined a cowering Rahul in front of the firing squad. Her platoon was looking at her for the final call to 'Fire'.

Rahul and Harish both stared at Tania impatiently. The girl was coming across as a bit slow.

Harish broke the silence. 'What were you expecting?' he barked.

'An iconic instrument of love,' she said wryly, then quickly composing her features into studied eagerness said, 'Great. We'll make sure Dyson gets its money's worth.'

Rahul looked relieved. For a moment there, he thought stodgy Tania had shown a flash of temperament.

Tania put her zealous firing squad on hold and asked, 'Is it a presenting sponsor? Will the brand name be part of the property?'

'Of course, it is going to be called *Dyson X30 Love Calls—Are you hot enough?* You know Amrit...once he's made a commitment to the client, there is no way we can back out. The client was very particular about this tagline.'

Amrit Khanna was the head of sales. For Amrit, every deal was a new fiefdom that his band of warriors annexed to the YTV Empire. Squat and bald, Amrit was a conqueror, a ruthless marauder who plotted and planned every sales deal like a war that had to be won. He was also a deeply religious man, and God was his client. God made shampoo, chewing gum, colas, handsets, cars, condoms, lingerie. God came in different forms but the path that God led him on was the singular path to increasing sales targets. And if God said a show had to be called *Dyson X30 Love Calls—Are you hot enough?* then, by God, it would be called that. After all God was paying for it.

Amrit had sent a typically Amrit Khanna email after adding Dyson India to his roster of sponsors. Except, as Aditya always said, 'A mail from Amrit is never a mere email. It is a missive, a battle cry, a petition, a call to action. It is anything but an email.' The latest epistle was no exception.

Subject: We return victorious

Friends,
One more new frontier is now ours. The sales team is proud to welcome Dyson India into our family of clients. This is the first time Dyson is advertising on a channel of our profile and we have a premium deal from them on our new love show with Vrushali Salve. It is our unstinting duty now to take this relationship to new heights—to gratify the immense trust they have shown in our brand.

Let us pledge to give them full satisfaction and to abide by all their commitments. The phone, Dyson X30, launch is only fifteen to twenty days away, and the client's expectations from our show are sky high. Let us demonstrate to them that when YTV promises, it delivers like none can. Let us help them drop other channels by the wayside—let the competition be dust on our feet that we shake off.

Time is running out on us, but I know you are with us

on this unprecedented triumph. The PPT on the list of client
commitments is attached. Please read it with due diligence
and let us sweep them off their feet. Let us endeavour
together to delight them like no other can.

Cheers,

Amrit

'The good that men oft do is interred with their bones. The
evil lives on.'

Only Amrit, thought Rahul, would write about
sweeping clients off their feet. Quite clearly his all-
conquering, numbers-driven exterior hid an absurdly
romantic soul.

Harish had a different take on it. He said, 'The fucker
has promised the client too many blow jobs.'

Rahul clucked at him in a mix of disapproval and
amusement, and turned to Tania who was smiling weakly
at Harish's latest salvo.

He gave Tania a printout of the mail and said, 'All
yours. Speak to Amrit. But don't let him bully you into
putting brand signage all over the set. Don't let this show
become the sales slut.'

Tania frowned. Handling Amrit was going to take a lot
of doing.

Rahul smiled at her reassuringly, 'If he gets out of
hand, you run to me. I'll deal with him.'

Tania gave him a glowing look of gratitude. And Rahul
suddenly felt heroic and equipped to sweep anything off
its feet. Especially pretty young supervising producers.

Harish suddenly felt hungry and equipped to eat anything. Especially a cheese and chicken laden sandwich. Both men left Tania's work station with pleasant enough thoughts.

———●———

Tania made her her way to Amrit's cabin. She wasn't looking forward to the prospect of dealing with his volatile impatience but even as she walked there she knew she wouldn't find him on his seat. Amrit, the war veteran, could hardly be expected to be sitting sedately at his desk. He spent half his day in client meetings and the other half pacing the corridors of the office—a bundle of nervous energy, glued to his BlackBerry, alternating between cajolery and coercion as he struck deal after deal.

Tania caught a glimpse of his bald head as he walked frenetically and talked frantically on his phone in one of YTV's corridors. She trotted after him trying to get his attention but he was in the middle of some heavy duty wheedling, so he paid her no attention. Tania spent a good forty five minutes on his heels and when he finally turned to her, offering no apology, she informed him curtly, 'Dyson. I am handling it.'

Amrit frowned. He didn't particularly care for Tania. He thought she was rather stolid and unimaginative, and if you asked Tania, she would probably say the same about him. He said brusquely, 'Please run the set design through me—brand colours are purple and black. Deep purple. Don't do some lilac shit.'

Tania bristled inwardly but replied pleasantly enough, 'I can usually tell the difference between purple and lilac but get me a colour palette from the client just in case. Any specifications on the black?'

Amrit snapped, 'Black is black!'

Tania considered that assertion for a good minute and then said earnestly, 'No. No, Amrit, it could be ebony black or coal black or grungy black. Best to be specific, no?'

Amrit glared at Tania, feeling slightly out of sorts. He didn't know what 'grungy black' meant and right up till now, he had had no clue that black could have so many variations. Tania, of course, had no intention of telling him that right up till now even she didn't know what 'grungy black' was or if any such colour existed. But she knew that she had put Amrit in a black fury and was pleased.

Tania looked at Amrit steadily. Amrit dismissed the fleeting suspicion that Tania was being a touch impudent. The girl was slow but she had a point—may as well get the colours totally right. He growled, 'Will get Ruchika to get the client to mail you,' and then stormed off in the general direction of yet another corridor.

Tania watched him go and allowed herself a little smile. Those forty five minutes of waiting were worth it just to see that flummoxed expression on that overbearing idiot's face.

A voice over her shoulder said, 'Chasing married bald men these days I see, Tani?'

Tania turned and smiled at Aditya. 'And why, may I ask, are you chasing me?'

Aditya said, 'Was wondering if you'd like a cup of coffee actually. I was thinking let's do black coffee... ebony black coffee or would you prefer grungy?'

Tania turned around nervously to check if Amrit had come back within earshot. He hadn't, and she turned back to Aditya and put a finger to her lips, laughing. Aditya smiled in amused appreciation.

———•———

That night, Tania awoke to an incessantly buzzing phone. Since she hardly received texts or calls that late at night, she wondered who it could be. She reached out for her phone and flipped it open and was even more puzzled when she saw whom the text was from.

As she read the message, her eyes widened in horror. The horror of the message could have only one befitting, and for her a fairly uncharacteristic, response.

'Fuck!' she exclaimed in the dark.

A Pox on Her!

Tania was in office earlier than everyone else. She waited for Rahul to come in so she could tell him personally about the mess they were in. When he did arrive two hours later, with Harish in tow, she popped her head into his office and asked, 'Busy?' And before he could say anything she walked in and continued, 'Vrushali has chicken pox.'

Harish let loose a string of Hindi expletives.

For a mere fraction of a heart-stopping second, Rahul forgot all his masterful expletives and said, 'Oh gosh!' and stared at Tania.

Only Harish understood the full implications of Rahul's 'Oh gosh!' He knew they were in deep shit.

Rahul's loss of bearings as evidenced by the use of a tame 'Oh gosh!' lasted only infinitesimally. He stood up and barked out, 'That is a fucking bitch of a situation. This has got us by the balls. Doesn't it take fucking three weeks or something to recover?'

Tania, feeling utterly miserable, said. 'She is out of action for the next ten days at least. It is a debilitating disease and she'll be quite weak even after that. She said she's getting her doctor to put her on the strongest antibiotics possible.'

Rahul paced around his cabin a very worried man. Carol strolled in looking slightly bored as usual. Rahul glanced at her cursorily, Harish's gaze lingered appreciatively at her legs, shown off to perfection in a pair of snug fitting shorts, and Tania frowned distractedly in her general direction.

Tania continued, 'Carol was supposed to do fittings with her today. But since it is contagious, she obviously can't.'

Carol shrugged her shoulders in casual acceptance as she lounged near the window in Rahul's cabin.

'Vrushali should have had the good sense to get over with chicken pox in her childhood. I got it when I was six,' Harish said with an air of singular achievement. Then he asked Carol in a tone of great surprise, 'Even you didn't get it as a child? That's strange.' There were not many occasions in Harish's life that he felt superior but this was certainly one.

'What to do, Harry? Not everyone is as smart at planning things as you are. It was stupid of me not to have scheduled chicken pox sooner. But now that I haven't, no way in hell am I going to go and get it from that chick. Not with my vacation coming up,' said Carol.

Harish looked dismayed at Carol's visible lack of commitment to YTV. He turned away and said confidingly to Tania and Rahul, 'I got it as a child, but man, those behenchod scars stay. I still have one or two scars. On my left arm.'

'Scars!' said Rahul and Tania in unison.

'Yeah,' said Carol and laughed darkly.

Harish, happy to get their attention, said proudly, 'Yup. Scars,' and started rolling up his sleeve to show them off.

But Rahul and Tania weren't looking. Till then, they had only been thinking of the delay that Vrushali's illness would cause on the shoot. But now, a more horrifying post-illness vision sprang up—their hottie covered in scars. On those impossibly long legs. On her thunder thighs!

Carol intervened. 'I guess we could ask the make-up guys to go heavy on the concealer and the bronzer. That should cover the scars.'

Harish, who was examining the faint scars on his fore-arm, said indignantly, 'Na. No concealer. I am not a vain guy. I don't even use moisturizer. My wife says I should, but come on, it's such a girly thing to do.'

Carol said pointedly, 'Everyone should use moisturizer. With SPF 30 at least,' and then thought clinically that, in addition, aloe vera face cleansing tissues could perhaps curb the problem of Harish's conscientious sweat glands. Tania looked at Rahul with a hint of desperation.

Rahul snapped. 'Harish, I am glad that you are looking at the funny side of this, but chief, this is very serious!'

Harish looked up from surveying a bell-shaped scar, and dutifully schooled his rotund face into an expression of concern. Suddenly, a storm burst of enlightenment hit him. He cried out, 'Oh god! Fucking hell. The girl will be covered in scars. Has anyone even thought of that?'

Carol shook her head in bemusement. Rahul paid him no attention.

Tania said urgently, 'The problem is we need to shoot the pilot day after. And now we can't. If she recovers in ten days, we will have to shoot the final first episodes in one go. A batch of them, since it's a daily. We will be going in blind without having tested the format or anchor. Can we push the launch date?'

Rahul said, 'No. Our sponsor will back out. The launch of the show is coinciding with the launch of their product. Plus communication around the show has started, with Vrushali being central to it. They are very excited about her. Teaser promos, with the hotline number being flashed constantly, are on air. We've got some press, not too much, but an adequate amount, on how YTV has a brand new face.'

Tania said what she always said whenever a crisis loomed large and she felt particularly clueless; a frequent occurrence in her two-year career at YTV, 'So now?'

Carol looked at her in sympathy and tried to help. 'We need time to figure out her look, dude. We should do at least two or three look tests before we finalize it. You want this babe to be hot—we have to work on it. We should push for more time,' she told Rahul.

Rahul tried not to look worried, 'We launch in whatever shape she is then. We have to. You were going to shoot final episodes on the twenty-fifth. We don't change that. That still gives us seventeen days for her to recover.'

Carol let out a low whistle. 'That is really cutting it too fine. We're launching a new face, it should be near perfect. You shouldn't be going for trial and error on air.'

Tania said nothing. She looked at Harish for a chance in hell.

'Of course. No roll back on the launch date,' he said.

Carol shrugged again and trilled, 'Okay suit yourself. I will get the clothes when we are good to go.' She looked at Tania and said, 'Dahling, best of luck, you're gonna need it,' and strolled out after waving cheerily at the men.

Tania was much too numb to react. So much so that even her perpetually ready firing squad sat forlornly instead of springing into action.

'Alright then, I'll send the final set design to both of you. Amrit wanted a lot of purple and black in the set. Deep purple and ebony black. Brand colours.' She left the room with a distinct air of deftly reined-in suffering. On her way out, she met Bose, who was striding into Rahul's cabin. Bose gave her a cursory smile. Tania knew she ought to feel grateful because Bose usually looked through people unless there was something specific he wanted to say. However, today she surprised him, and herself, by looking through him. The imminence of definite martyrdom had given an edge to sedate Tania's personality. Bose was mildly piqued—no one at YTV ever looked through him.

When Bose walked into the cabin, he was just in time to hear Harish felicitate Rahul, 'Brand colours are purple and black? Sir, using purple on the pitch PPT to the client was a stroke of genius.'

Rahul looked up and waved Bose cheerily to a chair.

Bose preferred to lean against the wall, from which position he surveyed Harish with amused contempt. He drawled lazily, 'You are never at your place. We could use the space for an edit bay instead.'

Harish replied with a sneer, 'Hi Bibo. We could do the same with your station since I never really see you in office either.'

Bose scowled. He hated being called 'Bibo'. It was a throwback from his gawky intern days, when his long winded name was ruthlessly truncated to the doltish sounding 'Bibo'. It reminded him of a time when he was the general dogsbody at the channel. But then things changed for Bibo five years ago when the supervising producer of YTV's biggest show quit in a huff and he was suddenly left to handle it. The show was YTV's stand-up comedy challenge, and it remained to this day one of the biggest success stories of the channel, and Bibo's.

Things changed almost overnight after the first season of the comedy challenge. Bibo metamorphosed into Bose. He developed a supercilious way of speech—cool and superior. His pimples disappeared as did his nervous giggle. The only thing he retained from his Bibo days was his crew cut, with one significant difference. Turn Bose around, and there hung a braid that extended from his head down to his waist. It was a quirk that Bose had cultivated after deep thought—so deep that it could even qualify as soul searching. But that was easy, because Bose didn't really have too much soul to begin with. And that was at the core of Bose's biggest regret. Bose didn't have a deep artistic angst—a brooding dissatisfaction that, in his mind, marked out all men of genius. His persona then became an impatient striving for that tumult of creativity that eluded him—and fortunately for him, the quest to seek angst passed off as angst. So much so that Rahul would say in awe, 'Bose is just such a crusading soul. You know the creative genius types.'

Harish, of course, thought that Bose's angst could be the result of a painful and protracted constipation, but wisely kept his thoughts to himself. After all, as Harish often said, 'I am a shallow, crude sort of guy, not at all soulful.' He often threw in a burp or a belch after that for effect.

Bose was a method actor. He had played the part of moody genius for so long that in his head now, he was one. But every time someone called him 'Bibo', a painful reminder of his former, not so exalted, self came to mind. Harish, who was incapable of such in depth psychographic profiling, just knew that calling him Bibo always hit a raw nerve. So he persisted with schoolboy-like glee.

Rahul defused the tension by quickly telling Bose about the new show. Bose paid full attention, pretending that it was the first time he had heard of it. Rahul, too, made it seem like he thought it was the first time Bose had heard of the show, although he didn't doubt the efficacy of the YTV grapevine.

Bose heard Rahul out and said, making sure to get in a note of slight boredom, 'On a conceptual level, isn't it a bit old-style TV? You know, maybe ten years ago, kids would have been excited about a woman wearing next to nothing and taking love calls. But now they can watch much bolder stuff on the net. I mean, just how spectacular are these legs anyway?'

Rahul laughed suggestively and winked at Bose.

Harish thought of the fleshy thighs and blurted, 'Very!'

Bose peered at him intently. Rahul stopped laughing and felt distinctly uncomfortable. Bose knew that he had succeeded in shaking Rahul up, and continued to look at him.

Rahul laughed a little too heartily and said, 'This country will never be tired of fucking sex symbols.'

'You're the boss,' Bose drawled.

For a fraction of a second, Rahul suddenly wished he weren't but he smiled at Bose cockily and dismissively.

'Need to book you in an hour's time. Have some reality concepts to discuss with you. The life swap show is looking good on paper,' said Bose.

Rahul's confidence crumbled the minute Bose left the room and he was left feeling quite unnerved. He was about to turn to his devoted deputy for reassurance, but was interrupted by his extension buzzing intrusively.

It was Bhosle. He wanted to know if omelettes made of only egg whites could be included in 'Food Incidentals'. Rahul put him on speaker phone as this situation demanded the intervention of Harish, who had strong convictions on the wastage of food and said they needed to find a way of utilizing the yolks. Neither Bhosle nor Rahul had any solutions to offer.

The situation was clearly spilling out of the realm of a mere con call. So Rahul decided that it was best that the meeting be reconvened in the boardroom in the next ten minutes.

The two men then strode out, armed with their laptops, towards the boardroom.

Validation for their existence had just been found.

Tragedy struck Tania again. Carol left with the parting words, 'It is the season for a sabbatical, dahling', leaving Tania with the assistant stylist, Garnet Patel of the coordinated clothes, bag, shoes, and eye shadow fame. Garnet Patel; who had just finished fashion school six months back, and who wore a multiplicity of buttons, bows, and ribbons with every outfit. She was as green at her job as the green gladiator sandals that she wore ever so often. Short legs and gladiator heels together was a reprehensible fashion crime but that was the last of Tania's worries. She was more concerned about the person who was wearing those heels.

Bhosle, the genial godfather who gave 'breaks' to greenhorns and newbies, told a worried Tania, 'We should give young people a chance.' To Bhosle all fresh, young talent was part of the amorphous mass that went under the heading 'low cost resources' in his excel sheet; three golden words to any production person worth his budget.

Tania was too weary to protest. The plot was getting too convoluted for her sedate taste—iconic phones, diseased anchors, a stylist who looked like a flower shop on heels —everything was coalescing into a painful blur in her head already. Tania, not the most cheerful of people at any given time, now moped around office weighed down by the burden of the show. There was a hint of fatigue around her eyes and she often bit on her lower lip in anxiety. All of this ensured that her confidante, Aditya, maintained a healthy distance from her.

Aditya was of the firm opinion that Tania enjoyed the melancholic, that she liked being sad. He had once told her, 'Your default setting is martyrdom. You want to climb on that stake *and* help with the burning.'

In Aditya's opinion, martyrs were nice enough people but he didn't rate their sense of humour too high. So he steered well away from the spiritless Tania. She noticed Aditya's withdrawal but was too caught up in the imminence of deeper tragedy to pay too much attention to it. Bose's growing admiration also eluded her notice completely. Tania looked like some private demon was consuming her insides, and Bose, who had been trying in vain to get some manner of gluttonous private demon going, was taken in by this kindred soul swamped in a creative morass. It helped that the kindred soul was quite easy on the eye as Bose was beginning to notice.

Tania's spirits would have lifted had she known the impact she was having on the head of the temperamental talented. Bose was considered a pretty good catch among the impressionable young female workforce at YTV. But Tania construed Bose's stray pats on her head as he walked by her workstation as condescension. So she barely acknowledged them or him, and in the process enhanced her elusiveness and appeal. Bose, used to the puppy-like adoration of most pretty young things in office, was befuddled with the almost reflexive rebuffs. Tania seemed not to notice or care for his fledgeling interest, and therefore piqued it further.

———

In the meanwhile, Garnet Patel had been handed over the responsibility of keeping tabs on Vrushali. Like Harish, Garnet Patel also had an admirable constitution. She too had had chicken pox as a child, and so was safe to visit Vrushali.

Garnet was a conscientious visitor, and with each visit brought back tidings to Tania. The only good news was that Vrushali's face had escaped the scourge. The rest though was enough to put Tania in a chronic state of manic depression.

'She has marks on her chest—not very visible, but we will have to see about the cleavage. Halters are out. There are prominent marks on the shoulder blades. The doctor has advised her not to use any make-up. And she can't wax.'

This last bit of information finally managed to shatter Tania's barely-held together stoicism. She hurried to

Rahul's cabin and blurted out this profoundly life-altering fact. The final shoot was still three days away.

Rahul chewed on this bit of information, and repeated slowly, 'She can't wax.'

Tania shook her head. 'Apparently, there will be a chemical reaction because of the wax.'

Rahul's head was spinning furiously and then he questioned hopefully, 'Can't she shave?'

Garnet Patel who had followed Tania into Rahul's office piped in, 'No. That will give her major in-growth and screw up the texture of hair growth later.'

Harish blurted out. 'She must be removing the hair every month. So how does it matter whether it grows fine or coarse?'

Garnet Patel said patiently, 'If the hair removal is not done in a proper way, she will end up being stubbly forever.'

Harish nodded in enlightenment. He looked at Rahul who was shifting in his chair uncomfortably, not knowing what to do.

And then it happened. It took everyone, most of all Rahul, by surprise. There comes a moment in every leader's life when he has to stand-up to the odds, take a situation by its horns and turn it around with strength of his resolve and tenacity. This is often called the moment of reckoning.

Rahul's moment of reckoning had come; it had walked in on him on a pair of potentially hirsute legs and waited for him to take charge of it. He had to take control before the situation slipped out of his hands irrevocably.

He took a deep breath, stood up, and said firmly, 'If Vrushali Salve wants to be the new face of YTV, she will have to find a way to get here on the morning of the twenty-fifth with hairless legs. That is not the problem of my creative team. I hope that is understood. This is the end of the discussion.'

Propelled by some unknown larger force, Rahul quietly repeated, 'Understood?' and then grimly added, 'It better fucking be.'

Tania, Harish, and Garnet Patel trotted out. Tania felt like a zombie. It was just her luck to end up with a hirsute, scarred host who needed to transform miraculously into a Playboy centrefold. Garnet Patel blabbered about getting Vrushali an epilator. Harish was internalizing Rahul's inflection just before he said 'Understood' for the second time. He was dreaming of a situation where similar mastery would be demanded of him. Back in his office, Rahul found that his knees were shaking slightly; he had managed to overwhelm himself.

With a few stutters, Garnet Patel got on the phone with Vrushali in an attempt to get her to use an epilator. It didn't work, so Garnet was deputed to visit a convalescing Vrushali in person. Bhosle was sent along with her to monitor things as the seasoned production controller.

Five hours later, Bhosle stomped into Rahul's room. 'The bitch wants us to buy her the epilator!'

Rahul said weakly, 'Oh! What did you tell her?'

'It is a crisis, so I didn't have a choice. It costs five thousand rupees. But I insisted that she return it to us after the schedule,' Bhosle ranted.

Rahul nodded approvingly. There wasn't too much practical utility in hanging on to a used epilator but, like Bhosle, he was more concerned about the moral victory.

Bhosle then said conspiringly, 'I am going to send her one of those Chinese ones that you find at Crawford market. Will come at half the price. If it's good enough for the Chinese, it'll be good enough for her.'

He strode out purposefully, thrilled at the prospect of saving money.

Harish told Rahul that it was his belief that the Chinese were not nearly as hairy as the Indians. Rahul gave the matter careful thought and pronounced that it was probably their diet that made them less hirsute. Harish countered that it could be the climate.

The rest of the morning passed in this fruitful conversation.

———

The set came up resplendent in purple and black; the purple was repainted thrice till the Dyson brand manager was convinced that it was, in fact, the same shade as his handset. No one else saw the difference and there was none because each time the brand manager said, 'Almost there. Just make it three and a half percent lighter,' the set design team repainted it in the same shade without any variation.

Purshottam, the head of the design team, was a veteran of all manner of sets and all manner of brand managers. The prototype of the brand manager didn't change too much—they were almost always fretting, unimaginative, and annoying men. As Purshottam told Tania, 'These brand manager types probably wear undies in their brand colours. The trick is to indulge them and then do exactly what you want to do.'

Tania, whose mood had lifted after the godsent gift of an epilator, smiled genuinely after a long time.

The pre-production work for the show was going along well. Tania had already started screening calls and callers who would make it to the final show. The teaser promos were on air with the hotline being flashed incessantly. Tania planned to make a shortlist of the best callers and problems for the final shoot.

The hotline number rang incessantly. Shimla, Shillong, Siliguri, and Secundarabad—the whole nation, apparently, was in the throes of love and its varied pitfalls. Except they weren't that varied. Most of the callers had a universal problem—pimply teens who had fallen in love with the girl or boy across the street, they had been staring at each other for two years, but now didn't know what to do.

Tania was taken aback. She asked Aditya, 'Where are all the kids who make MMS clips of themselves having oral sex? Kids who start doing it at fourteen? These problems here are from my dad's generation!'

Aditya smirked. 'I'd be disappointed if illustrious and enterprising kids like those called in to talk to a bimbo in a short skirt. Why would they call her? C'mon, Tani, talented kids like that could teach your hottie a thing or two. You're only going to get these nerds.'

Tania, whose sense of humour was recuperating, laughed, but she remained slightly concerned.

But at YTV, there was enough to keep her occupied, so she didn't get that much time to dwell on the staid love problems that were coming her way. The skirmishes with Bhosle, for instance, took up most of her time. He refused to install an answering machine for the hotline. 'We'll need ten thousand rupees for it. There's no budget.'

Tania asked angrily, 'Who is going to take those calls and make a shortlist of the callers? I can't be in office all the time.'

Bhosle said calmly, 'I have a solution, just hear me out.'

Typically, Bhosle's solution was one that involved no money. He got Tania's interns to take the calls. Tania decided she needed to vet these interns before she could put them on potentially sensitive calls. As it turned, out not too many of the interns that Bhosle had lined up were too sold on the idea of a love show. One told Tania jauntily that 'taking calls from losers was not my scene'. The other would only do it if 'steaming hot' Zain was the host.

Tania told Bhosle grimly, 'They don't get it, do they? They are interns. How can they be this picky?' Bhosle shrugged off the problem.

Finally, Tania found an intern willing to work on the show. Amend that—she found an intern who deigned to work on the show. Seventeen-year-old Vaidehi yawned out her acceptance. 'Dude whatever, I need to get my ass out of home before my mom decides this is a good time for me to learn how to cook.'

Vaidehi was far from ideal but she would have to do, thought Tania. Anyway all she needed to do was take calls and note down the numbers.

The strict instructions to Vaidehi were to take down the name and number of the caller as well as the nature of the problem, and hang up with a promise to get back to the caller if their problem made it to the shortlisted calls. However, Tania soon found Vaidehi doling out generous doses of profound love advice—some of it dangerously radical.

'You cannot,' Tania told her sternly, 'you cannot tell some caller that she should put a laxative in her crush's drink before he goes on a date with someone else. He could fall ill. Plus it's not right!'

'I think it rocks. Dude, everything is right in love,' Vaidehi said defiantly.

Tania took to monitoring almost every call that came on the hotline. As this took up a lot of her time, it left her feeling irritable and ill used. And so finally when Bhosle informed her curtly that he would not give her an STD facility on the hotline and that she should ensure that she made calls only in Mumbai, Tania Shah threw her first legitimate, full-fledged tantrum in her two years at YTV.

'You,' she hissed angrily, 'will give me an STD line. Otherwise there is NO show. You will give me what I want—STD, ISD, fax—whatever. I don't care how you do it—attach the line to your ass for all I care. Otherwise let's scrap this show.'

To her great surprise, Bhosle told her affably that he would stretch his budget and fit it in. And then he slunk away.

Tania felt for the first time the power of the tantrum. It was a heady feeling.

She smiled to herself, and found Bose looking at her oddly. He had walked in right before her tantrum and had witnessed it. Since she was feeling rather enervated after her first display of temperament, she gave him a warm smile.

Bose stood there transfixed. He had found his muse.

———

Tania's frosty equation with Vrushali persisted. She was always far too tired to be briefed about the shoot.

She confidently told Tania on the phone, 'I am like a professional persons. In five minutes you are giving me brief, in two and a half minutes I am getting yeah.'

Tania gave up. She just hoped God was planning to play a starring role on the first day of the shoot. She headed to Aditya's desk; as the shoot date inched closer, he had become her ten-minute daily sanity break and sounding board. He had a unique spin on all of her problems and in his company, none of them suddenly seemed that insurmountable. As usual Aditya had his own theory on Vrushali's exasperating behaviour.

'It would help, you know, if you weren't pretty,' said Aditya. 'Good looking people don't like other good looking people. See the entourage that film stars surround themselves with—most of them have faces that only their mothers would love.'

Tania smiled. 'Did you just give me a compliment, Aditya? It didn't sound like one!'

Aditya grinned. 'No, just stating a fact. It would have been easier for Vrushali to work with you if you were plain or just odd like that Christmas tree stylist of yours.'

Tania scoffed. 'There is no comparison, Aditya. Vrushali is a model and I am...well...look at me.'

Aditya's eyes twinkled as he looked at Tania steadily. He said softly. 'I am.'

Tania was disconcerted. Aditya was not the resident heartthrob of YTV in the way Bose was but he had an easy charm with women. Tania and he had started out as buddies, and that's the way she liked it. No complications, just easy companionship. She had to admit though that his latest utterance had given her an unexpectedly pleasant, semi-wobbly feeling in her knees. But her practical self took over almost instantly as she mentally scolded her errant knees into standing still. Her love life would have to wait till she sorted out the love lives of teenage India. The potential martyr in Tania had subconsciously made *Dyson Love Calls* into a noble mission.

More importantly, Aditya was not at all the kind of man she generally fancied. She liked them more intense, more serious, a bit like, if she were totally honest, Bose. She was no longer impervious to Bose's growing attention to her but wasn't entirely sure whether it was scary or flattering. 'You silly girl' thought Tania, 'this isn't the time to be thinking of men. Any man! Snap out of it.' So she laughed off the moment. 'Okay, I am glad you think I am a raving beauty, now I'll get my beautiful self some coffee.'

'Raving beauty is overstating the case a bit, Tani. Your right profile needs serious work!' said Aditya narrowing his eyes for effect.

Both of them burst into laughter at that and sauntered off to coffee together.

Silicone Pads,
Camera, Action

The big day arrived with a bright and sunny start. Tania heaved a huge sigh of relief and headed to the shower. At 8 am, she was on the floor. Roll time was three hours away, and the camera and lighting team were hard at work. Tania made a mental calculation—she had to shoot seven episodes, with at least half an hour of content each, that would finally be cut down to twenty-minute episodes. With seasoned anchors such as Zain or Natasha, this would have been a tiring but manageable affair. But Vrushali was an unknown quantity, so there was no telling.

The unknown quantity was at that moment sitting in the make-up van. Tania knocked on the van's door and a muffled voice said, 'Come in.'

With rollers in her hair, Vrushali was lounging around in a short dressing gown. She had lost weight and was low on energy. Tania peered at Vrushali's legs. Her left leg had escaped with minimal scarring, but the right leg still had visible scars. The much-discussed thighs could not be used for this schedule as the marks on them were prominent. The doctor had advised against the use of heavy make-up, so the concealer had to be kept to the minimum. Vrushali followed Tania's gaze and said, 'By next shoot all will be going only yeah.'

Tania gave Vrushali a tight smile, but didn't tell her that the first batch of episodes were the deciding ones, as she continued to survey Vrushali's anatomy dispassionately.

Tania decided it would be best to make the most of her legs and her chest. The shoulders were scarred as well—so no halters or straps. Tania thought it was perverse that she had a sex symbol on her hands and that her main preoccupation was not how much to reveal, but rather how much to conceal. Just then Garnet Patel came stumbling in through the van door. Tania gave her a disapproving glare and said curtly, 'You're late. You have one hour to get her ready.'

She then sought out Akaash, her director of photography, to discuss the issue of the scars and how much would be visible onscreen. Akaash came up with an idea. They would need to seat her in a way where the left leg was crossed over the right constantly. So whether she had her legs propped up on the coffee table or she huddled on the bean bag, the placement of the left leg was pivotal. Tania nodded her assent and then looked at the set. It was a small, flat set in shades of purple and black. There was a couch, a bean bag, and a coffee table.

A laptop sat on the table and the Dyson X30 lounged on the couch.

Tania looked at Akaash urgently. 'Please get one camera team to focus just on that phone. Take nice close shots.'

Akaash laughed. 'Don't worry. I'm lighting up the set only for the phone to look good. Doesn't matter how your lady looks.'

Tania looked at him slightly worriedly, but smiled when she realized that he was teasing. Akaash was an easy guy to work with, and Tania was grateful that he was on the set.

Just then Tania was urgently summoned by Garnet Patel to the make-up van. She had been called in to make an important decision. Garnet Patel and Vrushali had spent half an hour trying to get cracking but had now given up.

Garnet Patel said through giggles, 'We have lost objectivity. And so you have to be the final decision maker.' Garnet Patel gestured at Vrushali's newly expanded chest. 'What do you think? Too big? Too fake?'

Tania Shah took a deep breath. She was to decide on how full Vrushali's bust line should be and on the size of the fake 'boobies' that Vrushali would thrust down her marginal bosom.

What Vrushali and Garnet called 'boobies' were 100 percent pure silicone gel breast pads. Tania was spoilt for choice with the brand new options that lay strewn on Vrushali's dressing table. There were size enhancers, which could make her two cups larger, in two colours— nude and transparent. These were washable and re- usable. Then there were the disposable enhancers with a soft inner layer of wood pulp. Tania felt rather pleased at the thought of grown men turned on by wood pulp. There was some sort of bizarre justice in this 'boobies' business after all. One particular type of breast pads claimed to warm to your body temperature and mould to the natural shape of the bosom. Garnet Patel was particularly taken in by these but Tania had visions of the harsh lights in the studio playing havoc, and rejected it after careful thought.

Tania finally settled for the extreme push-up breast pads, which were 'anatomically curved and tapered to hug breasts securely with a unique shelf that sits below the breasts to instantly boost cleavage'. Vrushali expertly put the pads down her bra and stood there in her undergarments. She propped up her already propped up bust with her hands and looked at Tania. 'Yeah baby!' she said with a pout.

Vrushali's modest bosom had taken on a life of its own. Two mounds of creamy flesh delicately spilled out of a lacy bra, and the cleavage smiled out tantalisingly. Garnet Patel and Tania beamed proudly. Whatever Tania's feelings for Vrushali may be, she had begun to feel that her bust line was her protégé. And the protégé had risen to the occasion.

But through the ages, history has testified that the lives of martyrs are fraught with unrelenting crises of faith. The moments of joy are short lived and hard to find. Tania's little bubble of happiness, naturally, was not destined to last more than one minute and forty seven seconds.

For at that precise moment, the Dyson Brand Manager, who had arrived for an inspection, had a paroxysm on the sets. This convulsion was commonly called the 'but where is my brand' fit. It generally always took place half an hour before the shoot and was almost always accompanied by threats to withdraw sponsorship. This was an extremely common and contagious ailment among the tribe of brand managers. In YTV production circles, the code word for it was 'swine flu'.

When Tania returned hurriedly to the set, she found the Dyson Brand Manager jabbing away on his BlackBerry and jabbering away in some degree of passion. He glared at Tania and said, 'Madam, there is no Dyson X30 on this set. Where is my brand?'

Tania looked around mutely at a set which could be mistaken for a Dyson hoarding. A plasma screen in the background played the Dyson logo non-stop. The phone itself occupied pride of place on the patent leather couch. She looked at him and said sarcastically, 'You mean we have actually missed a spot where there is no Dyson presence? How is that possible?'

Sarcasm was the wrong wary to deal with him. If brand managers could get sarcasm, they wouldn't be brand managers. After all, these were men who spent a large part of their youth, getting an MBA degree only so that they could spend the rest of their lives in meaningful relationships with a series of lifeless products.

He snapped, 'My phone is looking too small! It's getting lost in your set. This will not do! This is a very special launch for us. You guys have to do better! Where is Amrit?'

Tania said quietly, 'That's the size you guys have made it in. Give us a bigger size and we'll use that.'

The Dyson Brand Manager glared at her and said hotly, 'Bigger size? Have you understood the brand values? It's for people on the move. We deliberately want it to be small, sleek, and compact. Its streamlined shape fits into the palm of your hand, combining cutting-edge technology with never before mobility. Business or pleasure—this is your mobile on the go. Don't you get the brand promise, madam?'

Tania was relieved to see Harish waddling in. Whatever his faults, Harish was a genius when it came to dealing with brand managers. His mantra was simple and uncomplicated—lick ass. Since this was a skill set that Harish was born with, he eagerly lapped up the job of handling these gentlemen. In any case, no one else wanted the job.

Harish clasped the Dyson Brand Manager's hands in his and said, 'We are so lucky to have a progressive client like Dyson on board. It inspires us to put our best foot forward—the kind of breakthrough brand integrations that we have thought of, it can only happen on YTV. We have only done this because we know we have a client who thinks out of the box.'

Nobody really knew the exact nature of these 'breakthrough brand integrations'. Not even Harish, but he continued confidently, 'We've kept our set small and compact so that it's totally in keeping with the brand. The temptation was there to go for size and scale, but where is the brand fit? So we went for intimate with an undertone of sensuality—just like the phone. Both blend in seamlessly.'

Tania looked at Harish admiringly. The man had utility after all.

The Dyson Brand Manager softened slightly and said, 'I appreciate that. But my product is not going to show. I believe when the calls come, it will be on speaker phone. We want Vrushali to constantly hold it and show it off. On speaker, it will lie on the table and it is looking too small there.'

Tania interrupted, 'But how else do we hear the caller? Vrushali can't be having a private conversation.'

Akaash who was in the vicinity suddenly said, 'We will take close static shots of the phone. Like really well lit product pack shots, and on the edit, Tania can keep intercutting between close shots of the phone and Vrushali.'

Harish thought this was a stellar suggestion. 'Yup. Bung

in close shots. Cleavage, then Dyson X30. Legs—Dyson X30. A bit of the thigh, and then a bit of the phone. Almost like hide and seek.'

The Dyson Brand Manager gaped in awe. He was almost completely won over when Harish delivered the winning stroke. 'Tania, when we have that flash of panty, make sure it is a purple and black panty—the Dyson brand colours.'

Harish had closed the deal. The Dyson Brand Manager clasped Harish's hand warmly and was incapable of further speech.

It was noon and Tania was behind schedule by an hour. It was time to roll. Akaash had out done himself; he had managed to make the rather garish purple and black look good. Most of the set was in shadows with only Vrushali being lit perfectly. The mood was sensuous and cosy.

The Dyson X30 glinted on the couch. And sitting next to it was Vrushali Salve—the hot new face of YTV. She wore a gold, sequinned, knee length dress with a deep, plunging neckline. Her left leg, crossed over her right, showed an expanse of bronzed flesh. Her eyes were smoky and her hair fell in careless curls. She looked the part of the temptress as she parted her full lips and looked into the camera.

Harish peered intently at her décolletage, approving its ampleness. Unaware of the large role that the silicone gel pads had played, he ogled appreciatively, wondering why Vrushali's well endowed status had missed his discerning eye earlier. Tania, noticing his reaction, felt her own bosom swell with pride. But before she could fully enjoy the moment, she heard Akaash saying, 'Rolling.'

She heard a clear voice ring out. It was her own. It said, 'Action.'

Dyson X30 Love Calls—Are you hot enough? was all set to become a momentous chapter in Indian television history.

Of course, nobody knew that then.

The Faith Healer in a
Short Dress

The first episode took three hours to shoot. Three minutes into the first call made by a young fifteen-year-old from Nainital who was having commitment issues with her thirteen-year-old boyfriend, Harish hollered, 'Cut!'

Harish was staring at the monitor. He called Tania urgently to his side, and whispered in her ear, 'Oh God! She has wonky boobs.'

Tania snapped, taking it rather personally, 'She so doesn't. Show me.'

The next five minutes saw a very worried Tania and Harish examining Vrushali's bust from every conceivable angle. Akaash adjusted his camera angles to give them a better perspective. He also suggested that Harish was imagining it. Harish, affronted by the suggestion, said that his imagination was more versatile and vivid than that. 'If I had to imagine things, I wouldn't be imagining crooked breasts, let me tell you that, gaandu,' he snapped at Akaash.

Tania yelled out for Garnet Patel, who came looking flustered and frazzled. They congregated around the monitor and discussed the problem in whispers.

The caller was told that there were technical issues and that the call had to be disconnected. The rest of the crew decided it was a good time to have a cup of tea.

Vrushali kept demanding to know what the 'problems' was but was not paid any heed to. So she occupied herself with swinging her leg as the whispers gradually reached an intense crescendo. The consensus was that Vrushali's left breast did look slightly askew. Harish, showing uncharacteristic delicacy, whispered urgently, 'How are we going to tell her that? It'll be a shock. Tania, please take her aside and tell her. Be a bit sensitive though.'

Tania grabbed Garnet Patel and gestured to Vrushali to head to the make-up van. However, Vrushali stayed put. Garnet Patel whispered the issue to Vrushali, who peered down her cleavage, and then thrust one hand down her left breast. 'Oh my left boobies has slipped a bit yeah.' She pushed up the silicone gel pad and then said loudly, 'Harish, check now?'

The crew lost interest in the tea, and Harish Swamy lost his voice and composure. He left embarrassedly for his workstation, wondering all the way how the adjustable breasts of women were a fact of existence that had so far eluded him. Harish Swamy had had a life-changing experience and he would be forgiven if he left for home early that day.

Tania didn't notice or miss his absence. It took another fifteen minutes to get the caller from Nainital back on the line, and the shoot resumed. Vrushali spoke to her in English that defied all existing laws of grammar, syntax, and tense. Tania cut a few times and asked Vrushali to speak more in Hindi. Vrushali obliged with ill grace. Her Hindi was almost as confused as her English. Tania wished again they had had the time to shoot a pilot and figure out some basic diction classes for the hottie.

Inexplicably, though, the caller had no issue understanding Vrushali, and to Tania's surprise, seemed to warm to her babbling incoherence. The call went on for fifteen minutes with Vrushali refusing to take a cut.

'So,' blabbed Vrushali inanely, 'the men yeah. They is there to be breaking our hearts buddy. All our lives—break, break, break—break promise, break trust, and everythings. It is like being a hobby with them.'

'Yes,' said the overwrought fifteen-year-old, 'now I will break his balls.'

'Ah,' said Vrushali wisely, 'if we is to be going around breaking all balls of all men there is going to be only women left. Buddy—no breaking, just pushing little bit. They will give commitments then yeah.'

The caller said in confusion, 'Pushing what? His balls?'

Vrushali said airily, 'Whatever buddy!'

'CUT!' yelled Tania finally. She motioned to Vaidehi to cut the call.

'Poor things! How we can tell to her to be shutting up yeah, when so much she is going through. Kinda mean,' said Vrushali with a toss of her hair.

Tania said firmly, 'Next time I call cut, we cut. Simple. Also follow the brief—you can't be telling a fifteen-year-old that men have commitment issues. Her boyfriend is thirteen for god's sake. And the two of you just went on and on, moaning about men. And balls—we will anyway have to beep that out. Can't use balls on air. That won't do.'

Vrushali said nothing. She looked sullenly at her bosom, and then thrust it out defiantly. Tania was about to continue when Vrushali suddenly smiled. Rahul had just strolled in. He asked amiably, 'How's it going? Everything is looking wonderful.'

Vrushali simpered. Tania smiled professionally and pleasantly. Or so she thought. Rahul couldn't tell the difference. All he saw were two attractive women simpering at him. That was enough to put him in a good mood. He exchanged gushing pleasantries and left, saying that he must not get in the way of the creative team. He had already, but nobody was going to tell him that. The shoot resumed.

The next two calls were almost as painful as the call from Nainital. One was from a boy in Siliguri who had met a girl on the Geetanjali Express. He told Vrushali that it was love at first sight. They had exchanged numbers before leaving but now she wasn't taking his calls. He was sure the grief would kill him. Vrushali handled the problem with little sense and little sense of tense. She gave the caller a homily on the power of faith and love. She airily concluded, 'When you are loving somebody yeah, you tell to the somebody: "Go, I am making you free yeah. If the somebody came back, he is a kept man... yours forever. But if he is running far, you can never be keeping him. Okay, buddy.'

To which the caller said emotionally, 'But I am loving a girl not a him, madam.'

'In love, there is no sex buddy,' said Vrushali wisely.

At which point Tania went blue in the face shouting, 'Cut! You can't be giving them these proverbs. You have to be firm and if the problem is a rather silly one, you have to tell them off. You don't meet someone on the train for twelve hours, and then get suicidal because they are not taking your calls. And what do you mean by "in love there is no sex"?'

Vrushali said piously, 'You are loving to a girl or to a boy. Love is love yeah. How does the sexes matter?'

Comprehension dawned on Tania. She said, 'Oh' and then, 'just don't say it like that. This is a show with a sexual undertone.'

And that happened to be the next big problem. There was no sexual tone—undertone or overtone—in the show. Vrushali was coming across as a faith healer in a short dress. Tania figured it had everything to do with her body language. She was not acting sexy. Tania said,

'Pretend you are on the ramp. Throw in a few pouts. Jut that hip out. Smoulder at the camera.'

Vrushali agreed, but in the middle of her rousing spiel on love and selflessness to a caller from Bhuj, she forgot to arch her eyebrow or pout her lips. Tania tried to give her non verbal cues by acting out sensuous gestures but Vrushali paid no attention to her suddenly pouting and smouldering producer. The crew on the other hand was much amused. Tania gave up and sat in a corner of the set, resigned to her fate.

After the first episode shoot, Tania had a brainwave. She told Vaidehi to quickly make a series of large cue cards. The text on the cue cards read in bold:

'THRUST OUT'
'POUT'
'HAND ON YOUR HIP'
'LEAN OVER'
'CROSS YOUR LEGS'
'NARROW EYES'
'PART LIPS'
'BITE LIP'

For the rest of the shoot, the intern was to sit next to the camera and hold up the cue cards for Vrushali to see. Vaidehi shrugged and said, 'In what particular order and when?'

'Use your discretion,' was Tania's curt reply.

The second episode began at 4 pm. The first caller was from Surat. The malaise of the young Indian pubescent male had struck him as well. He was in love with his neighbour. He said mournfully, 'For two years now, we are looking at each other. She is looking away but I know she feels the same about me.'

Vrushali kept it short, and dispensed with the boy by telling him that he should write her a letter or try to call her. Showing rare sensibility, she also added, 'She is not looking to you yeah. How then you can tell it is love that she is feeling? You gotta get like a real checks done, dude. Otherwise, two years you are looking at a girl who is not looking to you. Maybe buddy she didn't have known only that you are looking with love buddy. Cos you know Indians men like to be looking all the time and not with love all the times yeah.'

The Surat caller lapped up this garbled piece of common sense with profound gratitude and hung up. The next call came in from Jabalpur. A young hysterical girl whose boyfriend was not taking her calls. Her friends told her that he had found someone else, but she couldn't give up on him. She sobbed heartbreakingly. Tania thought of the promo she could make out of this heart rending call and smiled.

She waited for Vrushali to hold forth in her absurdly philosophical way. Instead to her horror, Tania witnessed some rather disconcerting behaviour from the siren. As the girl sobbed her heart out, Vrushali thrust her bosom out, bit her lower lip, and narrowed her eyes. This was followed by a quick succession of equally baffling acts—Vrushali suggestively put her hand on her hip and pouted most provocatively. This at a stage when the Jabalpur caller's voice had broken most tragically as she spluttered, 'W-what d-do I do? I gave him my everything!'

Vrushali, who hadn't listened to a word of what the hapless girl had said, purred, 'Uh huh…' The girl then said utterly baffled, 'Huh?'

Tania realized what had happened. Vaidehi, who had slept through the first call, had had a conscience attack. So she had frantically and rather zealously flashed the cue cards all at a go, and Vrushali had followed the instructions with equal zeal. Tania snatched the cue cards from Vaidehi and called for a cut. She banished Vaidehi to the farthest corner of the set, and told Vrushali angrily, 'I know she was flashing those cue cards at you but you should have used your head. Are you mad? The child was crying while you were behaving like a tart. For god's sake, Vrushali!'

Tania regretted the words the minute they were spoken. It was a cardinal rule of television that the on-air talent must at all times be handled with sensitivity and tact. After all, they were the face of the show, and if something upset them it would show on the show. This brings us to the other cardinal rule of television—the magnitude of the tantrum was always inversely proportional to the magnitude of talent.

Quite naturally, then, Vrushali Salve threw the mother of all tantrums. Take it back another generation. It was the grandmother of all tantrums. She let out great gasping sobs of anger. Tania watched in horror as the tears washed away her eye make-up, which then ran in black streaks down her cheeks. The bronzer remained in blotches and her natural fair skin peeped out. A lock of her hair dramatically got stuck on her lip gloss and Vrushali made no attempt to extricate it as she spoke through the corner of her mouth, 'I am so passionate about everythings. You telling me be sexy yeah and I'm putting all my passions. How I am knowing not to be sexy when you is telling me to be sexy?'

There was profound reasoning in this grammatically muddled piece of emotion so Tania hastily apologized. But this continued for another twenty minutes. Tania apologized and counselled in vain, as Vrushali's spluttering sobs took on a ferocious intensity.

Then the moment visited Tania. It was identical to the one which had strolled into Rahul's cabin during his crisis of faith about Vrushali's potentially hirsute legs. The moment that demanded to be taken charge of. Quite clearly, these moments had taken to stalking the corridors of YTV frequently.

So Tania said quietly, in a tone that she scarcely recognized herself, 'Vrushali, for the last time, I am sorry for shouting at you. But if you don't stop crying, I will announce a pack up and we will not have a show to put on air. I will deal with the repercussions but we will not shoot today.'

The word 'repercussions' was not part of Vrushali's limited, and largely self-taught, English vocabulary, but she intuitively understood its essence. She stopped crying immediately and said she would be back on the set in ten minutes.

It took a lot longer than that as Sammy, the make-up man, surveyed and fixed the ruin that used to be her make-up. Tania sat numbly, sipping from a tumbler of tea. Vaidehi spent her time texting messages furiously—the teenage state often has the happy condition of being completely cavalier and self centred. Vaidehi showed no guilt for the part she had played in the tragedy of the afternoon.

An hour later, Vrushali breezed in—the emotional and physical ravages of her recent trauma quickly blanked out. It was tougher for Tania who actually had a soul that plumbed to great depths of despondency and then took time to recuperate.

It didn't help that the Jabalpur caller had pretty much had her catharsis in the first aborted call. So the second time round, she didn't shed a single tear and instead sounded fairly cheerful about the fact that her voice would be on television. She said airily, 'I can't tell mummy but maybe my friends can watch. I am so excited.'

The shoot finally ended at 6 am the next morning. Tania could only shoot five episodes instead of the planned seven. But as she crawled into her bed, broken in spirit and body, she found that she was too tired to care.

Just as well because as things turned out in the next few days, sleep would be elusive.

Rahul was thrilled with the first few episodes, with one exception. 'We need to show more thigh. Once the marks go, so do the clothes.' Stetson was still abroad but he had been emailed a few stills of Vrushali along with the promo, and seemed appreciative enough. Like Harish, Rahul too noticed the enhanced bust, and that boosted his confidence in the show. Tania told him that she had personally supervised the silicone gel pads. 'It was a helluva decision. Three cups larger was so in your face and two cups was too subtle. Finally we got it to two and half cups larger.'

'Excellent, Tania. They look real and all credit goes to you,' Rahul said warmly.

Tania blushed. Harish flushed, and forgot to tell Rahul about the part he had played in setting things straight on the weighty matter of Vrushali's bust. He was much too caught up in the embarrassment of being conned by a pair of silicone gel pads. The only consolation was that the rest of randy India would also be taken in by Vrushali's on screen avatar.

Vrushali's off screen avatar though was set to give Rahul some serious heartburn. Rahul's mental faculties, which had initially weakened in the haze of hormones that Vrushali triggered off, were back to normal. That had a lot to with Vrushali metamorphing from a giggly, gushing bimbo to a regular all-purpose pest. As the launch date approached, her phone calls to Rahul became more persistent and petulant. Vrushali was convinced that the channel was not doing enough to publicize the show. The simpering gave way to shrill demands and all attempts at grammar and coherence were abandoned.

'You say me there wills be hoardings and outdoors. Not one poster also you are putting up! I am somebodies in the world but no press on me being on television for the first time.'

Rahul stopped taking her calls, and his standard text template, 'Sorry. In a meeting. Will call later', filled Vrushali's inbox in record time. Three days before the launch, Vrushali stormed into his office, accompanied by her newly appointed publicist-cum-manager, Nair.

Mr Nair was one of the oldest film publicists in Bollywood. At his peak, all A-list Bollywood films had him as the official PRO. But soon BlackBerry-wielding, power dressed celebrity managers left Mr Nair to handle B-grade soaps and Bhojpuri films. Before Vrushali signed on with him, his only other significant client was Charlie Angel. Nair had helped construct Charlie's sob story—he was an orphan who grew up on the Ghats in Varanasi.

The truth was that he was from a middle class family in Meerut, which now wanted nothing to do with him. But Charlie's sensation value was wearing off, and Vrushali as his new client was a godsend and a definite upgrade for Nair. He was determined to make the most of it.

There is a certain stereotype of the old school Bollywood PRO—white safari suit, oiled back hair, folder under arm, fixed broad smile displaying tobacco stains, and addressing everyone as 'Bhai' in tones of ingratiating familiarity; 'Salman Bhai', 'Aamir Bhai', and so on, with the exception of Sanjay Dutt who was destined to be the perennial 'Baba' even if he was pushing sixty. Nair did nothing to bust the stereotype. In fact, it would be accurate to say that he had invented it. He now sat across Rahul's desk looking disconcertingly smug.

Rahul smiled uneasily at Nair after Vrushali airily introduced him as her 'publicity manager'.

Vrushali cooed, 'I know buddy, you are not having enough time—so I am helping you yeah. Mr Nair will get the show all coverage.'

Nair beamed and leaned over on the table. 'Already, Rahul bhai, we have created a tehelka. I have circulated Vrushali's pictures with little bit write up, and sent to all the papers.'

Rahul relaxed visibly and said in a slightly superior tone, 'That is something our corporate communications would have handled. Typically, just a photo and a write up is boring and done to death. A more novel approach

94

is to start the publicity once viewers have sampled the product. But for what it is worth, thank you.'

Vrushali bristled. She hadn't understood much of what Rahul had said, but she instinctively knew when she was being talked down to. She turned to Nair, who was not flustered in the least—he hadn't survived Bollywood for decades without having the hide of many generations of rhinos.

He winked at Rahul. 'You and me, Rahul Bhai, we are thinking just the same. I know what these presswalas want. They want little sensation, and I have sent them such mind blowing photos of Vrushaliji that all will carry and all will watch your show also.'

Vrushali glared defiantly at Rahul and gave him a tight, cold smile. Harish walked in on cue, much to Rahul's relief. He took a deep breath and asked politely, 'What are these mind blowing photos? Ideally we should have sent publicity stills from the show.'

Mr Nair smiled a little too broadly and said, 'Beg your pardon, Rahul Bhai, but photos of Vrushaliji just sitting on sofa who will carry? She is a housewife or what? Like you said, boring and dead!'

Rahul interrupted, 'I said done to death, not dead!'

Harish, who had taken position behind Rahul, sensed his boss' burgeoning panic. He stepped in smoothly, 'Nair Sirji, we are on the same page. But what are these photos? Do you have copies?'

Nair took out his folder and spread half a dozen stills

on the table. There wasn't too much variation in the photos. The setting and pose were identical, only the magnification had changed in a few photos. Rahul and Harish stared at the stills and were left speechless.

Nair cackled. 'I told you they were mind blowing. Sexy but not vulgar, because Nair knows his job. In the industry, you want to be sex symbol—you have to be very careful about image, otherwise no difference from being a junior artist.'

Rahul paid no attention to Nair's rambling. He was completely riveted by Vrushali's stills. In his entire career, he had not come across anything so grotesquely ludicrous. A fully made up Vrushali stood there pouting suggestively at the camera. She was wearing a pair of black skinny jeans and stilettos. She was completely topless, except for a big fish that she strategically held over her breasts.

There was deathly silence in the room. Rahul tried to say something but found that his throat was strangely constricted. Harish gaped. Nair looked smug and Vrushali preened.

This was an opportune moment for Aditya to walk in. Aditya knew Nair well—Nair had worked in turns with Charlie Angel to convince him to sign Charlie on as a show host on YTV. Aditya had no plans of ever enlisting Charlie but found Nair delightfully amusing. He took in the situation in one glance and was happy for the diversion on a slightly dull day.

Aditya picked up the photos and whistled loudly.

'Nairji, this has to be your work. Mind blowing!' Aditya, by virtue of having worked with Bollywood closely, knew that the ultimate accolade there was 'mind blowing'. If it wasn't blowing your mind, it just wasn't good enough.

Nair cackled again in glee. Rahul looked exasperated and Harish glared.

Aditya ignored the latter two and focused totally on Nair. He asked in all seriousness, 'How did you decide on the fish? Super to use it as a prop like this. But why a fish? Why not a hen or a puppy or a kitten?

Nair smiled condescendingly and said, 'It had to be sexy. Kittens and puppies are for kiddie shows. Not for the sex show on YTV.'

Aditya said thoughtfully, 'Yes. Dead fish are known for their sex appeal. Putting an eminently edible fish in front of a woman's prime assets will drive men wild. And the beauty is that you are confusing them—is it lust? Is it hunger? What do they want to grab? The fish or what lies beneath? Even they don't know. What a masterstroke!'

Nair beamed, not understanding a word of what Aditya had just said. 'Yes. Sex show needs different kind of marketing.'

Rahul said quickly, 'Love show not sex show.' His head spun with the imminence of show cause notices from the I & B Ministry. He also day dreamed briefly about giving Aditya a golden handshake, in fact a double impact golden handshake which went right up Aditya's posterior.

Nair leered and said, 'Same thing na, baba. Aditya

Bhai understands. Anybody can send a photo but when Nair sends a photo, people know something explosive is there.'

Aditya gave him a look of deep understanding while Rahul squirmed. He had noticed his demotion from 'Bhai' to 'Baba'. 'How many publications has this gone to?' Rahul asked wearily.

Nair crowed, 'All!'

Rahul looked helplessly at Harish. Harish looked uneasy—the photos had disturbed him profoundly. His insides were a quivering mess. He finally spoke firmly and fiercely, 'Nair sir, I wish you had consulted us before doing this.'

Rahul nodded. He was glad Harish was taking the lead on controlling Nair.

Harish continued, 'How could you? That fish, sir, is of very poor quality. And it's at least two days old. The fish should have been fresh; I could have got you some great deals at Crawford market. Stale fish is a fucking crime.'

Nair was taken aback by the ferocity of the attack. He started to say something but was interrupted by Rahul who was staring in disbelief at Harish. He said, 'Harry, are you fucking insane?'

Aditya stood there expressionlessly; his stomach ached with the effort to curb the laughter that was bubbling up inside.

Harish looked mulish. He said, 'Sir, this fish is not YTV at all. We are upmarket—we should have used pomfret or salmon or something. We have gone and used a SEC D fish – a working class fish; this only low income groups like drivers and maids eat. The brand messaging is all wrong.'

Aditya burst into loud laughter and thumped Harish on his back. 'Bro, just when I think I figured you out, you out do yourself!'

Harish glared at him as he wiped his red, sweaty face. Vrushali twisted her tendrils; this wasn't going as planned.

Nair looked subdued for the first time and said ingratiatingly, 'Sorry, Bhai, it is my mistake. Next time we will use better quality fish. We got this from Dadar market.'

Harish shook in anger, 'From Dadar? We could have gone to the docks and got top quality fish.'

Nair said in a subdued tone, 'My mistake.'

Rahul spoke, exasperation in his voice, 'Next time, just let's approve photographs before we send them out. Please. It is a request.'

A chastened Nair and Vrushali left the room—Aditya asked them to coffee in the cafeteria. He wasn't done with his quota of entertainment yet.

Rahul asked Harish quietly, 'Besides the poor quality fish, you were completely okay with the stills?'

'Sir, all I saw was that stale fish and my blood boiled. YTV sending out stills with poor quality fish is unacceptable,' Harish said heatedly.

Rahul sighed. It was comforting to have a stooge and a yes man at his beck and call but he sometimes wished Harish had at least an iota of grey matter that he could count on sometimes. 'I hope no publication carries those awful photos. And God alone knows what write up he has sent.'

Harish shook his head in distracted fury—his mind was still on the fish.

———

Rahul's wishes came true. No mainline publication carried the photos. One or two tabloids used them in their gossip pages. One serious journal used them to talk about the degeneration of television. To Harish's excruciating relief, no food magazine picked up on the sub standard quality of the fish. So eventually, the photos didn't quite make the 'tehelka' that Nair had predicted. That was reserved for something else altogether because the next day on Haji Ali, flanked by the sea on one side and a bustling mall on the other, there stood a giant sized hoarding of a quasi celebrity, holding a huge SEC D fish. Vrushali Salve made it to a hoarding which was funded by one of her middle-aged 'admirers'. The hoarding bore the legend—Congratulations Vrushali Salve on LOVE CALLS on YTV. Call her on 1800-432-001 (the hotline number).

Rahul had a busy day. It was one day to the launch and his BlackBerry buzzed incessantly. The corporate communications department was miffed about being kept out of the decision to put up a hoarding. The competition was in a flutter—it wasn't like YTV to come up with something so decidedly tacky. Was *Love Calls* a spoof show on dating and phone sex lines? How could they have missed out on something so pivotal happening right under their noses? Dyson made its nth threat to withdraw sponsorship. The Vrushali hoarding had no brand signage or mention of the sponsor. Rahul delegated that particular crisis to Amrit.

Meanwhile the other 'talent' on YTV decided on a show of temperament. Zain refused to show up for his shoot. He was the most popular face on YTV and no one had ever put up a hoarding for him, while the 'dentist's wet dream' (a reference to Vrushali's gummy smile) hogged prime space. Natasha made one of her excursions to Rahul's cabin dressed in her skimpiest denim shorts and a singlet. She played the little girl to the hilt—she pirouetted, pouted, and preened in an effort to win back what she thought was Rahul's lost affection. In normal circumstances, Rahul would have been pleased with the attention but at that point he was trying to cajole Zain to come to the shoot floor and fending off Nair's triumphant texts. So he delegated, with trademark dexterity and Harish Swamy became the willing recipient of Natasha's attentions.

Just when the storm seemed to have abated, it took a turn and turned into a full blown cyclone. On the afternoon of July 31 , there was news that Stree Atyachaar Roko, a Mumbai-based women's rights organization, was all set to move court against the telecast of *Dyson X30 Love Calls* based on the 'objectionable hoarding which was demeaning to women'. Animal rights activists mulled over the rights of the fish and whether its life had been curtailed due to the photo shoot. Fortunately, that remained at the mulling stage unlike the women's activism which resulted in a legal notice. The legal department lumbered into action with an indecipherable counter notice, while Rahul looked for a compromise solution.

As a mere spectator to the drama, Tania had all the time for some armchair pontificating. 'A woman has a right to stand with a fish blocking her breasts if she wants to. Why should her right to do that demean the rights of every other woman? She is a thinking adult and knows what she is doing.'

Aditya, who had taken to hanging around her desk lately, declared firmly, 'You need a break. You just called Vrushali "a thinking adult!"' That put an end to that particular bit of pontificating.

Meanwhile, Rahul managed to black out the hoarding and save all of womankind from abject debasement. That is, all of womankind with the exception of one—Vrushali Salve who cried herself to sleep the night before the launch of her television career. Nair's assurances that this was the start of many big things to come didn't comfort her.

There are not too many times in the history of television that a show gets a unanimous verdict on the first day itself. *Dyson X30 Love Calls* was one of the rare few to have a single united opinion on it.

The show was a complete disaster. Or so the talented temperamental said. The dead fish, they said, had more sex appeal than Vrushali, and could probably give her diction and grammar classes as well. Everyone opined that it was suicidal to put a show on air without first testing the format and screen testing the anchor.

Tania wisely decided to ignore the chatter and thought they should wait for the ratings, which would come in only a week after the first telecast.

Rahul was brainstorming to find a quick fix solution to the ratings disaster that, he was by now quite sure, *Dyson X30 Love Calls* would be. He called a meeting with Tania and his shadow.

'None of the men—and we have horny guys here—find Vrushali sexy. That's the problem,' the furrowed lines on Rahul's forehead grew deeper.

Tania said quietly, 'But you do? Don't you?'

Rahul laughed uneasily. 'I think she'll grow on people. This country is not about subtlety. Make them three cups larger with deeper necklines.'

Tania said pensively, 'These days people get to watch really radical stuff on television—some item queen choosing a husband or some teenager confronting her cheating boyfriend—why would they be interested in some random people blabbing on a phone line about love? It is not Vrushali. Maybe we need to work on our content.'

It was a noteworthy moment. Tania Shah had spoken her first words of any importance in all of her television career.

Harish yawned. Rahul shrugged. The moment passed—its significance lost on everyone, including the speaker.

Rahul said, 'You have too many down market people calling in and they just *sound* ugly as hell. Nobody is interested in the love lives of ugly people on television,' and added with a touch of magnanimity, 'of course they are welcome to fall in love otherwise—no issue with that.'

Harish beamed at his boss' largesse.

'But these are real callers and I think the genuineness of their problems comes through. And oddly, Vrushali reaches out to them,' said Tania.

Rahul said, 'Get better sounding people. Mix it up—a few real callers and a bunch of better sounding people.

You can make-up some exciting problems. Do your casting and get me drama.' He continued reprovingly, 'You know, Tania, half of these issues wouldn't have been there if we had just tested the format with a screen test or a pilot. Plus, her look would have been in place and we could have worked on that ghastly accent. This is a lesson for all of us.'

Harish nodded and looked at Tania pointedly. Tania's heart sank. She knew Rahul had softened the blow by saying 'we' and 'all of us' but he had clearly meant 'you'. She also knew that it was pointless to remind him that those decisions were not taken by her. Bosses and convenient memory lapses were inseparable. And there was no benefit in proving the boss wrong, especially when appraisals were a month away.

'Yes, it's a lesson for all of us. Let's try and fix things in the second schedule,' she said. Her firing squad in the meanwhile took position and looked at her in hope. Tania shook them off with a defiant toss of her head and walked out of the cabin.

Later she complained bitterly to Aditya, 'I told them right in the beginning that we need to have a pilot. I love how it is my fault that we didn't listen to me.'

'Do you have this chain of communication on record?' said Aditya.

Tania said, 'No. I mean how do you do that? These were conversations we had had among ourselves.'

Aditya countered calmly, 'The same way you tried

105

to cover your crisis on the pet show by marking a mail, which should have only been to me, to everyone?'

Tania flushed and instantly denied any such hidden motivations. 'God! Aditya, you know me better than that. If I were that calculating, I wouldn't even be doing a stupid show on pets in the first place!'

Aditya explained. 'Tani, it is not about being calculating. How can you have such selective instinct for self preservation? Your pet had not shown up, my department had goofed up, and you were letting the powers know. You will follow corporate protocol for some silly pet show but when it comes to this make or break show, you will sit back and feel persecuted.'

Tania was annoyed now, partly because there was some truth to what Aditya had just said. She snapped, 'So should I cc all mails to Stetson? Go over Rahul's head? That is a great way of keeping me employed. Thanks!'

'No,' said Aditya, 'you are being dense. Just make sure that the system knows that all of Rahul's decisions are his own and, not yours. If that means having a record of everything, so be it.'

Tania looked pensive and sighed, 'Okay, I'll do what I can. Now I need to figure out my second schedule and get exciting sounding callers.' She brightened slightly. 'Hey! How about you calling in? You will sound upmarket and non-ugly and you can invent any problem. Will you?'

Aditya laughed. 'Sure. I am always game to productively waste time. I would love to.'

The stage was set for another eventful second schedule of *Dyson X30 Love Calls*. This schedule had to go on the floors within four days of the first, as Tania had to build on her bank of episodes. The ratings for the first batch had still not come in.

This time round she commissioned 'speaking parts' to whoever was willing and able within YTV. So from Aditya Menon to Vaidehi to the receptionist Stella, everyone was roped in as love struck and heart sick callers.

It was an unmitigated disaster. Aditya, heartbroken over a two timing girlfriend, laughed heartily in the middle of Vrushali's incoherent ramblings on the healing power of love. Vaidehi sounded sleepy and bored—this when her problem was supposedly that of a physically abusive boyfriend. Tania wished heartily that it were the truth—she would have paid to have Vaidehi pummelled. Only Stella, the middle-aged receptionist, acted her heart out. The only problem being that like all great thespians, she didn't know when to rein herself in.

As Radhika, the girl who discovered her boyfriend was gay but continued to love him, Stella took over the show. She started falteringly with her problem, listened impatiently to Vrushali's vague utterances for all of ten seconds, and ruthlessly cut her out from thereon. She went from being a betrayed lover to theorizing on how sex was not that important in a relationship. Her voice broke and then it took on a firmness of resolve, as she decided that she was going to marry her gay boyfriend.

'After all,' she said with great feeling, 'how many of us marry people who we can talk to and be best friends with?'

It was a surcharged performance, but it reduced Vrushali to the position of a gaping prop on her own show. Tania decided to get back the real callers, but while Vrushali did better with them, it wasn't quite the same. Stella's stellar histrionics had unnerved her and getting back her composure took some time and doing.

If Vrushali's vague love talk was tepid this time round, the smoulder and sizzle department was doing even worse. It wasn't because of lack of effort though. Following instructions to perfection, Vrushali's cleavage was a gaping crevice between two mounds of flesh. Practically the entire length of her legs was on display, and Vrushali trilled happily, 'I am wearing next to nothings yeah!'

But Tania knew by then that even if they divested Vrushali of all her clothes and sat her there, she was not going to be the sex symbol of Rahul's fantasies. She knew that as soon as she had heard the reactions of the male callers—they were all grateful and appreciative, but not one of them had sounded even mildly turned on. None of the mails that came in said anything remotely sexually explicit about Vrushali.

The final and most damning indictment lay hidden in the *Dyson X30 Love Calls* feedback inbox—an email from an eighteen-year-old in Bhopal, which arrived on the morning of the shoot. It said, 'Dear Vrushali didi...'

Tania recoiled from those cruel words. Silicone gel pads, mood lighting, left leg draped over right leg, flash of panty, bronzer—all of that had combined to create *Vrushali didi*?

Ninety-nine percent of the time, you could depend on the Indian male population to be perverts. This one time, they had decided to be perverse.

It was left to the indubitable genius of Aditya to sum up the sorry situation. He cackled with glee and said, 'We wanted a hottie, and we got an aunty.'

Hot or Not?

The ratings surprised everyone. *Dyson X30 Love Calls* was not a blockbuster but it had opened decently. There was a fifteen percent jump in viewership in the 6 pm slot. On a twenty-minute show, the average time spent was six minutes.

'Which is okay,' said Vishal Budhiraja, the head of the strategy team, 'nothing to throw a party about but we can put a little extra sugar and cream in our coffee.'

He laughed approvingly at his own joke. Rahul and Harish joined in. A year back, forget laughing at his feeble jokes, not too many people would have known what Vishal Budhiraja sounded or even looked like. He was the most nondescript of men, and he liked being nondescript, at least for the most part of his thirty-four years he had been happily reconciled to an existence where nobody paid him the slightest attention.

But since Rahul's rise to eminence a year back, Vishal's fortunes had changed radically. Rahul put great store by Vishal's number crunching abilities, and refused to take a single programming decision without consulting him. Viewership data, gross rating points, stickiness of content, reach, penetration—Vishal could glean all this information just by running his eye over excel sheets containing numbers.

To say then that Vishal's status was rather exalted in the scheme of things would be a gross understatement. To say that Vishal was many things at different times— harbinger of happiness, prophet of doom, and general all purpose oracle—would still be an understatement, but closer to the truth. His pronouncement on Love Calls' above average performance lifted Rahul's spirits.

Rahul said hopefully. 'Should we make a presentation for the board?'

'A lot of the walk-ins may be because of the novelty factor. This was an absolutely dead slot with negligible content. We have something that has rated slightly higher than the ads that played out at the slot earlier—I would think it too premature to make a presentation. But I'd be glad to help if you need to,' said Vishal.

Rahul said quickly. 'No. Without you totally convinced I don't want to do it. Let's wait then.'

Vishal felt a rush of power and smiled placidly at Rahul. To Rahul, Vishal was the human embodiment of the ratings—he cared little for his powers of perception, cognition, and interpretation. But Vishal, of course, couldn't tell the difference, and the last year at YTV had been an edifying one for him.

Rahul walked out of Vishal's cubicle—the ratings had emboldened him to meet Bose, who was waiting. Ever since the launch of the show, this was a meeting that Rahul had tried to put off. He hadn't wanted to deal with Bose's constant air of slightly sneering condescension—not when *Love Calls* looked all set to be a massive flop.

But it wasn't a massive flop and therefore Rahul greeted Bose cheerfully enough. 'Hey there, Bose. Good set of launch numbers for Love Calls. Better than expected.'

'You're happy with a marginal jump of fifteen percent?' Bose said coolly.

'Well, yes, considering you fuckers had written it off completely,' Rahul said defensively.

Bose said, 'I never wrote it off. We haven't even spoken about the show after the launch.'

Tania who had also been called in for the meeting looked surprised, but said nothing. She was on her guard—none of her earlier shows had ever merited a meeting with Bose.

Rahul acknowledged the truth of the statement. He had taken considerable effort to avoid Bose post the launch. 'Yes, been really caught up. Internally, the feedback was quite bad but I am happy you liked the show,' he said genially.

Bose said, 'I never said I liked it.'

Rahul squashed the irritation he felt but before he could say anything further, Tania surprised herself by stating coldly, 'Maybe we should talk about the show once you have resolved your feelings about it. Your feelings seem to be rather multi-layered and complex. Once you have managed to distill them, and break them down into simple, understandable emotions such as like and dislike, maybe then we can resume this discussion about *Love Calls*.'

Tania was in a cold fury. Most people when furious cursed, shouted, or raved and ranted. Some women were also known to vent their spleen in torrential tears. Not Tania. When Tania was furious, she spoke in chaste English. And she spoke in paragraphs.

Bose smouldered. His intense gaze was on Tania's slightly flushed face. She thought he was furious, and the initial bravado, spurred by anger, crumbled. She was off the mark; Bose was furiously in love. He had finally found what would complete him. That which would stir a soul which so far had obstinately refused to be stirred, leaving him to despair that he perhaps had none. He was struck by the intensity of her fury and the innate nobility in it. She was supremely lofty in her anger.

While Bose strung together an ode to Tania in his head, Rahul caught on. Not to the lyrical longing of Bose's thoughts, but to the rather basic emotion that governed all such thoughts. He thought to himself, 'Bose has the hots for Tania!'

Rahul was not a romantic like Bose but he was incurably randy. After all, Rahul understood the hegemony of hormones in the constitution of all men. Of course, he would have phrased it differently. He would have said, 'All men are horny.'

Bose recovered from his momentary stupor and said quietly, 'I don't think the show is working in its current format, but it could work if we tweak it. However, I don't mean to interfere so I'll keep my suggestions to myself.'

Tania, realizing that she was risking alienating the demi god of the talented temperamental, said, 'No. Please carry on,' and threw in a smile.

Bose was transfixed but to his credit, he showed no change in expression. Instead he said to Rahul, 'Vrushali is no sex symbol. She won't turn on a light switch.'

Rahul spluttered. He looked at Tania for support, but Tania was suddenly very pre-occupied with the paperweight lying on Rahul's table.

Bose continued, 'But I have noticed that people seem to want to talk to her. They reach out to her.'

'Okay?' said Rahul testily.

Just then Harish walked in after an extended loo break. No one paid him any attention as he plonked himself on one of the chairs. He looked at Bose curiously.

Bose ran his fingers through his close cropped hair and said, 'We haven't got reality right yet. None of our reality shows have clicked.'

Rahul interrupted, 'Yes, but with the life swap show, we'll probably fix that. Anyway, what does reality have to do with *Love Calls*?'

Bose said nothing. He narrowed his eyes and stared

into the distance. That look always worked for him; it made him look every bit of the intensely creative whiz kid he was touted to be. He knew that and held on to the look for a fraction of a second more than necessary. The extra effort was for Tania—it always impressed the women.

Tania would have been impressed but she was far too busy being relieved. She was glad that she wasn't the one breaking the news about Vrushali's non-existent sex appeal to Rahul. Bose noticed the lack of reaction or at least the reaction he was hoping for and perversely fell deeper in love. He continued, 'Before the life swap show, which is our big ticket, goes on, we should and could try out some reality on *Love Calls*.'

Harish decided he needed to contribute to this conversation. He stated most intelligently, 'Whatever we do let us make sure that brand YTV is intact.'

Bose said impatiently, 'Real people, real situations. Get people in the studio with Vrushali. Let them break down there. Call their partners on the show—get conflict. Make it edgy and intense.'

Rahul listened intently. Harish tried to read his expression and pre-empt his thoughts but Tania broke the silence and said, 'That's great but isn't that another show altogether? We're supposed to be this flirty, naughty, light-hearted show—that, at least, is the brand personality I have been given to understand.'

'Sure, but the flirty naughty thing with the hottie is

not really working. TV is about constant change. Seduce your viewer with something new each time,' said Bose.

'Within one week of the launch of the show, we go from naughty hottie to Oprah? Isn't that too much of a paradigm shift?' said Tania.

For a minute, the use of the words 'paradigm shift' almost led the three gentlemen in the room to believe that they were making something worthwhile. Creating, in fact, a legacy of enduring television. But Rahul quickly dispelled the illusion with a chuckle, 'Fucking morons watch TV. They are not going to care how the show changes as long as they like what they see.'

Tania held her ground. 'Even if there has been just a fifteen percent jump in viewing, it is a jump. Can't we just fine tune the format instead of experimenting with it immediately?'

Rahul said slightly impatiently, 'The deal is to pre-empt the viewer; Don't let him settle down into a pattern. Hook him with something new each time. Titillate the fuckers so much that they keep coming back for more. I think Bose has a point there.'

'So now?' asked Tania.

Bose took charge. 'Get real people in the studio.'

Tania spoke slowly. 'Except that Dyson X30 is paying us a lot of money to get Vrushali to call people using their handset.'

Harish had been out of the conversation for far too long and he felt every second of his diminishing clout.

So he rushed in with a suggestion. He said eagerly, 'We can give Vrushali one handset and the case study another one. They can sit side by side and talk to each other on the phones. Dyson will be happy—we are using two handsets instead of one.'

Rahul burst out laughing. 'Brother, your sense of the ridiculous rocks. No one can ever tell when you are joking.'

Harish felt ridiculous; he hadn't been joking but he played along by grinning proudly. Tania felt obliged to laugh too, which she did politely. Bose, under no such obligation, just looked impatient.

He turned to Tania and said, 'I'm not suggesting that you get only real people in the studio. Mix it up. Get some real people and some callers.'

Tania looked at Rahul, 'And when people come into the studio, should she try to seduce them?'

Rahul laughed uneasily, 'Subtly.'

'I thought people in this country don't get subtlety,' said Tania.

Rahul pretended that he hadn't heard that.

'You know like when she is leaning over to maybe hold someone's hand to comfort them, if there is a glimpse of cleavage that will comfort the fucker even more,' Harish interjected helpfully.

Tania suddenly spoke with a glimpse of dormant humour. 'Maybe she can hold his hand to her heart and say "I feel your pain". She can feel his pain; he can feel something else! I guarantee he will forget his pain completely. Which reminds me, I am the one who is going to be looking for him, so do excuse me.' She laughed darkly and left the room.

Harish said to no one in particular, 'Surprising how so not hot Vrushali is. The packaging is all there but she doesn't turn you on.'

Bose narrowed his eyes and stared at Tania's retreating back in brooding longing.

The Hairstyle has
an Idea

Tania had a new assistant.

A young associate producer fresh off the boat from Chandigarh, Mohit was outsourced to her from the ranks of the talented temperamental. Bose had hired him purely on instinct. Like all creative geniuses, Bose had his quota of whimsical hires—all based on some intangible 'something'. Mohit had the good fortune to fashion his mop of hair into an unsightly Mohawk before he had come along to meet Bose. And Bose believed that men capable of hairstyling quirks were men out of the ordinary. The propensity to experiment with one's hair showed an inventive mind—a mind that was keen to think out of the box. Rahul had also endorsed his choice, and said that indeed Mohit *looked* like a lateral thinker. Of course, the only lateral thinker in the scheme of things was Mohit's hair stylist who, on a whim, had snipped his hair off much to his horror. But no one needed to know that, not when the Mohawk was the key to getting him the job.

Tania suspected that, in fact, the Mohawk was his only talent. In his two months at YTV, he had acquired a reputation of being a motor mouth and the nickname Mohawk. And precious else. But since the logistics on *Dyson X30 Love Calls* were steadily becoming more complicated, Tania was glad of *any* help that came her way. She put Mohawk in charge of getting real life case studies on the show. With Vaidehi to help him out, it was a combination destined for disaster.

Vaidehi stormed out in two days declaring frostily that she refused to be an intern to a person who was not fit enough to be *her* intern. Mohawk preached to Tania on the dangers of cultivating pesky juniors. 'You must,' he said, 'keep them in their place right from the beginning,' and then resolutely stonewalled any attempt by Tania to follow his advice.

Tania told Aditya half laughing, 'The problem is that he doesn't think he is a junior. He thinks he's a trouble shooter sent to bail me out, so all he does is tell me what I should and should not be doing.'

Tania also stumbled upon Mohawk's secret ambition. The reason why he showed no inclination or aptitude for television production was simply because the only side of the camera that Mohawk was interested in was the front. Yet another small town aspirant with hopes of television stardom!

So everything Mohawk did was with the purpose of fulfilling that ambition. 'And,' Tania said in disbelief, 'he

does it with the subtlety of a—how do you say it— yes…
sledgehammer. The other day he told me that we should
balance out Vrushali with a male presence, and then
went on to describe how this male host should look…'

Aditya interrupted, 'Let me guess, the presence of a
Mohawk was an important physical prerequisite for this
male host?'

Tania said drily, 'Genius, how did you ever guess!'

The two of them burst out laughing.

Bose watched them with a growing sense of discomfort.
He wondered how Tania could encourage the friendship
of a shallow hustler like Aditya. He decided to improve
her mind and her friend circle. Unaware of the plans
being hatched for her redemption, Tania smiled across at
him and Aditya waved jauntily. He ignored both of them
and walked past.

Tania looked after him in surprise. 'He just looked
through us. Back to being his snobbish self, I see.'

Aditya said, 'But only after he had had a good look at
you, darling.'

Tania said hastily, 'Don't be silly. I'm not his type. I
don't wear eyebrow rings and my hair is not coloured. But
honestly, he's been rather helpful on *Love Calls*. I mean,
I'm sure he thought lending me Mohawk would help.'

'Well, I wonder why he's being so helpful. It can't be
because of his regard for Harish,' Aditya said in mock
seriousness. Tania said nothing but felt her cheeks grow
warm. 'So tell me this,' said Aditya looking at Tania's tell

tale blush. 'The resident heartthrob of YTV clearly has a thing for you and you are totally unaffected by it?'

Tania blustered, 'Why is that so hard to believe? He's not some Greek god.'

'No,' countered Aditya coolly, 'but I know you, Tani. You are not some hardnosed, detached ice maiden, and such intensity of attention is quite flattering.'

Tania flushed and said reluctantly, 'Yes, well, it is flattering. But I don't want to be flattered into doing something stupid.'

'Has Bose proposed something stupid that you might be considering?' asked Aditya, a little too quickly.

Tania said in a rush of confusion, 'He hasn't...I haven't, I mean not in that way. Shut up, Aditya!'

'Sweetie, don't play dumb. The only problem is that you won't have him with only smiles for too long. Sooner or later he'll expect more action! Quite distasteful but it beats sleeping with Harish. That won't get you anywhere,' said Aditya in an exaggerated drawl.

Tania laughed and punched him on his arm, 'Stop sounding like you're in some B-grade film. Hate to disappoint you but I don't intend to sleep with either. Bose is just being helpful and I would never need to sleep with Harish. Sex is not a priority for him, not when he can have butter chicken.'

'Rahul then? He'll give you a power point proposition and ask you to power his points,' Aditya said smoothly.

'Ugh! How vulgar you are!'

'Thank you! I work hard on it.' Aditya winked at her.

Tania walked off, wondering when she would ever be able to tell when Aditya was being flippant or serious. Was there an off chance that he was bothered by Bose's interest in her? And why should that bother her? Just that she liked being friends with him and didn't want to lose out on that. YTV would be a dreary place without Aditya's wisecracks. As for Bose, life was much too complicated to deal with him at the moment.

Right now the more immediate concern was to get hold of Mohawk.

Only two days remained to the shoot, and not a single lovelorn case study, willing to be on camera, had been found. Tania was worried.

When Tania found Mohawk, he had his legs propped up on the hotline desk and was guzzling a chocolate milk shake, gabbing away with his girlfriend back home in Chandigarh. He waved at Tania and continued to exchange inanities over the phone. Tania no longer saw the humour in the situation. She went across to him and pulled out the wire from the phone. Mohawk sat up and said defensively, 'I was going to hang up. Just two minutes more. It's not easy being alone in this city. You need some time off for your family—'

Tania interrupted, 'I can't imagine they miss you much. Have we found even one guy willing to come on TV for the show? Or girl? A guy is preferable for the chemistry with Vrushali but we'll even settle for a girl.'

Mohawk looked at Tania triumphantly, 'We found a guy.'

Tania said excitedly, 'That's great. Get him over tomorrow, we'll see how TV friendly he is and prep him.'

'Oh, he's very TV friendly, very photogenic, and talks well,' said Mohawk.

Tania suddenly had a dreadful suspicion. She hoped she was wrong. 'Does the case study have a Mohawk by any chance?' she asked hesitantly.

Mohawk grinned. 'Right you are!'

'Look here, I am not in the mood for a joke. Cut it out. Let's get back on the phone. We only have a day now,' glowered Tania.

'I'm not joking. Why can't I go on? Give me any love problem, and I'll do it. I'll fake it. I have no issues about it. That is the least I can do for the channel if it needs me to do it,' he pleaded.

Tania said mock appreciatively, 'You are doing this for the channel? That is really selfless.'

'Why else? Why would I want to be on air looking like some ass who needs love advice from a girl? But hell, I'm small fry compared to what this can do for the channel. Bose sir wants reality and I'll give it my best shot,' Mohawk said righteously.

Tania looked at him levelly. 'Will you take up any love problem?'

Mohawk bobbed his head in all earnestness. 'Anything!'

'That's generous of you. You're on then. Your problem will be erectile dysfunction. You haven't been able to tell your girlfriend, but you can't get it up and she is getting impatient for some action.'

Mohawk paled. 'I can't do that!'

Tania said quietly. 'Think of the channel. We will make a promo around it.'

Mohawk said something incoherent. Tania suspected it was a suppressed expletive. She was enjoying herself now.

She said helpfully. 'We can blur your face.'

He said weakly, 'That won't help me,' and then groaned, realizing that he had almost given away his master plan of making that glorious television debut, which would be his ticket to being discovered. A lovesick case study was admittedly not terribly glorious but he had planned a noble, heroic role for himself—a man who had lost the girl he loved in an accident, and just couldn't get over her. Erectile dysfunction somehow didn't fit into this potential tearjerker. It wasn't noble or heroic enough.

He tried his luck one last time. 'Can't I play a guy who has lost his girlfriend in an accident and can't find love again? People will cry.'

Tania said thoughtfully, 'You could. That is a nice touch.'

Mohawk looked relieved and said, 'I will do a good job—'

Tania cut in. 'The trauma has given you erectile dysfunction. I think that's super!'

125

Mohawk gaped speechlessly.

'It'll help the channel. Thank you, Mohawk. It's brave of you. I'll get the stylist to give you a nice, cool look. You may have erectile dysfunction, but you still need to be well dressed—golden rule of television,' said Tania as she walked out on a spluttering Mohawk.

On her way out Tania bumped into Harish who asked her, 'Any luck on studio guests? Found any?'

Tania smiled grimly, 'We haven't yet. But we will now.'

In the next hour, studio guests miraculously lined up for *Love Calls*. And at the end of the day, Tania was in the happy situation of having three confirmed guests. She then told Mohawk, 'Great, we have at least three case studies. But none of them is even half as exciting as your erectile dysfunction problem.'

Mohawk blubbered, 'B-but with these new case studies, you don't need me anymore.'

'The more the better, and with you, we can script things completely. It may be fun.'

'I'd rather help you on the shoot. Don't want to be distracted,' Mohawk said shakily.

Tania pretended to consider it deeply and then finally after a few tense (for Mohawk) moments sighed, 'I guess you are right. We are getting in guests for the first time… will need you to handle them. If we run short of guests in the next schedule, you can come in.'

Tania was not usually clairvoyant, but one thing she

could see clearly in—she was not going to ever run out of guests on *Dyson X30 Love Calls* as long as Mohawk continued on the show.

She ran into Aditya and told him without stopping, 'I'm turning into you! I am getting cheap thrills!'

Aditya smiled back. 'There is hope then.'

Things were falling into place for the third schedule of *Dyson X30 Love Calls*. In the meantime, the second week's ratings had come in. The show had not dropped but there was no spike in the ratings. The surprise success of the season for YTV was another new show—the low budgeted and zilch publicized show on celebrity pets. This show had twice the ratings of *Dyson X30 Love Calls*.

The Indian television audience had evolved—it preferred watching cocker spaniels get a pedicure to a semi nude siren on a couch. Tania took this sudden coming of age of TV audiences with her usual stoicism, and directed her energies on *Love Calls*. She was unusually hopeful of the reality factor swinging things for the show.

One of her guests, at least, was a winner—Prem, a baby-faced boy, whose skin was marked by the ravages of over active sebaceous glands and his soul, by the ravages of an over active romantic disposition. He wore his heart on his sleeve, his collar, and on his shoelaces. Prem also had the delightful ability to start crying almost at will, with heart rending, gasping sobs torn out from his inner core. The first time he met Tania, within a minute into his story of heartbreak, he sobbed his heart out. Tania scared that he would exhaust all his tears off camera, did her best to divert him. But she needn't have worried because Prem had an inexhaustible source of tears and didn't need too much stimulus. He even cried when the pantry boy asked him how much sugar he wanted in his coffee.

This ability made up for the otherwise mundane nature of his story—his girlfriend kept breaking up with him, and this time round it seemed like it was finally over. She had stopped taking his calls and deleted him from her Facebook friend list. In a seemingly irrevocable move, she had also changed her relationship status to 'Single' on her Facebook page. That had led Prem's fragile heart to finally break. He wanted to be on the show so that he could beg her on national television to take him back. And so when Prem took his place next to Vrushali on the couch, the stage was set for a potential melodrama.

Except that when the lights came on and Vrushali, a vision in white silk and bronzed flesh, began speaking to Prem, he transformed into a coherent, poised, dry-eyed boy. He narrated his story of heart break and betrayal in a matter of fact way, and even rounded off the story by saying that if his girlfriend didn't want him back, now was as good a time as any to declare that he, too, was single. After that, he smiled appreciatively at Vrushali, who laughed coquettishly back at him.

Tania called for a cut. She rushed across to Prem and

said that his being so unemotional and matter of fact would not get his girlfriend back.

Prem who was beginning to feel very much at home on the sets confided to Tania, 'Suddenly, I don't feel so sad anymore.'

Tania hissed, 'That's fine but if you want other girls to feel sorry for you, you can't be so casual. You have to show some emotion.' She wished she could shake him hard and make him cry, but resisted the urge. She limited herself to whispering furiously in Vrushali's ear, 'You have to make him cry.'

Fortunately for all concerned, Prem finally did cry. The trigger was unexpected and came at a time when Tania had nearly given up on him shedding a single tear.

After a series of questions that got the most placid responses, Vrushali asked Prem what his ex girlfriend's favourite song was. He sniffed suddenly and said shakily, '*My heart will go on* from *Titanic*.' His eyes became watery and he said, 'We would go to Bandstand, stand on the rocks in that *Titanic* pose, and she would sing for me.'

Vrushali spurred by an unexpected intuitive genius said softly, 'You want to show me how yeah?'

Prem's gangly frame was now racked by sobs. He stood up and pulled Vrushali to her feet, and stood behind her with his arms outstretched, tears running down his face. Vrushali extended her arms out and sang completely off tune, and a little too cheerily given the sombre nature of the situation. 'My heart will go onnnnnn...' she sang full throatedly. Prem winced and sobbed some more. Tania exhorted the cameraman to take close shots of his face. Mohawk bit on his finger nails to clamp down the lump in his throat.

Then Vrushali said, 'Let's call your girlfriend only on my Dyson X30.'

Prem was too overwrought to speak. The girlfriend came on the line, and Prem spoke to her breaking down every two seconds. He went down on his knees and said, 'Please, baby, please come back.'

The girlfriend was resolute in not wanting to renew the relationship. She said impatiently, 'I have even changed it on Facebook. Too much trouble now to change it again.'

Prem sobbed furiously.

Vrushali said quietly, 'Okay, one last time you will be singing for him yeah? My heart will goes on...nothings for you, but making him so happy yeah.'

The girl, quite chuffed with the possibility of her singing ability being discovered on national television, happily obliged.

So she sang, 'Once more you open the door and you will see, my heart will, my heart will go onnnnnnn...'

Prem said emotionally, 'All doors are closed,' and buried his face in Vrushali's lap and wept. Vrushali's left strap slipped and her dress hitched up, revealing her right thigh as she leaned over to comfort him. The silicone gel pads rose to the occasion.

On the sidelines of the shoot, Mohawk wept and ogled with equal intensity.

Tania took a deep breath and she declared hoarsely, 'If after all this, people still prefer to watch dogs being shampooed—I can't do anything!'

Enter the Nation

Not very far away from the YTV office, the newsroom of YNN—short for Your News Now—was buzzing with activity. The fact in itself was not remarkable as newsrooms are prone to buzzing. No self respecting newsroom would call itself one if people didn't sprint across it perpetually or constantly yell at each other across it. But today, the buzz was more in the nature of stage whispers. And the subject of that buzz was Rajneesh Tiwari—the forty-something, managing editor of YNN, its primetime anchor, and best known face—also known as 'the nation' to YNN insiders for reasons that will soon unfold.

'So,' said Vaibhav Trivedi the head of the night desk, 'is it my imagination or is the mood of the nation a tad subdued today?'

'Subdued?' scoffed Akruti, the studio producer. 'The nation is in depression. He let Neha read out more than just the break links. You should have seen her face…joy, pure joy.'

The condition called megalomania is rife in the news sector. It afflicts most news editors because the poor souls, in the process of reporting the news, often assume that they are, in fact, the news. As a breed then, editors live and breathe in the rarefied clime of self importance, which nurtures their egos to unmanageable levels of obesity. Megalomania therefore is an acceptable occupational hazard in the business of news dispersal.

But Rajneesh Tiwari took the phenomenon to a complete new level—he extrapolated his feelings, emotions, and desires on to a whole nation. So if Rajneesh was angry, the headline through the day would read 'Nation outraged'. If Rajneesh was sad, the 'nation was numbed'. If Rajneesh was constipated, the 'nation was frustrated'. Of course, valid enough 'newsy' reasons were always found for the varying mood changes of the nation, but the fact was that the mood of the nation, on any given day, depended hugely on Rajneesh's mood when he woke up in the morning.

Today, the nation was unusually mellow. Rajneesh had been rather pensive through his flagship primetime show at 10 pm. The show, 'The Mood of the Nation', was the definitive last word on current affairs in the country, and Rajneesh ensured that no one else got in a word. Not his impressive panel of guests and definitely not his ever-changing co-anchors.

Rajneesh was very clear about the job description of his co-anchor on the show—a decorative prop who would

133

read out the break links—except that this job description was never spelt out. It was left to the co-anchors to find out by and by. They did always find out though, and would soon quit the show and the channel in a huff.

His current co-host, the lovely Neha Chitre, suffered from no such inconvenient ideological hang ups. She was in the right place at the right time. After the defection of his second anchor in the space of six months, Rajneesh noticed the pretty young intern with her peaches and cream complexion and jet black hair. The dimple that appeared at the groove of her mouth tilted the scales completely in her favour. She also had some sort of journalism degree but that wasn't important to Rajneesh. Neha was not too sold on being a journalist, but she had always wanted to be an anchor. In Neha, Rajneesh found the ideal foil.

Of course, Neha's sudden elevation and obvious good looks did give rise to some degree of speculation on the nature of her relationship with Rajneesh. But this speculation was unfounded and baseless, pretty much like most of the news on YNN. As Vaibhav, the cynical newshound of many years said, 'Rajneesh is so into himself that he prefers masturbation. The man is in love, and lust, only with himself.'

Truth be told, Rajneesh had no time or inclination for affairs of the heart or hormones. He had a wife and a daughter tucked away and each had their functional utility. His wife made sure he ate just right—the right proportions of carbohydrates and proteins were carefully calculated by her for his daily dietary intake. And the daughter gave Rajneesh someone else to love besides himself. He adored her primarily because she was an extension of his impressive genes.

Today, Rajneesh was pensive and perturbed. It had been a month and he had not been able to find a 'driver' story. The success of YNN was largely due to the 'driver' story formula; a story with an emotional hook that drove the fortunes (read ratings) of the channel. A story that was over and above the regular news mix—politicians going on rath yatras, the budget, the Indian cricket team—all of these regulation stories were given the Rajneesh Tiwari spin. Emotionally over-pitched rabble rousing, with the right degree of righteous incredulity thrown in. Rajneesh had got his delivery just right—he always sounded like the voice of God as he thundered impressively every night: 'Let us ask ourselves today, does Dhoni deserve the trust of the nation?' 'Can India handle another ostentatious political gimmick?' 'Is the nation's blood boiling?' 'What, Mr Finance Minister, are you doing to make my home loan easier? The nation is asking you today.'

Rajneesh made news on YNN a personal crusade. Old fashioned journalistic attributes such as objectivity and detached reportage were anathema to the functioning of YNN. Rajneesh often declared, 'We are a fast-paced, aggressive news channel and we set the agenda for the nation.'

The nation seemed quite happy outsourcing its agenda to Rajneesh Tiwari, given the success of YNN. It was also fortunate that the nation had lax libel laws and lumbering litigation, which meant that YNN's heady mix of drama, emotion, and minimal facts went unchecked. It was among the top two English news channels in the nation, but was in a neck to neck battle with its competitor. Rajneesh wanted a knockout blow—a story that would hook the nation and take him far ahead of the competition. His obsession with finding that one story, on which he could whip up emotion and sentiment, had whipped him up into quite a frenzy.

He had convened an editorial meeting earlier in the day with his think tank but it was an exercise in futility. The think tank had gotten so used to being told what to think that any attempt now at independent thought was destined to tank. Finally at the end of a three-hour meeting, Suketu, his deputy news editor, said hopefully, 'Maybe some other kid will fall into a pit.'

Rajneesh scowled. 'And nobody will give a rat's ass. The first time that Prince fell, it was full on drama. But now kids keep falling down pits and people tune off. It has to be something new and controversial.'

The meeting dispersed with no resolution in sight.

Rajneesh wracked his brains after his show was done; maybe a story from the world of entertainment. The nation was filmstar struck. But what? He knew it was pointless to summon his entertainment editor, Surbasree

Mandal. She wasn't just a recruitment mistake, she was a recruitment disaster.

Surbasree Mandal was a certified flake, and she also had the ability to unnerve him. The silly girl had no sense of news. He recalled his last conversation with her. He had asked her what was new and interesting in the world of cinema and Surbasree had smiled and answered, 'The Pan India hit is dead. Multiplexes have so fragmented the audience that in C class centres there are no new Hindi film releases. A lot of the people there have no clue who Hrithik Roshan is because they only watch Mithun re-runs. Fascinating, no?'

Rajneesh didn't think it was fascinating. He thought it had the ability to put the nation to sleep. 'What about Chandralekha's marriage being on the rocks?'

Surbasree looked at him steadily. 'Is Chandralekha a friend of yours?'

Rajneesh laughed. 'Sure, the superstar of the '90s who moved to England after her marriage will definitely be a friend of one lowly journalist. I don't have your contacts, sweetheart.'

'Then how do you know that her marriage is on the rocks?' she had asked disinterestedly

'It was in the papers how she had admitted her children in a play school in India during her summer holiday here.'

Surbasree laughed, 'Papers or tabloids? And putting them in a play school means there are cracks in the marriage? A lot of people on a longish holiday do that. Plus, even if the marriage was on the rocks, why should we care?'

'Because you are an entertainment journalist!' An exasperated Rajneesh had spluttered.

Surbasree said calmly, 'Sure, but I didn't sign up to be the paparazzi,' and then she walked out on him.

No, thought Rajneesh, those would definitely be the wrong quarters to requisition for a burning hot, sensational story. Something will come up, he hoped as he left for the day.

And something did come up; from the unexpected quarters of Neha Chitre.

Every night after the primetime bulletin, Neha would call her boyfriend Biplab in Delhi. Biplab and Neha had studied in the same journalism college. Neha was the prettiest girl in the batch and he was the cleverest student. It was an unlikely coupling but Neha was smitten by Biplab because he had never paid her the slightest attention.

On the few occasions that they had spoken, he had talked about Chomsky and manufacturing consent. About how America had perpetrated lies to carry out the horrific bombing of Hiroshima. Neha, whose worldview till then was confined to her pretty little toes, was totally taken in. The truth was that Biplab was like any other slightly precocious journalism student spouting borrowed wisdom, but Neha didn't know that. To her, he was someone whose life was governed by a larger purpose, and the fact that he took time out for something as trifling as her affections won him her devotion.

Biplab's motivations were easy to read too. Men with larger purposes often have egos that match the purpose in size. Biplab revelled in having a trophy girlfriend like Neha. He liked the envy her presence on his arm aroused, more so because she had eyes only for his smarmy and not very likeable self. He strengthened her devotion by treating her with a mix of condescension and indulgent affection.

Today as usual, Neha called him at eleven fifteen, right after the primetime show. Biplab let his phone ring about six times and then drawled, 'Child, you actually spoke on today's show. Viewers must have been happy to know you have a voice too.'

Neha laughed. 'Yes, but for some reason, the boss was off colour.'

'But how long are you going to be happy doing this? Sitting like a dummy next to him?' Biplab asked seriously.

Neha turned defensive. 'Not everyone gets primetime visibility so soon...and I have. I thought you would be happy. You know I don't want to save the world like you. I'm not made that way.'

Biplab scoffed, 'Don't be such a dunce, child. What is the point of being a pretty, empty headed thing on a news channel? You should have become a veejay or something.

139

You know, like on that awful channel YTV, where they have this model type chick, Vrushali something, in hot pants, crossing her legs. At least she is making more money than you.'

Neha was surprised. 'You watch YTV?'

'No, lady, have you heard of a phenomenon called channel surfing? Also there is no harm in consuming products of mass culture from time to time. Anyway, the point is that it would not be farfetched to equate you with that Vrushali chick on YTV at this time,' Biplab bristled.

Neha was hurt. It wasn't the first time that Biplab had talked down to her, but being equated with some scantily clad tart on a trashy channel was a first.

The rest of their conversation was a blur for her—Neha was suddenly determined to watch this Vrushali girl on YTV. Neha, like most women stupidly in love, was masochistic. She wanted to see Vrushali for herself; so that she could cry herself to sleep over the deep injury her Biplab had done her. She wanted to magnify the hurt and let it eat away at her—she liked the concept of being in a complicated, layered relationship as opposed to all her teenage romances. This was all so adult.

So Neha made it a point to tune into *Dyson X30 Love Calls—Are you hot enough?*

'Incest,' declared Rahul, thumping his table. 'That's what we need. That'll do the trick.'

Harish wasn't quite sure what Rahul was proposing this unnatural deviance for, but he would not deviate from his natural instinct to agree instantly with anything that Rahul said. So he agreed immediately—yes, incest should be the order of the day. In fact, if Rahul wanted to push for legislation that decreed incest mandatory, he would be there by his side to lobby for it. Of course, he didn't say all of this—everything was implicit in his vigorous nod.

The ratings for the third week of *Love Calls* were in and they had gone up marginally. The show was not a washout and, in fact, optimists would even call it a semi-hit. But the managing board of YTV was not made up of optimists, and Rahul knew that they would probably call it a semi flop.

Tania roused herself from the inertia she was feeling

and managed a slightly curious expression and repeated, 'Incest?'

Her heart should have been sinking at this dire utterance, but after the Prem fiasco, her heart was no longer in the show. Or, for that matter, in anything at all. She was a listless being who wafted across the corridors of YTV. This doomed show; nothing ever went right on it.

As was expected, the Prem episode had got in the eyeballs and the emotion. In the office itself, Tania had noticed usually blasé YTV employees in tears. Prachi, the head of studio production, was still wiping tears when she came up to her after the show. She gasped, 'Tania, what a killer episode! Absolutely super! When the two of them stood up together and sang, I almost peed in my pants!' And she laughed hysterically again, like the rest of the office, which had had an orgy of mad mirth through the show. Tania noticed with grim amusement that Mohawk laughed the maximum and the loudest.

If the aim was extreme emotion, *Love Calls* had definitely scored with the Prem episode. 'But,' as Aditya told Tania, 'you shouldn't get too anal and go about classifying the emotion. You wanted a reaction and you got one. Now don't get greedy and dictate what the reaction should be. Plus, the best thing about ratings is that while they may be completely illogical, they are also pretty emotion neutral. They will just tell you how a thing rated, not why it rated the way it did. So, there's no need to get pissed off if Prachi can't hold her piss.'

Tania stopped being cut up about Prachi's urinary incontinence and saw the eminent logic in what Aditya had to say. She reconciled herself, with a fair degree of equanimity, to the episode which she had dubbed 'The Prem Affair'. The mood continued into the next day when she breezed into Harish's workstation. 'Great reactions to "The Prem Affair". You caught it?' she asked pleasantly.

That was when Rahul had thumped his desk and brought up the issue of incest. Tania repeated quizzically, 'Incest?'

Rahul had a distinct gleam in his eye now and spoke in low, excited tones. 'Losers who want to get it on with the neighbour's daughter. We want reality. Let's go dark—extreme and edgy. Incest, paedophilia. Let's get the bastards on. We shock people with really hardcore stuff.'

'On the same set with the same host?' Tania asked.

Rahul snapped, 'Yes. Is there a problem?'

Tania said with a flash of irritation, 'So on a show called *Love Calls* you have Mr Paedophile walk in. Vrushali flashes cleavage. He tells her he likes little children, so not to bother. And she says what precisely, then?'

Rahul gestured impatiently, but Tania was now on a roll. She continued in a very passable imitation of Vrushali, 'Loves is love yeah, buddy. Don't matters if it is someone little or big, yeah.' She paused then and said calmly, 'That will really get the ratings up.'

Harish beamed appreciatively. 'That was a very good Vrushali, Tania.'

'Thank you,' said Tania in mock gratitude.

'I was talking victims, Tania. Victims,' Rahul said defensively.

Tania held her own. 'Is being a victim of incest or paedophilia a love problem? Can Vrushali handle such scarred people? We'll need a clinical psychologist in the mix. This is serious stuff.'

Rahul backed down and said very pleasantly, 'Of course, I didn't mean actual incest or paedophilia.'

Tania snapped, 'What is fake incest? I am sorry. I don't understand.'

Rahul, taken aback by Tania's unusual aggression, said pleasantly, 'Tania, you are getting worked up unnecessarily. My bad. I should not have taken extremes like incest and paedophilia. But just make your problems a bit more complicated. You know...my girlfriend is sleeping with her boss, or I have the hots for my best friend's mom and I think she likes me too, et cetera et cetera.'

When bosses make concessions, it is the closest they ever get to admitting that they have goofed up. Tania was aware of this, so she promptly and enthusiastically agreed to Rahul's watered down version of extreme love problems. That is the concession subordinates make after catching bosses on the wrong foot—be extremely compliant with the next suggestion that comes up. Reassure them subconsciously that their authority remains not just unchallenged but also revered and worshipped unconditionally.

Tania successfully conveyed this subliminal message to Rahul—fortunately, her instinct for self preservation was still intact...so far.

Rahul beamed in a mixture of relief and triumph, as Tania marched out of his cabin all set to revamp *Love Calls* yet again.

Suddenly Harish was hit by a storm burst of enlightenment, which was always a dangerous event. He summoned Tania and asked her to shoot a special schedule of two episodes with only studio guests. 'And,' he said excitedly, 'shoot them in silhouette; in darkness.'

Tania asked, 'Even if they are quite willing to be shown openly?'

Harish said impatiently, 'Yes. It will add to the drama. And don't bother finding real cases. Just get people from office and make-up some radical problems. Get that sales girl Ruchika for sure. She has great legs.'

Tania argued, 'How will the great legs show up in darkness?'

Harish had not thought of that. 'Arrey I can't do all the thinking. You figure it out!' And he waddled off pleased with himself.

Tania convened an emergency meeting with a bemused Aakash. 'We can do it. It will look weird but it is possible. Her torso will be in darkness, but the rest of her can be fabulously lit,' said Aakash.

Tania wearily gave him the thumbs up. Aakash smiled at her sympathetically. She wasn't the most gifted of producers, but she was definitely the most earnest one he'd come across, and that spurred him on to making things slightly easier for her.

Buoyed by the genius of his plan, Harish insisted that they shoot the episode the next day. Bhosle, thinking that the budget that would go off track unless they shot a batch of episodes in one go, opposed the plan. Finally, it was decided that time and studio space would be borrowed from Bose's comedy challenge schedule. Tania thought of the prospect bleakly—the comedy challenge series had a congregation of gigantic egos. Bose was the creative director and Zain, the host. The sets were hallowed grounds and would be defiled by the presence of a low rung, floundering show such as *Love Calls*. Surprisingly, Bose agreed to share space and said he would take a three hour break in his schedule, without any trademark display of temperament. His feelings for Tania had a starring role to play in the decision.

Constraints of time meant, however, that only one special episode would be shot on the day. Ruchika, the ditzy sales executive, was all set to make her television debut. 'I wish you guys had given me more notice. I could have done some extra squats and lunges at the gym,' she moaned.

Harish reassured her. 'They are fabulous legs, Ruch. They will kick ass.'

Ruchika pouted and walked away, swinging her hips ever so slightly. Harish thought it was a shame that they could not capitalize on Ruchika's shapely, taut bum as well. He sent Tania a text, 'Figure a way of getting Ruchika's ass on the show. Even one fleeting back shot will do.'

Tania held her head in her hands and contemplated a career change. Maybe she could be a telephone operator or join the housekeeping department. How stressful could it be to scrub toilets and shine window panes?

Ruchika was going to play 'Preeti', a twenty-something executive who was sleeping with her much married boss. She had a devoted boyfriend she intended to marry and now her conscience was bothering her. The conscience-stricken Preeti would be appropriately clad in a short mini and pencil heels.

Tania, the pop sociologist and theoretical feminist, took over briefly. She told Aditya, 'Mass culture and its stereotypical imaging—if you wear skimpy Western clothes, you are more likely to sleep with the boss as opposed to if you wear a salwar kameez.'

Aditya looked at her in amusement and said, 'Tani, you must speak like this in front of Bose. His Bong pseudo -intellectual side will want to take you home to meet the parents.'

'You are just so pointless,' said a stung Tania.

Aditya continued to laugh and steered the conversation into a slightly less sociological realm. He asked her what they should order for lunch—a subject that Tania definitely had more expertise in. Pan fried noodles and kung pao chicken effectively blanked out mass culture and its stereotypical imaging.

The next day of the shoot, a combative Vrushali arrived dressed in a silken pair of shorts and a peasant top. All she had been told was that they were going to shoot a special episode. No other details were forthcoming. Vrushali was restless—her television debut had got no attention. Forget glowing reviews, no television critic worth his while had even deigned to bash the show. The show was an inconsequential blip in the universe of big budget reality shows and grandiose soaps. Vrushali was disgruntled and determined to be difficult, petulant, and quite the prima donna. The only positive in this bleak scenario was that she didn't need to try very hard to be all of that and more. A super ingratiating Nair accompanied her. He had fallen slightly out of favour as he had not yet delivered on his hyperbolic promises. So far, all he had got her was an item number in a Bhojpuri film, which Rahul had nixed saying it was far too down market for a YTV host. He was determined to fan Vrushali's general petulance in the direction of the channel.

To complicate things further, both Zain and Bose decided to stay back for the shoot. Bose felt the need to lend moral support to the woman who was beginning to take over his waking thoughts. Zain felt the need to mark his territory as YTV's most popular face.

To Tania's great relief and surprise, Aditya walked into the shoot as well. She raised one amused eyebrow and said, 'Aditya, it is 6 pm and you're here in office, on my shoot. Here to lend me support?'

'No,' said Aditya cheekily. 'I am here to lend my support to Ruchika's legs. Long legs are my area of specialization.'

Tania smiled. A part of her wondered if Aditya was there to lend support to her very own not so long legs but she dismissed the thought. Aditya was way too detached to do that. But his sense of the ridiculous would make sure that he didn't miss out on this particular circus.

Whatever the compulsions, she was glad he was there. 'Isn't this channel just great? Men here get paid to lech!' she joked.

Aditya laughed and then took Tania aside to tell her in an undertone, 'Tani, just make sure you don't let your siren know that Ruchika is here purely for her legs. It's the worst thing you can do. And, by the way, Zain's being here can only mean trouble.'

Tania nodded gratefully. Aditya was right. Bose, who stood at a distance, stiffened in resentment. Tania didn't look grateful in the least that he had stayed back—her pretended indifference was captivating most times, but when she chose to couple it with whispered conversations with Aditya, it was annoying. He stood there quietly seething.

Zain, in the meantime, lounged around the set demanding Chinese food and cigarettes. This threw production into a tizzy, and a harried production manager came charging up to Tania demanding to know which show would foot the bill for Zain. 'See, Tania madam,' said Subbu, the production manager, 'he is not here for your show and he is not shooting his show, so from which budget can we take the money for his food?'

Of course nobody dared suggest that Zain pick up the tab for his own expenses. On-air talent have a really short shelf life and in that lifetime they want to stock up the shelf with as many freebies as they possibly can. In short, there was no way Zain was paying for his food and cigarettes.

Tania took out two hundred rupees in a rush from her purse and distractedly waved Subbu aside, 'I'll pay for this. Just please don't bother me now.' Subbu stood his ground. 'Madam, if you make a voucher for this later, then I can't tell Bhosle sir to sanction this. Hope you are understanding?'

Tania shooed him away in a mix of exasperation and annoyance. Trust Bhosle to saddle her with Subbu, one of his most ineffectual production cohorts.

Vrushali had come onto the set and could be heard asking Akaash, 'Why everythings is so dark dark?'

Tania rushed to Vrushali and reassured her that they were just experimenting with the lighting to make the show look even more glamorous. Vrushali was suspicious but was instantly distracted by Zain, who sauntered across and lazily saluted as he came closer. Vrushali transformed into her giggly carefree girl avatar as she always did in the presence of anything that looked remotely male.

Zain let out a low whistle as he beheld Vrushali in a cream short dress. 'Vrush baby, finally the look is right. You know these things always take time—first few times everyone looks a bit strange, but then you get comfortable in your skin and it shows,' he said.

Vrushali's giggles subsided, as she realized what he was saying. 'I was looking strange in the first episodes yeah?' she said coldly, and then she looked at Tania with mounting hostility.

Zain drawled, 'No, sweetie, don't get me wrong. You would look hot in a sack. It's just that the sequinned dress in the first episode was a bit cabaret no? But don't worry too much. They say, in television, the first impression is the best impression but honestly I don't care too much about that. I think even if you put off people the first time, there is always a next time. You grow on people and in fact, sometimes, it is great if your first few times are a disaster coz that sticks in public memory.'

Vrushali shuffled her feet uneasily and gave him a strained smile.

Zain continued blithely, 'We are going out to such a critical, unforgiving audience—they make no concessions at all. It is unfair to newcomers but now what to do?'

Vrushali gave Zain a tight smile and snapped at Tania.

'Why we are experimenting with lights now? First not getting the dress right, now we have dress right then lights will be wrong.'

Zain smirked slightly at this incoherent display of insecurity. Tania fervently wished that Zain would choke on the hakka chow that she had paid for. Before she could say anything though, Zain continued philosophically, 'As the faces of our shows, we should not bother about technical stuff, Vrush, but we should listen to feedback and try and filter constructive criticism from it. People will keep telling you that your accent sucks or that age lines show on your neck and near your eyes in the close shots. You fix what you can and take the rest in your stride.'

From a vague feeling of unease, Vrushali promptly transited to total horror. She blanked out on the 'accent' part but the stray 'age lines' comment chilled her to the bone. She told Tania urgently, 'I need touch up on my face yeah.'

Tania tried hard to assure Vrushali that her make-up was perfect, but there was no way that Vrushali was going to listen. She rushed off to the make-up van. Tania stared at her back in frustration and glared at the smoking Zain. 'Zain, you know smoking is not allowed on the shoot floor. You could start a fire.'

Zain laughed and said cryptically, 'If I haven't already!' He walked outside to continue his smoke.

Aditya came up to Tania and said, 'He is a natural born bastard but paying for his meals is not a great idea. Next time, if production has an issue just overcharge on some other overhead.'

Tania looked at him in exasperation. 'You think, with all this happening around me, I'm going to think of ways of siphoning a Chinese meal off this organization?'

'You keep at the siphoning long enough and it could pay for a vacation in China. Let me see what I can do about him though,' said Aditya and went to distract Zain. Soon Zain and he were seriously considering if gummy women were any better at blow jobs than non-gummy women. It was exactly the kind of risqué banter that would keep Zain out of Tania's way.

Then Bose summoned Tania—Aditya's constant excursions into the studio and his mind space were aggravating him. He told her shortly, 'Lady, you have three hours. Your anchor is not here yet. I think you should speed things up instead of chatting with colleagues who don't need to be here in the first place.'

Much to her irritation, Tania felt her eyes sting. She nodded quickly and walked away. Bose noticed the glint of tears and instantly regretted being short with her. He resolved heroically to bail out the helpless damsel of his dreams.

Vrushali finally arrived on the sets in another half hour. Tania noticed that she was wearing more foundation than usual, which made her look caked up and much older than she usually did. Tania cursed Zain again and wished him an extreme case of food poisoning, but she knew her feeble curses were destined to bounce off Zain's thick hide. Vrushali sat down petulantly on the settee, and peering suspiciously at the corner where the guest was supposed to sit asked, 'What is being so special about this episode?'

Right on cue, Ruchika walked in. She had outdone herself. Instead of a short mini, she was wearing a barely-there pair of hot pants. Her legs looked fabulous—toned and impossibly long. Vrushali gaped at her and looked at Tania accusingly, 'This one has a love problem? This one?!'

Tania came across to Vrushali and whispered urgently, 'Yes, her problem is that she's sleeping with her boss but now is regretting cheating on her fiancé.'

Vrushali cast a withering look at the legs and wrinkled her nose as if to suggest legs like those could only lead you to walk on the path of moral turpitude. Tania remembered something vaguely about mass culture and its stereotypical imaging but promptly squashed it—there was way too much to think about in any case.

Aditya had exhausted his impressive repertoire of blow job jokes and Zain walked back in. He hooted enthusiastically, 'Ruch darling, you're wasting yourself in sales. You should be on air. Those are the sexiest legs I've ever seen.'

Ruchika giggled and blew a kiss to Zain who made a great show of catching it and winked flirtatiously at her. Vrushali sat up straight and pretended not to notice.

Nair barked out orders to a spot boy to get 'Madamji' some coconut water and told Tania impatiently, 'We were told this will take only one hour. This is not part of the dates that Madam gave YTV—we have made special favour for you. So please be serious now.' He stared pointedly at Zain, as Vrushali coldly and expressionlessly sipped her coconut water. Zain ignored him and continued to smile approvingly at Ruchika.

Aditya, who had strolled in by now, decided that now he should just be a spectator although he felt a twinge of sympathy for Tania.

Tania wisely chose not to say anything. She asked Aakash if they were ready to begin. Aakash told her he needed five more minutes for the final touches on the lighting for Ruchika. Vrushali bristled when she heard that and glared at Tania.

'Vrushali, she is going to be in silhouette, erm…in darkness. That needs special lighting,' said Tania to a stiff and mollified Vrushali.

Finally, it was time for Tania to say the golden word. But just before she could, Bose sprang into action. He said quietly from the corner of the studio that he was lounging in, 'Just a minute there, if this episode is about Ruchika's legs, as I have been given to understand, the lighting is great to showcase them, but we need something more to make sure that they really stand out. They should be the only fucking thing that people notice on the show.' He clicked his fingers at a servile make-up man who, on cue, ran into the frame and slathered Ruchika's legs with baby oil. Bose said with the complacence of a genius, 'Now that will make sure no one misses those legs.'

Bose was pleased with himself. It was all so effortless; the way he had stepped in the crucial last minute to elevate the good to the great. He glanced at Tania for some well deserved gratitude. Tania wasn't looking at him—she was staring at Vrushali who was glaring at a pair of long legs being polished fervently.

Aditya grinned at Bose cheerily and whispered, 'Bro, good job!'

Bose ignored him. As far as Tania was concerned, there was the small matter of the final nail in the coffin, which was duly hammered in by Zain. 'Genius! This is what the show always needed. Finally some sex appeal—look at those legs man!'

Vrushali walked off the sets with Nair trotting after her. Zain laughed to himself and sauntered off. His job was done. Bose sat there bemused; he wasn't quite sure what had happened. Tania chased after the duo and caught up with them in the vanity van. Much to Bose's discomfiture, Aditya followed her. Vrushali was enraged and Nair was fanning the rage rather effectively.

He said, 'Madamji is very disturbed. She is not in the frame of mind to shoot. Taniaji, this is insulting. The star is being treated like an extra. You never told us that this show was about some other madam's legs. This is her show.'

Tania spluttered, 'Don't be stupid, Nair. One pair of random legs does not stop it from being Vrushali's show!'

'Madamji's show—only Madamji's legs. Why has third party come into it?' Nair said firmly.

Aditya coolly interjected, 'He is right, Tania. The deal was that we will only exploit Vrushali's anatomy. It was an exclusive deal. You really can't have other random body parts floating along. I understand, Nair saab.'

Vrushali looked sufficiently self righteous and sniffled approvingly at Aditya.

Tania looked at Aditya incredulously and threw up her hands but Aditya smiled reassuringly at her.

Nair beamed, 'See, Aditya Bhai, we should only be interacting with you. You are knowing how this industry works.'

'Yes absolutely, you should put in an exclusivity clause in the contract. But until that is done—think of it Nair, those legs are like the item number in a film. Item numbers are never more important than the heroine no?' said Aditya.

Nair softened but was not giving up that easily. 'That all is okay but you people are rubbing oil and all and making them shine. You must decide who is the star and whose legs are more important.' He added sternly, 'And all this should be done before Madamji comes on the sets. No right thinking person will tolerate like this behaviour. Though Madamji is very humble and professional.'

The humble and professional Madamji glowered.

Tania said quickly, 'Yes, but Ruchika is not lucky. She doesn't have the natural glow that Vrushali has. But if Vrushali wants oil on her legs, she just has to say it, and we will put all the oil she wants.'

Vrushali finally broke her silence. 'Same oil like you are putting on the girl?'

Tania said, 'If you wish. Or any other oil that you want.'

A defiant gleam came into Vrushali's eye. She said, 'Eucalyptus. I am having allergy to other oils.'

'But we don't have that in the make-up room. Someone will need to get it. It'll delay the shoot. Come on, Vrushali, I thought you wanted to go home early,' she pleaded.

Vrushali said sweetly, 'For benefits of show, I will be making the compromise yeah? Whatever delays there is you can keep polishing up that girl's legs. So no time is being wasted.'

Tania looked at Aditya for help but he smiled ruefully. He knew that Vrushali would now only come to the sets with eucalyptus oil or not at all. Years of managing celebrity egos had taught him when to back off.

Tania gave up. Nair helpfully opened the door of the make-up van for her. A production person was dispatched to procure eucalyptus oil and in the intervening period, Ruchika's enthusiasm to have her legs on air ebbed rapidly.

With the result that it was two grumpy, leggy women who shot for *Dyson X30 Love Calls*, two hours later for a tepid episode.

On the other hand—their legs shone like hell.

The Anatomy of
a Contract

The Ruchika episode created a stir even before it went on air. The next day Rahul wearily trudged his way to the legal department. Nair had taken Aditya's advice and was insisting on the exclusivity clause being added to Vrushali's contract.

Rahul sighed heavily at the prospect of dealing with the legal department. He could have mailed them but then it would take forever. Harish usually dealt with contracts but he was not in office yet. The legal department was a blur of bald, bespectacled men, and for the life of him, Rahul couldn't remember any of their names. So he said to no one in particular, 'We need to change Vrushali Salve's contract. One extra clause...and we need to get this done now.'

Everyone looked at Rahul impassively. He said impatiently, 'Let's change it today itself. Basically the clause has to say that we have an exclusive understanding with Vrushali, that the only skimpily dressed person on the show will be her. So if we need to show skin, we can use only her legs, her cleavage, her thighs...her whatever.'

This was an unprecedented clause in the history of legal contracts, but the legal department seemed impervious to the history being made. They continued to register no change in expression on their collective blur of faces.

Finally one of the bald bespectacled droned, 'We would advise a rethink on the usage of the word "whatever". Her "whatever", which we take to mean the "service provider's whatever", is too open ended a term to be to be incorporated in a contract. It is subject to interpretations which may be detrimental to the interests of the contractor.'

Rahul gulped, 'Who the hell are the contractor and the service provider?' And then comprehension dawned. 'Oh, you mean Vrushali is the service provider and YTV, the contractor. I don't really want you to put in "whatever". It's just a figure of speech. I leave the definition to you guys. I mean you can call it...' Rahul paused as he visibly struggled for the right word, and then, in a burst of inspiration said, 'You can call it...whatever. Whatever you want...' He trailed off weakly and was rewarded by a quelling look of collective legal contempt.

Rahul thought fast. 'Okay, just call it "Body Parts". That works?'

Another nameless, hairless legal beagle piped up. '"Body Parts" could also include eyes, nose, ears, cheeks, hands. Does this mean all other guests on the show will be covered from extremity to extremity?'

Rahul's head spun. Where the hell was Harish? 'No, of course not. Just the obvious body parts like what I told you earlier,' he snapped.

'So the contract is for mutually decided body parts and not the whole body. Body parts with the expressed and explicit objective of titillation. That is the purview of the new clause. That is your complete and final petition.'

Rahul winced at this brutal legal honesty but said plaintively, 'Yes. Yes. Please just draft it as soon as possible. We will review it once I see it on paper.'

By the end of the day, the legal department had put all of their bald heads together and drafted a contract that covered all possible loop holes. In its own right, it was a masterpiece.

Fm: Manoj Waghmare (YTV Legal)
To: Rahul Singh
Sub: RE: Additional Clause

Dear Sir,
Please find herewith the additional clause to be incorporated in the contract between the service provider (which expression shall, unless the same be repugnant to the context or meaning, thereof be deemed to mean and include Ms Vrushali Salve) and the contractor (which expression shall, unless the same be repugnant to the context or meaning thereof, be deemed to mean and include YOUTH TV).

162

It is stated that the service provider is in an exclusive agreement with the contractor to provide services to the television programme 'Dyson X 30 Love Calls' (Duration: 22 minutes. Genre: Romance Reality. Periodicity: Daily). The services will deem to mean and include in part, or in whole, explicit, exclusive, mutually agreed exhibition of body parts of the service provider. It is further stated thereon that the term 'exclusivity' will deem to mean, and include in its purview, the undertaking that the contractor will not approach other vendors for dispersal of similar services on the aforementioned show. The service provider is also deemed to refrain from providing services that conflict or could conflict with her obligations in relation to this agreement.

The service provider agrees that intellectual property rights, in all products of her services pursuant to this agreement, are the property of the contractor. The contractor reserves the right to use one or all body parts at its discretion. However, the body being used will belong solely and completely to the service provider for the duration of the agreement. This agreement extends only to the exhibit of body parts that are commonly identified with the objective of titillation.

Therefore, it must be stated that the eyes, nose, ears, hands, feet, and arms of other service providers/participants can be used wholly or in part by the contractor in the show and will not represent a conflict of interests with the spirit of this agreement.

This agreement will be governed by the laws of India and shall be subject to the exclusive jurisdiction of the competent courts of Mumbai.

Regards,

Manoj W.

Rahul quickly forwarded the mail to Aditya, asking him to vet it. Aditya doubled up with laughter—there was never a dull moment at YTV. He quickly jabbed Rahul's number and said eagerly, 'Works like a dream, bro. Not only do we have exclusive rights on Vrushali's titillating body parts but evidently they also qualify as intellectual property. Wow.'

Rahul said cagily, 'Okay, we'll go with it then but will you please handle Nair?'

Aditya agreed promptly. His conversation with Nair on this clause would give him the fodder for anecdotes for a lifetime.

Rahul was relieved. That was one thing less on his plate—but there was still Amrit left to handle.

Amrit had made an urgent call to Rahul. He was Ruchika's boss and she had told him about a special episode shot in darkness which had made him jittery. 'If the branding is not showing, then don't put it on air. Or let me get client approval—the market is bad. You don't want the sponsor backing out,' he said to Rahul.

Rahul told Harish to keep the episode on hold, which put paid to all his plans of heavy promotion and the resultant spike in the ratings. Harish grumpily tried to find a way of blaming Tania for the entire fiasco and drowned his sorrows in a cream and mango milkshake.

And then Bose stormed into Rahul's cabin blaming *Love Calls* for derailing the schedule of the comedy show. 'We don't have enough episodes in the bank. You don't want to be repeating your best rated show,' he bit out angrily.

To add to Bose's fury, he had just received a text message from Zain saying 'Dude, not shooting for the rest of the week. Bad Chinese food. Stomach fucked.'

Later Tania was to tell Aditya in the best spirits, 'God must be someone like you—the one time he decides to grant me a wish, he wastes it on that Zain.'

Rahul, reeling under this multi-pronged attack, told Harish shortly, 'Forget all this silhouette stuff. Forget studio guests. Just keep it to phone calls and keep the calls edgy and controversial. That's it. Stick to it.'

Tania was duly instructed, and she briefed Mohawk about the new plan. She also told him a tad tartly, 'Since you refuse to step into the edit bay, this is now your baby. Find slightly controversial problems. Real ones would be great but you can also make-up a few. And get your friends to call in. Don't use office people—they have come on too often and are now recognizable. Avoid Stella who has almost become the voice of the show. Also we really need her to answer office calls instead of constantly being on a love call.'

So the actor in stodgy Stella, the receptionist, after a glorious run of three weeks, was shown the door. Stella took it in her stride, but Aditya noticed that her tryst with television had left its mark. He told Tania, 'Call the YTV board lines at different points in the day. She has a new voice and a new delivery to say "Good Morning.

YTV" or "Good Afternoon. YTV". Depending on the time of the day she changes her tone and modulation. I think in her head she is still playing different characters on '*Love Calls.*'

Tania laughed, 'Aditya, you really need to find yourself a job. Oh wait, I forgot. You *have* one!'

Aditya laughed heartily. At times like these he liked Tania…*a lot*.

Bose frowned furiously. At times like these he disliked Tania…*a lot*. He was still fuming over her complete lack of gratitude for his intervention on her sets. He stomped off, his braid swishing violently behind him. It was the wrong angle to present to a girl he was trying to impress. Tania caught a glimpse of his departing braid and thought he looked like an angry cow trying to swat flies. It was a ludicrous sight and she laughed to herself, but refused to share the joke with a very curious Aditya and walked off.

———

Mohawk did a half decent job in conjuring up problems and lining up an impressive contingent of friends who would call in. He gave himself two speaking parts as well. Tania didn't see the harm in that, so she let it go. His list of love problems was assorted and complex. Tania quickly skimmed over the first set of problems.

Problem 1: I found condoms in my girlfriend's bag. A half used pack of condoms. We are sexually active, but she does not get us the condoms. I do. So I don't know what to do!

Problem 2: My first cousin is marrying my ex-boyfriend. We had a live-in relationship but one day he just upped and left. Now six months down the line he is marrying her. What to do?

Problem 3: I find my best friend's mom very hot. His father is always on tour, and she is very nice to me. Should I tell her my feelings?

Tania nodded approvingly, 'We're finally on the right track. I don't need to go through all the problems. Just make sure you have the right voices lined up for all of them.'

Sometime in the immediate future, Tania would regret not going through all the problems. But at this point, it was an eternally effusive Garnet who got her attention.

Garnet had retained all her enthusiasm through the one month of *Love Calls* and had become fast friends with Vrushali—a bond spurred by similar levels of vacuity. Tania wasn't complaining, though, for it made dealing with Vrushali on her styling requirements that much easier.

'Tania, you know, let's experiment with the silhouette,' Garnet gushed.

Tania laughed. 'I would be careful about using the word "silhouette" anywhere near this show. Enough trouble as it is.'

Garnet stared blankly.

Tania sighed, 'Never mind, it was a joke. Go on. '

'Let's make it more fluid and flowing. You know maxis are back in a big way with huge floral prints. We should try that on Vrush—she is very comfortable with the idea.'

Tania smiled. 'Well, if *Vrush* is so comfortable with it, go for it, I guess. Just don't compromise on the sexiness.'

And again, sometime in the near future, Tania would partially regret these words as well. But now, she sauntered off to the edit bay feeling unusually light headed.

———

The fourth schedule of *Love Calls* came up in the next two days. The running of the show, Tania thought, with an air of self congratulation, was on auto now. The set had come up, the callers were lined up, and Vrushali had cracked a degree of coherence in her speech. The best part about the schedule was that Nair was missing, which meant there would be no delays because 'Madamji' was looking tired or needed coconut water. All in all, Tania had a good feeling about it. Maybe, she thought wistfully, from the next schedule onwards she could just hand over the entire show to Mohawk and volunteer to devote her life to the fortunes of Tiger and Googly. She often thought of her former pet project with a pang of regret.

Tania continued in this trance-like state for the first two hours of the shoot. Everything was going like a dream anyway—Mohawk's callers were bang on, Vrushali did the best she could with them, and her wardrobe changes were taking a maximum of five minutes.

It was too good last. And it lasted for a good five minutes more. The peace came to an abrupt end when Vrushali glided in for the third episode shoot.

Tania sat up straight in her chair, stared at Vrushali in disbelief and hollered, 'WHAT IS GOING ON HERE?'

The Belly of the Beast

A few days later, away from the purple and black set
on which a woman with a faux bosom presided, Tania's
words found an echo.

'WHAT IS GOING ON HERE?' hollered Rajneesh at
the morning edit meeting.

Everyone respectfully kept quiet. Rajneesh didn't
really expect an answer anyway. He continued, 'Give
me that one story, guys; something that belongs only to
YNN. Something we break first and own. How can you
guys call yourselves journalists? There is not *one* of you
who can find a story that can get us the attention. How
long do you expect my perfection and genius to bail you
out? What if I am run over by a bus tomorrow... How
will you run this channel?'

Rajneesh's think tank looked suitably shamefaced even
as they longingly thought of the elusive bus that would
truncate Rajneesh's genius. Away from his line of vision,
some of them doodled furiously on their note pads. Others
who had their laptops open in front of them thought up

inventive Facebook status updates for their profiles. Most settled for 'Getting screwed, so what's new?'

Rajneesh, oblivious to all of this, spoke in tones calculated to stir his slothful news team into action. 'You have to realize, we are the emperors of news television. And I will not let any of you abdicate this easily. The emperor will not give up on his supremacy!'

The edit team nodded in hushed reverence.

The theatrics had been spurred by the Friday morning ratings. YNN had slid to second place. The difference between the top two was marginal but Rajneesh was an ambitious man.

'One story, guys. Give me that one story that will get people to follow it only on YNN.'

Geeta Khanna, the Chandigarh bureau chief, was bemused. Rajneesh was just a thunderous voice on the phone when she was in her cosy cubicle back home, something she had to deal with only for five minutes every morning. But Rajneesh in the flesh, with his overblown theatrics, was something else altogether. She was certainly glad that her two-week Mumbai operations orientation stint was coming to an end. She wondered for the nth time whether her move from a newspaper job to television, a year back, was the right one.

Rajneesh barked, 'Geeta, any ideas?'

Geeta broached, without hope, a series of stories that she had her heart set on, 'Chief, why can't we commission some hard hitting investigative stories? Like the state of government hospitals or how RDX can be smuggled in via sea so easily?'

Rajneesh said nothing. He hadn't, by and large, recruited the kind of people capable of that degree of journalistic depth. He had recruited acolytes, hangers on, and devotees—all of them with an allegiance to the shrine of Rajneesh Tiwari. Given these circumstances, this band of news hounds would not have the editorial maturity, or know how, to pull off the series that Geeta had just suggested. More importantly, Rajneesh knew that the nation was not interested in these stories and he was always right about the nation for *he* was the nation.

'Geeta, you're a senior journalist and I expect you to differentiate between perception stories and rating stories. These stories are good for perception and some schmuck will give us an award. But we are not in the awards game. We want ratings. So give me ratings—that is all that matters.' Rajneesh said curtly.

Geeta's face fell.

The ghost of the former idealistic journalist that still lurked in some deep recesses of Rajneesh's being said gently, 'Once you get the ratings, you can step away and do something for yourself. Be self indulgent and do the kind of stories you want to do but only after you have tasted success. Otherwise it is not acceptable.'

'Good journalism is self indulgent?' Geeta said quietly.

'On YNN, I decide what good journalism is. Get that

straight, my dear.' He clicked his fingers impatiently—a cue for the meeting to disperse.

That got everyone's attention. Except for Rajneesh who sat brooding, the room cleared out in minutes.

Neha Chitre strutted out of the meeting pouting furiously. She hadn't listened to a word. She was slotted for reading out the 6 pm bulletin and her only thought was to get out of it; 6 pm was when the show on YTV with that Vrushali would come on air. And there was no way in hell she was going to miss it.

She walked up to the executive producer, Shalini Sharma, and said nervously, 'Madam, today I can't do 6 pm—I am not well. My eyes are feeling watery and I won't be able to read off the teleprompter.'

Shalini looked at the perfect picture of radiant health that Neha presented. It wasn't like the girl to cry off an opportunity to be on air—she was gloriously vain and loved every minute of it. The viewers loved her too, especially when in between reading a serious news item, she suddenly either cocked her head or tucked in a stray tendril behind her ear. One viewer had even sent in a poem inspired by her live coquetry. Shalini usually would have let her off the bulletin because, except for Rajneesh, everybody was fairly dispensable. But today Rajneesh was rattled by the ratings and it would be the wrong day to be yanking off a popular anchor from 6 pm. 'I am sure you will manage. Rest your eyes one hour before the bulletin. It will be fine,' she said to Neha.

Neha's eyes filled with tears. 'Please, madam…I just can't. I won't go home. I will do the 7 pm. I will be there for 9 pm but I can't do the 6 pm slot.'

Shalini was slightly taken aback. There was a very real chance that the girl would be an emotional mess on live television as well—a chance she didn't want to take. She'd rather take a chance on Rajneesh's fury instead. At least that was a known quantity unlike this volatile sobbing mess in front of her.

Shalini said curtly, 'Don't puff up your eyes please; they will look like bags on air. Fine, I'll swap you with Suketu. But don't make a habit of this.'

Neha looked profusely grateful and walked away. The tears had stopped though—the possibility of puffy eyes on air was a deterrent. When Neha let vanity guide her she was usually on the right path. But today the love struck girl was thinking with her heart.

The rest of the day passed too slowly for Neha. The hours crawled and everything moved in excruciatingly slow motion. Finally at five minutes to 6 pm, Neha sprinted into the conference room and tuned on the plasma to YTV. Here she was assured of some peace and quiet.

Neha sat on the edge of her seat. The snazzy opening package with a husky voice cooing 'Dyson X30 Love Calls—Are you hot enough?' started. Neha bit her finger nails in nervous anticipation.

It started with a wide shot of a busty woman reclining on her couch. Neha squinted at the screen—her first impression was of long, bronzed legs. The host was wearing an impossibly short, blue dress, with a neckline that plunged to her knees. The leggy woman then said, 'Hellos peoples! This is *Dyson X30 Love Calls—Are you hot enough?* We know who is the one burning hot here, but the question is, are you the one too yeah.' She cocked her head and then demurely tucked a tendril behind her ear.

Neha recoiled in horror. This is what her Biplab had equated her with. This painted caricature of a tart! How could he? Did he think so little of her?

Almost to rub it in further, the host laughed a low deep laugh. Neha was generally a self obsessed girl, and in her current state of emotional tumult, the self obsession was magnified many times over. She thought angrily, 'She is taunting me! The bitch!'

Vrushali, callously oblivious to the emotional havoc she was wreaking, trilled, 'Love is calling on my Dyson X30...Hello, who this? Talk to me, buddy.'

A call had come in from Chandigarh on the show. At that precise point, Neha stopped listening to anything that Vrushali had to say. Her eyes filled with tears, and her petite frame shook slightly with sobs as she thought of Biplab's callousness. How could he? If only she had watched on, she would have had the satisfaction of seeing Vrushali's seductress act crumble completely. But as it were, Neha didn't notice that at some point Vrushali had stopped seducing the camera and was listening to the phone call with a look of faint horror. She had put a hand to her chest and was stammering incoherently. Something had happened to shake her completely. Neha missed all of this as she wept piteously.

—•—

Rajneesh, on the other hand, had seen everything. He had walked into the conference room to make 'a few confidential phone calls' (that was what he told his secretary but these calls were generally to his wife to discuss the dinner menu, which only Rajneesh knew. His weakness for food was a well-kept secret—he liked to perpetuate the belief that he had no human frailty), when he saw his primetime anchor sobbing her heart out at something she was watching on some entertainment channel. Neha didn't notice him, but unlike her, he listened to every word that Vrushali said or was trying to say. He observed the discernible change in Vrushali's expression and her shock. He noticed the impact on his furiously sobbing young anchor. And then it hit him.

Rajneesh, the emperor of television, would rise again. His big story had, most fittingly, just sprung out at him from a television screen.

And now for the back story, we return to a purple and black set presided over by a woman with a faux bosom.

'WHAT IS GOING ON HERE?' Tania shrieked.

Vrushali stopped short and froze in shock. She said coldly, 'What is problems?'

Tania sprang to her feet and rushed to Vrushali. She hissed furiously, 'What is this rubbish you are wearing? Garnet, get here right now!'

Garnet rushed to the scene and said tearfully, 'I checked with you. You said maxis are fine.'

'Yes, but why is she wearing this huge tent?' Tania pointed at Vrushali's billowy, floral outfit.

Garnet gulped, 'It is not a tent...'

Tania glared at Garnet. 'No, of course, it's not a tent. Even a tent would look sexier than this nonsense. Three Vrushalis can fit into this shapeless rubbish. Isn't your brief to keep it sexy? How are you achieving that by making her wear this? Even maternity clothes are better fitting! As it is people write in calling her "Didi" and

"Aunty"—don't know what they will call her if we put her on air like this!'

Vrushali then threw a tantrum as huge as the oversized maxi she was wearing. The tantrum was accompanied by a sobbing session of gargantuan proportions. Tania plonked herself on the chair, instantly regretting her words but making no attempt to console Vrushali. Emotions of an epic scale were therefore on display, and the result was an epic delay in the shoot.

It took three hours before Vrushali strode back into the sets defiantly. She was dressed in an impossibly short blue dress with a neckline that plunged to her knees. Tania said nothing. Besides a slight lift of her left eyebrow, Vrushali refused to acknowledge Tania's presence.

She reclined on the couch and hitched up her short dress even further up her thigh. She said coldly, 'Ready when you are.'

Tania whispered to Mohawk, 'Are your callers lined up? Is this a fake call or a genuine call?'

Mohawk gloated, 'Fake...but there is super emotion. Full on sobbing...'

He was interrupted by Vrushali shouting impatiently from her couch, 'You will be blaming me for delay but everyone can be seeing I am here, and nothing is ready yeah.'

Tania said hurriedly, 'Never mind. Just get the caller ready. Let's roll.'

Tania said 'action' in her firm, clear voice and

Vrushali's petulance vanished as the siren came to life. Stung by Tania's revelations that people were writing in with familial feelings, Vrushali gave the sex symbol act her all. She smouldered and cooed huskily, 'Hellos peoples! This is *Dyson X30 Love Calls—Are you hot enough?* We know who is the one burning hot here but the question is, are you the one too yeah.' She cocked her head and then demurely placed one tendril behind her ear.

Vrushali had never succeeded in being sexy but at least she had never been comical. That was, right up till then. Tania cringed.

Almost to rub it in, Vrushali laughed a low laugh. Tania winced and stopped herself from shouting 'cut' because she knew that that would be calling for more trouble.

Vrushali trilled, 'Love is calling on my Dyson X30... Hello, who this? Talk to me, buddy.'

A female voice came on. 'H-hullo...Vrushali.'

Vrushali pouted. 'Who this is, where you are calling me from?'

The voice said, 'Ch-Chandigarh.'

Vrushali laughed. 'Is it hot there? Hot like me?'

The voice said, 'I don't know. I don't know anymore what is hot and what is cold.'

Vrushali sighed and smouldered simultaneously. 'Love is being like that only, girlie—you will never be knowing yeah.'

The voice laughed bitterly. 'I don't know about that

but if you are dying, how does it matter whether it is hot or cold?'

Vrushali, focusing on her fluttering eyelashes, said inattentively, 'Love can be killing yeah.'

The voice now sounded slightly irritated. 'I am dying. I am going to be dead.'

That got Vrushali's fickle attention. She froze. 'Dying? Y-you are meaning exactly what?'

'I have cancer. I have two months to live.' The voice repeated.

Vrushali, totally shaken by now, put a hand on her chest and said, 'Oh! What is your name?'

'Jassi, but that is not my real name. I can't tell you my real name.'

'Jassi, this is being a love show. My dearie, I am not being sure how we can help you yeah with death and all that. Maybe there is another show for that, though I am not knowing.'

She looked at Tania for help and Tania gesticulated to her to keep the conversation going. She liked the sound of it.

Vrushali grimaced slightly; she didn't like the sound of this conversation. Dying girls were best left alone. Her usual platitudes of 'life is short, move on yeah', and 'there is so much living and loving ahead' could be a little out of place here. And Vrushali had not invested too much time or effort in refreshing her armoury of platitudes.

She said gingerly, 'My dear, at this time you should be spending time with the peoples you are loving yeah.'

'The man I love doesn't want to be with me. I have only two months but he doesn't even want to pretend he loves me. He has left me…' Jassi said flatly.

Vrushali blubbered and looked at Tania for help. Tania gave her the thumbs up. She could see the teaser for this show forming in her head. She looked approvingly at Mohawk—he had finally lived up to the potential inherent in his maverick hairstyle. He beamed.

Jassi's voice broke, 'I am asking him for two months… is that too much after three years? I- I-I have no one. No one. I am going to die alone.'

'I am sorry but you needs to forget him. Your parents…' Vrushali said softly.

Jassi interjected, 'Parents? They died one month back in an accident. I have no one. Two weeks before they died, the doctors told me I had three months. I wish I had died too with them.'

Vrushali gulped in shock. This dying girl and her assortment of dead relatives were completely out of her depth. Tania frowned—clearly Mohawk had gotten carried away. He should have left it at her impending death and betrayal. Vrushali managed to say, 'I-I am sorry.'

Jassi was no longer listening to Vrushali. 'He cuh-could have waited for me to die, before falling in love with my cousin…they are getting married next month. They are not even waiting for me to du-die.'

Vrushali, who was hunting for the right thing to say, suddenly remembered a stock phrase that she thought might fit the situation. 'You can't be putting the time for falling in love. It is just happening yeah,' she said seriously.

Tania's heart sank. Stock phrases usually work fine, ninety nine on a hundred times, but there is that one time they blow up in your face. This was that one time.

'Is that all you are going to say, you...bitch?' Jassi bit out angrily.

Vrushali stuttered, 'I didn't mu-mu-eans it that way puh-please don't take to heart...'

But the intensity of the sobbing that followed clearly demonstrated that Jassi had taken it not just to her heart, but also to every bodily organ functioning in her dying being. Shuddering sobs mixed with angry and confused incoherence was all that could be heard. In television parlance, this was what you would call a royal fuck up.

Tania was furious with Mohawk of course, but more with herself. She should have checked all the problems before putting callers on the line. This one had become a sordid joke, which had spun completely out of control. Mohawk didn't seem to think so. He stood there, grinning at this riveting bit of television that he had created. Tania glared at him before quickly turning her attention to Vrushali, who was gamely stringing together comforting ineffectual phrases. The poor, hapless siren stuttered, 'You are having to be strong. Forget him and move on.'

This was the cue for uninhibited hysteria. Jassi yelled between heaving sobs, 'Move on to what? There is only death. I want to be happy for two months. How do I find that happiness? Please tell me how to be happy. Please tell him to love me again.'

Vrushali was now close to sobbing herself. The fact that her make-up man had forgotten to get his waterproof mascara along was the only thing impeding her complete breakdown.

She said, 'Must be s-strong my dear. Please don't be crying yeah...not for him. You must give thoughts to what is making you happy in the next two months.'

All she could hear was the sound of Jassi crying over the phone line. Suddenly the words of consolation that she had been grappling for came to her. She said, almost brightly, 'In two months time you will be meeting mummy-daddy again. Be thinking of that instead.'

Jassi spluttered. Mohawk spluttered. Tania spluttered out a 'cut'. She asked Mohawk to put Jassi on hold and ran up to Vrushali.

'You can't say something like that. You just can't.'

'How else I am going to make her happy yeah? Stupid girl,' said Vrushali.

Tania sighed, 'This was such a bad idea. We have to drop this call...it's just too negative.'

Vrushali suddenly snapped, 'Is she not being a real caller? Is this being some sort of joke yeah? You is playing with my mind?'

Tania couldn't risk another epic display of emotion. So she quickly lied. 'No, this one is a real person. I am just saying that we are not equipped to deal with this problem. Get back on the line and tell her that we'll refer her to counsellors who will help her deal with the issue.'

'Yeah, I am not being able to handle her.'

Jassi was put back on the line. She was still sobbing. 'Just let me be happy for two months. That is it.'

Tania thought admiringly that whoever Jassi was, she was a consummate actor. Slightly too theatrical for her taste but perfect for mainstream television. Of course, there was no way of putting that thought to test, because Tania had decided to not put the call on air. It was far too grim for a light chat show. Plus Vrushali had not exactly handled it with any degree of finesse.

Vrushali said, 'I am sorry, Jassi. Tell you what, buddy, we are going to be getting you some help. We will get like professional peoples like...you know...' Vrushali trailed off—she had forgotten the word 'counsellor'.

Tania mouthed the word to her frantically and Vrushali caught a bit of it. 'Dear, we will be getting like consultants to be talking to you. To be making you happy. They will call you...stop crying.'

There was a pause. Then Jassi's voice rang out again shrill and clear, 'You are leaving me! Just like everyone else. You were supposed to help...you have to help me. Please! Please! Don't hang up on me. I have no one.'

Vrushali said ineffectually, 'We are there—we will be calling you the minute the show is over...the professional peoples. The dead consultants...you know...who will be talking about dying and all to you. Your problems cannot be helping like this buddy. Please we have to go now.'

Tania suddenly knew what Mohawk could do to pay for the excesses of his imagination. I'll make him line up dead consultants, that will teach the jackass, thought Tania with grim satisfaction.

Jassi said brokenly, 'How will dead people call me? This is a joke. I am going to be left alone.'

'No dead people is going to call you. Professional peoples is going to call you. Now we must be going... erm...you take care,' Vrushali replied crankily.

The last sound she heard was a series of fresh heart rending sobs before the phone line went dead.

Vrushali burst into frustrated tears, the lack of waterproof make-up notwithstanding. She said angrily, 'How am I going to help? She shouted so much at me. I am not knowing what to do if she is stupid enough to die so soon and can't hold on to a man!'

Tania thought that she wouldn't have put stupidity as the impelling reason for the tragedy that had just played out on the telephone line. But that wasn't relevant—the immediate wringing of Mohawk's neck was. In the hour that Vrushali took to deal with her excesses of furious emotion, Tania dealt with Mohawk's excesses of creative license.

'Are you insane?' she shouted. 'Do you know how fake that sounded? How can one girl have everything—cancer, dead parents, cheating boyfriend, and a disloyal cousin? Don't you know where to stop?'

'It can happen,' Mohawk said defensively.

Tania said between her teeth, 'Where...in the soaps you watch every day?'

Mohawk said stiffly, 'I watch *Grey's Anatomy* and *Prison Break*. I generally don't watch Indian soaps. I—'

Tania interrupted, 'Do I look like I give a hoot about your television viewing habits? The news is that we have wasted close to two hours on this call and we are not going to carry it. Think of that when we don't get any sleep tonight because we will still be shooting!'

Mohawk gasped. 'It was such good TV. We'll get ratings...'

Tania said coldly. 'Let me be the judge of that. I am not putting an obviously fake call, where my anchor comes across as a clueless ass, on air. The viewer is not an idiot. Let's leave it at that. I hope that is understood.'

Tania was wrong on all counts. Nothing was understood. Mohawk was not going to leave it at that and Tania was not going to be the judge of anything. More critically, Tania was hopelessly wrong about an immutable law of television. The viewer is, was, and will remain an idiot.

Two days later, Tania found herself in Rahul's cabin. Also in attendance were Mohawk and Harish. After an hour of concerted badgering, Tania said weakly, 'It's a very lame call and will just look weird on TV.' She tried very hard not to scowl at a silently gloating Mohawk.

'Let me be the judge of that,' said Rahul.

Mohawk didn't say a word nor did his expression change, but Tania could hear his whoop of delight loud and clear.

Rahul said slightly more affably, 'Tania, I am looking at it as a viewer. When I heard it for the first time I got goosebumps. That girl, whoever she is, was super. The crying...the fucking catch in her voice—it was all so real. It doesn't matter if people watch it to speculate whether it is a fake call or not. It still works for us. Put it on, make a teaser out of it. We'll promo like mad and I guarantee we'll get a spike in numbers.'

Harish nodded his eager approval, and added for good measure, 'Stop being a school miss, Tania. You are getting hung up on the propriety, the ethic of carrying a fake call. This is TV, sweetie.'

'*Love Calls* has a fifty percent proportion of fake calls since the second schedule—I am not stupid enough to suddenly get moral about that factor. But this one is just so contrived and fake. Plus Vrushali comes across as an insensitive prize idiot. There's something just not right about this.'

'I heard the call and I think she handled the issue with tact and sensitivity. Nothing to complain about there. She really has come into her own now,' Rahul said brightly.

'T-tact! You are joking, right? Sensitive? Are you serious? My left toe nail has more tact than two of her put together,' Tania cut in harshly.

She was right—it did seem that all of Tania's reserves of tact and restraint were currently focused in her left toe nail because the rest of her had just made a hash of the present situation. She had just told off her boss with the subtlety, sensitivity, and tact of a sledgehammer. The only visible effect of this massacre, though was a slight strain in Rahul's smile and a slight stiffening of his spine. He was now convinced of what he had to do, 'The call is going on air. Get operations to put together a promo.'

Tania's left toe nail took over—she spent the next fifteen minutes in an impressive display of charm, cajolery, and coaxing in an attempt to make him change his mind. But Rahul was a man operating with a mortally wounded ego and was left untouched by Tania's belated ministrations.

She walked out of the cabin defeated, Mohawk on her heels. He said, 'Dude, I know what you are thinking. But I swear I didn't tell Rahul sir about the call.'

Tania muttered, 'I know. It came to him in a dream.'

Mohawk blustered on, 'No. I had made a CD of it, and was playing it on my computer, when he happened to walk past—'

'Save it,' she headed to Aditya's workstation and spat out the whole story of Mohawk's perfidy.

Mohawk shrugged his shoulders—he couldn't help it if his ideas on television worked better than hers.

—————

Aditya chuckled and said, 'Tani, that freak of nature will run the channel one day. He is on the right track.'

Tania snapped, upset with Aditya for not being empathetic enough. 'Thanks, that makes me feel so good.'

Aditya smiled gently, ruffled her hair in affection, and said, 'You silly girl, just be cynical about employment. It's a way to pay the bills. Period.'

Tania continued to look put out.

Bose chose that specific moment to walk past, and once again felt betrayed.

Tania called out to him plaintively, 'Bose...I need to speak to you.'

Aditya stopped smiling as he suddenly found something on his BlackBerry to jab on.

Bose said coldly, 'I'm really busy. Can it wait?'

'It's about *Love Calls...*'

Bose interjected, 'Give up the chase—the show is not working. I don't have the time for it. Plus you need to deal with Harish and Rahul on that one.'

Tania shrugged her shoulders and said, 'Fine', and turned her back on him. Her eyes were suddenly stinging and felt a bit moist. Aditya noticed her reaction and felt a jab of irritation that Tania was letting that pompous idiot affect her. He continued, though, to look like he was fully occupied with his BlackBerry.

Bose spent an agonizing minute wondering if he should speak to her again. In the resultant battle between his ego and his heart, it was a landslide victory for the former. Of course, if Tania had not made the strategic mistake of turning her back on him, it would have been a different story. The sight of one's muse in tears would have melted even the most hardened ego. But it was clearly not Tania's day, so Bose turned on his heel and stomped off.

'You guys need to get it out of your system. Get a room and get it over with.' Aditya observed, with a slight edge to an otherwise drily amused tone.

'I'd rather die,' said Tania, too caught up in her misery to catch the inflection in Aditya's tone.

'Lovely. Now you are behaving like the star of a B-grade melodrama...well done! But I must say it's much better than your usual passive martyrdom. You must keep it up,

Bose clearly brings out the best in you.' Aditya gave her a cheery thumbs up.

Tania sniffed and walked off. Damn Aditya. Damn Bose. Damn Rahul and Harish, and lest she be accused of sexism, the chronically correct Tania damned Vrushali and Jassi too. And then threw in Garnet for good measure.

Aditya stopped grinning and looked thoughtful, but then smiled wryly and got back to his laptop. He was breaking his own rules of total detachment and getting too involved in Tania's affairs—it was time to retreat.

The Jassi episode made it on air two evenings later at 6 pm sharp. In the YTV office, the impact was negligible. It played out on a Friday evening when most people had already switched to weekend mode. So, very few people at Tania's workplace paid attention to the goings on.

———

But a few kilometres away, *Love Calls* was getting all the attention that it certainly could have done without. In the plush conference room of a leading news channel, its prettiest face was hunched over a chair weeping while its most influential face stood at the door, watching. Rajneesh Tiwari had just made a crucial decision—the heart rending plight of Jassi would become a national campaign on his channel.

'Justice for Jassi'—the tagline blazed across his brain, which was feverish with possibilities. He laughed triumphantly. Neha looked up in shock and stood up hurriedly. She thought desperately for a plausible reason for her visible distress and drew a huge blank.

She stared helplessly at Rajneesh and stuttered, 'S-Sir I-I-'

Rajneesh was looking fixedly at the plasma screen, his eyes visibly excited. He turned to look at Neha and grinned affably, 'Neha, my girl, I understand. Don't worry...I am also a very sensitive man. I am almost sentimental, in fact, and it can be a liability when you are in the news business, but one cannot change what one is.' He then turned and strode out of the room purposefully. His mission was to find Shalini Sharma immediately.

Neha stared after him. For once she was not a pretty sight with her tear streaked face and dishevelled hair. It didn't help that she stood there gaping for a full five minutes long after Rajneesh had made his dramatic exit.. No one can look remotely pretty if their mouths are open so wide that you can see the cavity in their wisdom tooth.

Just one of life's little tips.

Playing Dirty

Zahira Mehra sat across Rahul's table, gesticulating furiously. She was a bird-like woman with a thin, high pitched voice. But she was the kind of bird that would not inspire warmth in even the most passionate ornithologist's heart. A raucous crow, she demanded that you instinctively shoo her away.

Rahul was not an ornithologist, at least not in the dry, scientific way. But most would testify that he was an accomplished bird watcher, and bird brained females were his domain of expertise. Zahira Mehra, the head of corporate communications at YTV, didn't fall into this area, so Rahul groaned inwardly as she kept up a steady stream of chatter.

Zahira narrowed her eyes and chirped, 'So what do you want me to do about it?'

Rahul asked blankly, 'About what?'

Zahira was used to people not listening to her, so she said patiently, 'About this news channel YNN—they have been calling me non-stop over the weekend. They want to do a story on *Love Calls*. Something about how lonely young Indians are turning to television for guidance, and if the traditional family structure in the country is ill equipped to handle their emotional needs.' She faithfully rattled off the contents of the email that Rajneesh had sent her.

Rahul wondered whether news channels were in the happy position of being immune to ratings. What a patently boring story to do. Rahul asked with a flicker of interest, 'Do they want to interview me?'

'Not yet. They want a few clips of the show,' said Zahira.

Rahul was bored now. 'Give them the clips then. What's the big debate here?'

'We should investigate further. It is important that there are no negative repercussions on the brand image.'

Rahul snorted. 'With that boring fucking story that no one will watch? Give them the clips—a little bit of publicity never harmed anything.'

The clips from *Love Calls* were sent on a CD to the YNN office. Rajneesh had been in an exultant mood the entire day, with the result that YNN was hysterically happy the entire day about the junior hockey team beating Bangladesh in a minor tournament. The sports desk complained feebly but Rajneesh was pleased, and he decreed that the nation must be too. This inconsequential hockey triumph was the only positive bit of news in a news list dominated by farmer suicides, dengue outbreak, and Rahul Gandhi's sneezing fit in the Parliament. So while Rahul Gandhi made headlines on every other channel, YNN played up the hockey win. And now, Rajneesh Tiwari was all set to extend the edgy unpredictability further.

Most of Rajneesh's core team, with the exception of Shalini, were kept in the dark about his latest brainwave. Like all self-made geniuses, Rajneesh was deeply suspicious and trusted no one. He was also superstitious and didn't want to jinx his masterstroke.

On Monday evening, the 12th of September, six weeks into the launch of *Love Calls*, it was all set to capture nation's imagination beyond any stretch of imagination of its makers. YNN's flagship show *The Mood of the Nation* started with the usual theatrical flourish but discerning viewers would notice that the mood was especially heightened on this day. Rajneesh was ferociously happy and Neha's good looks blazed out of the screen—Biplab had made an unscheduled weekend trip to Mumbai, so all was duly forgiven and blanked out.

Rajneesh had thrown the competition off guard yet again, for just when most of them were sheepishly taking up the hockey story, he threw in his lot with the Gandhi story. Half of his show was devoted to a discussion on the Gandhi scion's sneezing fit. The discussion was provocatively titled 'Is Rahul Gandhi laying it on too thick?' Rajneesh glowered into the camera and declared, 'First, the waiting in line to eat canteen food, now the sneezing—is Rahul trying too hard to be one of us?'

As usual Rajneesh had an impressive panel of guests— the party spokesperson, image management experts, and even the opposition representative. The stage was set for an invigorating discussion. Yes, said the opposition, Rahul was playing the commoner card in an extremely gimmicky manner but it was so ham handed that the electorate would see through it. This was hotly countered by the spokesperson who said that Mr Gandhi's ailment was not meant as an image building exercise.

'Ah,' pounced Rajneesh, 'is the pressure of politics taking a toll on him then?'

'No,' said the spokesperson stiffly, 'he is of a robust constitution but is entitled to his sneezes like everyone else.'

Rajneesh, the consummate debater, sprung in, 'Yes, that is the point. Is he trying too hard to be like everyone else? Denying his privileged roots and trying to be common?'

The image management expert interjected that the fact that he constantly covered his mouth while sneezing, with an immaculate white hanky, undid the attempt at being one with the masses. For in India, the common man believed in a free and fair dissemination of his germs. The opposition then said bitterly, 'Maybe he thinks his germs are too good for the rest of us—a clear testament to how, deep down, he is a feudalist. Our leaders, on the other hand, openly belch and spit, but you media guys give that negative publicity.'

Rajneesh added that it was indeed an unfair world and perhaps the media, especially the English language media, was unduly concerned with elitist notions of sneezing etiquette. In all of this, Neha discreetly painted her nails a pretty shade of pink. In any case, the cameras, through the discussion, were never on her.

The discussion ended like all of Rajneesh's discussions—inconclusively and pointlessly. But it was never his intention to either make a point or seek a solution. His job was to entertain and that he did every weeknight at ten. But today there was still more to come. Five minutes before the show was to end, Rajneesh looked into the camera. On Shalini's instructions, the camera zoomed in closer. His grin disappeared, his tone softened, and viewers could have sworn there was a thin film of moisture in his eyes.

'That's it from us on tonight's edition of *The Mood of the Nation*. We hope you will now have a happy dinner with your loved ones. But there are people in this country for whom that is a luxury. We leave you with a young girl—helpless, friendless, and dying alone. In her desperation, she calls a television helpline only to be treated callously, and be shaken off like unwanted dust. If you have a heart, our next story will disturb you as it did me. Do keep watching.'

The camera lingered for a moment on Rajneesh's face—a lock of his hair crept out and fell dramatically on his forehead and his voice sounded oddly choked. Whatever his failings, the man was a class act when it came to playing to the galleries. As it was a special case, Rajneesh had done both the script and the voice over for the news story to follow. It played out then for all of its three minutes of running time.

Opening graphics: JUSTICE FOR JASSI
Fade to black
Visuals: Tinted visuals of *Dyson X30 Love Calls*
Voice Over: A desperate cry for help. A call in the dark throes of despair.
Fade in Audio: (Jassi) *You are leaving me like everyone else. You were supposed to help…you have to help me. Please. Please! Don't hang up on me. I have no one…*
Voice Over: That voice sends a shiver down your spine. Don't shut your ears to her loneliness and sorrow.
Fade in Audio: *You are leaving me like everyone else. You were supposed to help…you have to help me. Please. Please! Don't hang up on me. I have no one…* (echo effect in the voice, this time round)
Voice Over: Who is she? A young girl abandoned by fate, by God, by us… Hear her story in her words.
Fade in Audio: *I am dying. I have cancer. I have two months to live.*
Voice Over: And if only it had ended here…
Fade in Audio: *The man I love doesn't want to be with me. I have only two months but he doesn't even want to pretend he loves me. He has left me He cu-could have waited for*

me to die. Before falling in love with my cousin—they are *getting married next month. They are not even waiting for* *me to du-die.* Voice Over: Every instinct in you wants to tell her to stop. You are sick in the stomach listening but fate continues its cruel joke …

Fade in Audio: *Parents? They died one month back in an* *accident. I have no one. Two weeks before they died, the* *doctors told me I had three months. I wish I had died too* *with them.*

Fade to black (Jassi's voice is still echoing as the frame dissolves into black)

Cut back to Rajneesh, staring rheumy eyed, into the camera. He spoke, 'Truth is sometimes stranger than fiction. This young and helpless girl is somewhere in the country, crying out for help. Desperate, she calls a relationship hotline on an entertainment channel. Now watch the treatment that is meted out to her. My blood boils, but I pray to God that you are not as sensitive as me because otherwise there will be blood on the streets.'

Fade to black
Jassi's tortured testimony is played out for the nth time in a loop. Her words reverberate.
I am dying. I have cancer. I have two months to live.
The man I love doesn't want to be with me. I have only two *months but he doesn't even want to pretend he loves me.* *He has left me.*
He cu-could have waited for me to die, before falling in *love with my cousin…they are getting married next month.* *They are not even waiting for me to du-die.*

199

Parents? They died one month back in an accident. I have no one. Two weeks before they died the doctors told me I had three months. I wish I had died too with them.

You are leaving me like everyone else. You were supposed to help—you have to help me. Please! Please! Don't hang up on me. I have no one.

(Sound of the phone being disconnected over and over again).

Voice Over: Would you hang up? Would you turn your back on this child? Would you have no mercy? Would you be callous enough to yank her only lifeline? If the answer is a resounding no, what you will witness will shock and sadden you. It will revolt you to the core of your being.

(A visual montage of Vrushali preening, pouting, and looking visibly exasperated).

Voice Over: We are not passing a value judgement here but would you entrust the counselling of that hapless girl to this scantily clad lady here? If you think we are only going by her appearance, listen to what she had to say to this desperate case.

(Carefully selected audio snatches play out, interspersed with the sound of a tabla playing frantically).

Love is killing…yeah
My dearie, I am not being sure how we can help you yeah with death and all that.
Two months time you will be meeting mummy daddy again.

200

Be thinking of that instead.

No dead people is going to call you—professional peoples is going to call you.

(Sound of phone being disconnected—looped over and over again).

Voice over: Yes, this channel dealt with a poor, helpless child with utter callousness. Leaving her to fate which had already abandoned her.

Fade in: *You are leaving me like everyone else. You were supposed to help...you have to help me. Please. Please. Don't hang up on me. I have no one...*

Fade to black

(Cut to a visual of Vrushali completely in black and white, the only thing left in colour is her Gothic eye make-up and blazing red lipstick. Her voice rings out again).

Audio: *My dearie, I am not being sure how we can help you yeah with death and all that.*

(A visual of Vrushali from the first part of the show where she is tittering and fluttering her eyelashes. The sound of her laughter is intercut with Jassi's plaintive voice, in another endless loop).

Don't hang up on me. I have no one (sound of Vrushali laughter). *Don't hang up...* (Sound of the phone being disconnected)

Fade to black

(Audio of typewriter keys being rammed. One by one, the letters appear on a black screen—J-U-S-T-I-C-E F-O-R J-A-S-S-I)

(The black screen then crumbles and forms the sentence once again in bold red. The words flash across the screen

till they are screaming out at the viewer. JUSTICE FOR
JASSI)

The screen cut back to a glowering Rajneesh. He cleared
his throat and bit out each word. 'Nobody listened to
her. Not the host—not the channel. She was just another
case to be dispensed with. We are not taking the moral
high ground here. This channel must have its reasons and
compulsions to abandon this girl. But can you? Can I?
Can we go on with our lives and put even a morsel of food
down our throats, while this poor girl dies alone? Life will
go on—the Sensex will soar, the government will stay in
power, and the cricket team will win matches. But life
will not go on for Jassi—she has only two months. Can't
an entire nation of people—people with a conscience,
with a heart—do something for her? I leave you with
those thoughts.'

He looked down seemingly overwhelmed. The closing
packaging of *The Mood of the Nation* played out. Rajneesh
ripped off his lapel mike and whooped in exultation.
Neha sat there still feeling like Pandora or whoever it
was who had opened her box. Shalini Sharma pumped
the air in the control room, and the entire studio
production team broke out into spontaneous applause.
Whatever the general sentiment about Rajneesh Tiwari,
a truly thespian performance had to be acknowledged
and appreciated.

Rajneesh tucked into a huge ham and cheese pizza to

celebrate his spectacular performance. Histrionics always increased his appetite.

In a corner of Mumbai, Tania watched the *The Mood of the Nation* come to an end, her dinner lying untouched on the table in front of her.

Tania sat twisting a tissue, which she held to her dribbling nose. Lack of sleep always aggravated her sniffles. The shreds of the mutilated tissue that fell on the carpet invited a mildly disapproving look from Rahul. Aditya often said that Rahul had missed his calling in life—he should have been in housekeeping and maintenance.

At this moment, Rahul would have welcomed the career change. He had listened to all of Tania's quavering account of the theatrics on YNN last night without any outward change in expression. But his insides were quaking almost as much as Tania's tremulous voice. He had ignored Zahira's attempts to convene a crisis management meeting through the morning, telling her tersely and firmly, 'Don't blow things out of proportion. To manage a crisis, let's be sure that this is a crisis in the first place. Get a CD of the story first and then we can take a call.'

Rahul was right—it wasn't a crisis, it was a full blown calamity. Tania's testimony had settled that. Amrit

Khanna, who had an early morning panic call from Dyson, was pacing impatiently in the room, pulling his lower lip—his dislike of Tania growing by the minute.

Tania's voice trailed on, 'And then that annoying, pompous ass on YNN said something like he won't eat till they can make Jassi happy or something to the effect. The graphic plate they had was something else...On the right they had in capital letters—"Justice for Jassi".'

Amrit frowned, 'Sounds ugly. Why didn't they just pick up our packaging? That way we could have got the brand colours in as well. That may have pleased Dyson a bit.'

Tania sniffled angrily and blew her nose in disapproval. Amrit stared at her in open contempt and thought she was an eminently incapable woman. In his mind, she was now permanently etched as a constantly blubbering mess armed with disposable tissue. Rahul wasn't listening to Amrit. He said softly, almost to himself over and over again, 'Oh gosh. Oh gosh. Oh gosh.'

For the second time in their acquaintance, Tania felt that Rahul's reaction to a crisis situation was annoyingly tame and passive. What she didn't know was that Rahul was falling apart. He had blanked out. He couldn't remember a single masterful expletive.

But Rahul's knight in sweaty armour was just around the corner. Harish Swamy walked in, and Rahul was never happier to see his multiple-chinned accomplice.

Harish looked around and realized he had walked

into trouble. Tania looked like she'd been crying, Amrit looked irritable, and Rahul—the man whose fortunes he had a majority stake in—looked like he was ready to be burnt at the stake.

Rahul said in notes of despair, 'Harish, we have a situation, a…damned…awful situation.'

Harish felt a lurch of panic at the usage of the words 'damned' and 'awful'. Rahul was losing his bearings. So he charged in promptly. 'Fucking hell. Is it that behenchod show *Love Calls* again? What has it got up its motherfucking ass this time?'

Rahul staged a quick recovery. He felt the blood rush back to his head—the light at the end of the tunnel became a laser display. 'Fucking bastard on some third-rate news channel has made one big drama of that Jassi call. He's running a campaign against us, and Zahira has her motherfucking panties in a knot.'

He proceeded to spell out the sorry situation to Harish. Tania noticed that he punctuated each line with a new expletive, pausing to savour it once it had rolled off his tongue. She had not missed the look of gratitude that Rahul had dashed Harish's way the minute he had stepped into the room. Harish's presence gave him a swaggering confidence, and for once, Tania was appreciative of it. It was decided that Zahira should now be allowed to convene her crisis management meeting. She was urgently summoned on the intercom. She trotted in briskly and brusquely in a few minutes.

She said sharply, 'I do hope you realize we have wasted time. All the tabloids of the world are calling me for a reaction. Next time I tell you we have a crisis, do me the favour of listening to me. Now, what are we going to do?'

'You've been stressing about this the whole morning. You must have devised some plan,' Rahul said genially.

'We send out a press release saying that in the interests of Jassi's privacy, we strongly condemn the spectacle that has been made out of her life. And that it is her express desire that she be spared all this—we take a moral high ground. That is what we do,' bristled Zahira.

Rahul interjected, 'I think we don't do anything. We sit it out. It'll blow over. Some bomb will go off somewhere and this Rajneesh fucker will get off our backs. We send out a press release and that will mean more fucking media attention. Don't say anything. If people call for a clarification, say the channel will not react to false, twisted stories.'

Tania nodded, 'Yes, please let us not quote Jassi or anything. She does not exist. We will just make things worse.'

Zahira looked displeased. She shrugged her shoulders coldly. 'Sure, but I am going to put the advice of the communications department on record.' She walked out of the room stiffly.

Amrit said he was getting into damage control mode with Dyson and left as well. That left Tania, Harish, and Rahul in the room.

Tania said wearily, 'Please let's get rid of this show. From day one, it has just been a lot of trouble. I'm sick and tired of it.'

'You need some sleep. Go home early. It'll blow over,' Rahul said kindly.

Tania's shoulders slumped. She was sure that it wouldn't be as easy as that.

Rahul watched her leave thoughtfully and turned to Harish. 'So, brother, you think we are okay?'

Harish said promptly, 'Of course, sir. No point in reacting.'

Rahul relaxed visibly and hoped that everything would die down soon.

What they don't tell you about hope is that it has a very poor delivery record.

——

As Tania had suspected, the episode didn't blow over. It blew up. In Rahul's face.

Rahul, unfortunately, hadn't watched too much news TV before the Jassi fiasco. Rajneesh Tiwari's ability to stoke a non-existent fire to a blazing inferno took him completely by surprise. Every bulletin had the 'Justice for Jassi' campaign as an end piece. The three-minute story was truncated to a fifteen-second clip of Jassi begging to be heard. Each anchor would sombrely rattle off the lines, 'As we speak, we still don't know where or who Jassi is. Time is running out for her. Help us help you, Jassi!'

On the right side of the screen, a countdown clock ticked away. It was an electronic clock with flashing numerals which alternated with a heartbeat line. This was Jassi's countdown to death.

Shalini had her reservations about putting the clock on air. 'It looks a bit cheesy.'

Rajneesh laughed. 'We are a cheesy country. We love this shit. We love nautanki. And most importantly, I know what I'm doing.'

Even his most staunch loyalist would have found it hard to defend Rajneesh's hardnosed stance, which was bereft of all ideology. You could spin the readymade sentimental back story—that had he hung on to ideology or ideals, the big bucks corporation that owned YNN would have quickly shown him the door. But Rajneesh had never really put up a fight because all he had had, in the first place, was a perfunctory allegiance to nebulous text book ideals. He had cheerfully hand delivered his soul, gift wrapped and perfumed, and didn't want it back. A soul, after all, was a poor substitute for success.

And Rajneesh had made a habit out of succeeding because he had the winning formula down pat. 'Remember, we are an English news channel, but the aggression, our values, our tenor is more like a Hindi news channel—we are not the fucking BBC. We take a stand and we will be emotional and we will be in your face and loud. Because that is the way this country likes its entertainment. And make no mistake that news *is* entertainment.'

The latest installment in entertainment—the 'Justice for Jassi' campaign—was set to be a blockbuster story for YNN. The other English news channels steered clear from it rather squeamishly but the Hindi news channels lapped it up. Half hour shows discussing Jassi's plight in graphic detail with viewers calling in, played on every channel. The faceless Jassi seemed to have captured the nation's imagination.

Unfortunately for Rahul, terrorists, arsonists, hijackers, suicidal farmers, and even Naxalites had decided to take things easy, and nothing suitably disastrous had happened to take attention away from Jassi. The Indian cricket team, too, had unthinkingly been given a three-week season break. Unless Sania Mirza won a Grand Slam singles title, it didn't look like there would be any respite for YTV. Even the most radical optimist wouldn't be wagering on Sania, and Rahul was a realist. For two days, YNN had gone hammer and tongs at the Jassi story. The story had been juiced of every kind of emotion—grief, empathy, sympathy, commiseration, identification—and now, Rajneesh was steering it into an emotion guaranteed to treble the ratings. Anger.

At the end of *The Mood of the Nation* the night before, Rajneesh had demanded accountability. Supremely angry, he had blazed fury into the lens. 'We still don't know who or where Jassi is. What saddens me is the silence of the channel that let her down. Is its conscience dead? Fine, you don't want to tell us where the girl is. At least tell a worried nation what you have done to help her since you can access her and we cannot. If you have washed your hands off the girl, entrust her to an entire army of hands willing to take on the responsibility. I am confounded, confused, and angry. You should be too,' he had thundered.

After telling the nation what to do and signing off from the show, Rajneesh yawned sleepily. He smiled at Neha as she took off her lapel mike and told her about the PTA meeting he had to attend at his daughter's school the next day. Rajneesh liked attending PTA meetings because the other parents treated him like a figure of authority, occupying a higher moral plane than them.

Surbasree then managed to surprise Rajneesh by walking into his cabin. 'That Jassi story is good, you know.'

Rajneesh clutched his heart and said in tones of deep gratitude, 'You think so? Really? Thank you, I can retire now.'

Surbasree paid no attention to his exaggerated reaction. 'It's interesting that people are moving away from a certain kind of television viewing. The television soap is no longer the singular source of drama. New genres are taking precedence.'

Rajneesh sighed and said, 'Yes. So?'

'Reality—that is what we're getting addicted to. We want it real and raw. From a fiercely conservative society, we are changing into a country that wants to make an exhibition of itself. This Jassi case started out on a light chatty show. Clearly, in an effort to prop up ratings, the channel got in this extreme case, which, otherwise, is a complete misfit with the tone of the show. A fine example of blindly following a trend and having it misfire.'

Rajneesh fidgeted with the paperweight on his table. He had stopped paying attention after the first line of Surbasree's little speech.

She continued, 'There is a larger story on television and society that we can and should do. If you wish, I can take the Jassi story forward along these lines.'

Rajneesh was not a man given to keeping a wish list. But if he had any such inclination, any wish to give the Jassi story to Surbasree would have come a close second to his wish to be assaulted by a pack of rabid dogs. 'No. I have already assigned the story. You don't worry.'

Surbasree said calmly, 'I can help. Who has it been given to?'

'There is a team working on it. You really don't need to focus on this,' said Rajneesh.

Surbasree looked at him quizzically, 'You have a secret crack team working on this?'

Rajneesh said cagily, 'You can say that. It's a big story for us.'

Surbasree shrugged her shoulders, 'That is fine then. You know, I don't think this girl exists by the way.'

It was typical of Surbasree to introduce the most dramatic point of her discourse in this incidental manner. That was why she would never make for a good broadcast journalist. She never really broke news. She was much too matter of fact.

Rajneesh had not thought of that at all. 'How do you mean?' he enquired.

Surbasree said thoughtfully, 'A bit too convenient no? Channel has a flighty agony aunt kind of show. It's not rating to well so some wise guy decides to put in reality. And one of your first cases is an extreme case—where nothing has gone right for the girl. Not only is it too convenient, it is a bit too ham handed. Typical knee jerk reaction of not very intelligent channel programmers.'

Rajneesh decided to blank out whatever Surbasree had said—it would not work for him to have a fictional Jassi.

'Surbasree, you are too cynical. The suffering of the human spirit no longer moves you. Everything is dry, analytical, and academic. You are a journalist, not a sociologist. You need to report, not editorialize, my girl,' he said.

Surbasree laughed. 'I am cynical? I love your sense of irony. It's superb; so finely tuned.'

She left Rajneesh feeling as he usually did after a conversation with her—slightly overwhelmed and a bit undone. He wished that some foreign university would appear on the horizon and whisk Surbasree away to the safety of a dissertation on Indian mass culture. Her preoccupation with getting to the heart of the matter, of putting things in the right context, was an annoying trait and totally detrimental to the news business.

Stetson was back from his working holiday, and Rahul hadn't had a moment of sleep since then. How the hell was he going to get out of this Jassi fiasco? Stetson had shown only an absent minded interest in *Love Calls*—an interest which had soon degenerated into indifference after the indifferent ratings. In his last email, he had pretty much told Rahul to now focus on Bose's life swap show.

But this was before 'Justice for Jassi' had become the nation's agenda. Zahira had called Stetson to brief him about the ongoing crisis and had even asked if he needed Rahul to clarify further. His response was a quick, pithy negative. Rahul had been torn between relief and dread, but now, the moment of reckoning could no longer be kept in abeyance.

In fact, the moment of reckoning was flashing on his BlackBerry. Stetson was calling. Trying to steady his shaking hands and voice, Rahul said jauntily, 'Hello, sir, good to have you back.'

Stetson had no time for the banalities of social discourse. He came straight to the point. 'Good going on this *Love Calls* show. We wouldn't have got the kind of publicity even if we had paid for it. What's the plan now?'

Rahul was stupefied. 'Plan, sir...uh...we are hoping that the stories will stop if we don't pay them any attention.'

Stetson snarled, 'Hope is not a plan, Rahul. The stories won't stop on their own. Why don't you produce the girl? Let us have a press conference where she can tell people how YTV safeguarded her interests and was her only hope. We steal the thunder from this news channel.'

Rahul stammered, 'Sh-she doesn't exist, sir.'

Stetson said thoughtfully, 'Oh yes, Zahira had mentioned that. Get in an actress or something then. Make her sign a confidentiality agreement or something.'

'Except that she would have to die in a month's time. Will tell the talent acquisition department to get cracking on it though. I'll speak to Aditya,' said Rahul.

'Or just get a dying actress. Sort of kills two birds with one stone. Sorry, that was insensitive of me but you get what I mean.'

Rahul felt his heart lurch and sink into the deep recesses of his stomach. It kept slipping further and had just reached his knees, when Stetson spoke again after a pregnant pause.

'Find the girl and let's see how it goes. In the meanwhile, make sure no one on the show team blabs.'

Rahul took a deep breath and steadied his shaking

knees and voice, and jabbed at Aditya's number. It was midnight and Aditya had most prudently switched off his phone like he did every evening after 6 pm. Rahul typed him a quick SOS mail and spent a restless night texting Harish Swamy instead, who assured him that all would be well soon.

The next morning Aditya Menon found himself in the happy position of being the recipient of an email which said:

> Bro,
> Situation is spinning out of control. Urgently require a young teenage actress with a life threatening disease—she will need to die in the next one month or so. Stetson wants this done immediately. Get all of celebrity content on this. We don't have too much time.
> Best,
> RS
>
> PS: Please try and ensure that the girl looks YTV. Don't want some hick.

A lesser man would have possibly had a paroxysm at this point. But as has been established by now, Aditya was not a lesser man—he was Aditya Menon, the master of hustle and bluster. So without skipping a beat, he typed in his reply.

> sure thing, boss. will try to line up well groomed dying girl. I think it would make sense to look for someone skinny coz

you perceive dying as wasting away, etc. However if push
comes to shove, and the girl is slightly overweight, we may
just have to settle for that since it is crunch time.
AM

Then Aditya went back to lazily brushing his teeth.

It was a slur on the collective reputation of the entire talent acquisition team that in the next two days, they recorded no success in finding a young, dying actress. In a city teeming with young aspirants, not one seemed to be in any hurry to die.

'How is that possible?' fumed Harish. 'Have we become such a healthy country that people no longer die? Or has the mortality rate among females really improved that much? I don't think these fuckers are trying hard enough, sir. As usual.'

Rahul looked grimly at his strangely bloodless knuckles.

Harish, detecting an opportunity to run down the detestable Aditya's department, added, 'Even if we can't find a girl with a disease, how tough is it to find a suicidal girl? Saali, she is anyway going to swing from some fucking fan, may as well let it benefit someone. These guys are not trying at all. Remember how they didn't deliver Shahrukh for our dandiya party, and we got some third-rate television actor instead. Sir, don't mind me saying this but we are far too lenient with them. We should have put something up their ass a long time back.'

'Asses...plural,' said Rahul vacantly.

Harish nodded in agreement. 'Yes of course, sir.'

Rahul wondered if they should make the rounds of hospitals to find sufficiently dying and sufficiently poor girls who would agree to be Jassi for some money. He cursed under his breath as he remembered that the parents would also need to agree to die. The other big problem was that poor girls would look like poor girls and decidedly down market. Rahul's shoulders drooped and he only straightened up when Aditya and Mohawk walked into his office.

Aditya said breezily, 'We dialled all of Screen Video World, which is an actors' database, as you know. Besides an eighty-year-old woman who used to act in silent films, noone is in any imminent danger of dying. Even the eighty-year-old assured me that she is in pretty good health—she does yoga.'

Harish said, distracted instantly, 'Yoga? Really? My wife wants me to join classes. They have individual training as well as group sessions.'

'So you will probably end up paying group costs then... one of you equals quite a large group!' piped Aditya as he jabbed at Harish's belly.

Harish was suddenly quite happy that he had spent most of his morning bad mouthing Aditya. Mohawk, who was now touted as being the Harish Swamy-in-waiting, given the amount of time he managed to inveigle for himself in Rahul's cabin, grinned.

Rahul turned to him with more than a hint of desperation and said, 'That friend of yours...who made the call...she wouldn't be really dying by a long shot?'

Mohawk shook his head mournfully. 'Naah, she's the type who doesn't even get a cold, dude.'

Aditya noticed the 'dude' and the easy familiarity with which Mohawk had taken up residence in Rahul's cabin. He felt a sudden pang for the hapless and harried Tania; she was clearly not part of this cosy inner circle. He asked Mohawk casually, 'What is your immortal friend's name?'

He said a tad uneasily, 'Jasleen—Jassi.'

Aditya laughed, 'Oh well, at least that part of the story is true if nothing else. Is she going to keep a lid on it?'

Mohawk said, 'Yes. I've warned her. She won't say a word.'

Aditya looked intently at Mohawk. 'Can't we get her to record a message saying she wants to be left alone and send that tape to these channels?'

'She really doesn't want anything more with this situation. I could try and convince her but....' Mohawk trailed off, looking at Rahul.

Rahul was shaking his head. 'Good thought, but it won't work. These guys are not going to back off till they see Jassi. We either give them the girl or nothing at all.'

Aditya shrugged his shoulders, 'There is no girl though, remember?'

'I guess I'll tell Stetson that there is no dying actress available. The other problem is that the story is not going cold at all. That fucking channel just isn't stopping and some useless fifty-thousand fuckers have logged on to their website in support. There is going to be a candlelight vigil in Delhi. This is madness! I don't know where we can get off,' sighed Rahul. He continued worriedly, 'And then we have to control Nair too. He wanted to take Vrushali to one of these candlelight vigils because YNN has made her look like a vamp. I had to threaten to pull the plug on her YTV career before he backed off.'

Tania walked in, cutting a desolate and faintly resentful figure—she suspected there was a lot of activity going around her show but no one thought it important to keep her in the loop. Rahul and Harish didn't acknowledge her presence. Aditya looked at her thoughtfully. She glared at Mohawk sitting jauntily in a corner of the cabin and said to him sharply, 'Why are you never at the edit? The editor spends half his time looking for you.'

Rahul stepped in and told Tania pleasantly, 'Not his fault. I just wanted to pick his brain for five minutes. Crisis on *Love Calls*. We need to find an actress to play Jassi. Stetson's orders.'

Tania felt her spine stiffen in resentment—noone had mentioned this to her. She heard herself say tartly, 'Pity Jassi is not a man otherwise Mohawk would have happily

220

killed himself for the cause of the channel by playing her. He is very dedicated that way.'

Mohawk winced. Aditya smiled—Tania's words had triggered off an idea.

Rahul clucked, 'Come on, Tania, this is not the time to get territorial. We're all in this together. This is our problem to solve. He is just helping out.'

Tania looked at Aditya. He winked imperceptibly; it was so fleeting that no one else caught it. To everyone else, Aditya looked unusually serious and deep in thought. But Tania knew better. She knew that Aditya was hatching some scheme for his amusement. Her spirits lifted. She was going to enjoy being a spectator.

Aditya looked intently at Rahul. Very early in his career, he had decided on his role—he was always going to be like the chorus in a Greek drama, which is constantly present on stage but doesn't influence the course of events. It is a chronicler and a commentator, and pretty much in a comfort zone. Today, Aditya decided that he was going to step out of the chorus and join the main cast briefly. He wanted to see what levels of desperation Rahul and Harish could go to. This was a purely academic study, for malice never governed any of Aditya's motives. Plus it would cheer up Tania—he didn't like her looking so downcast.

So he cleared his throat and said, 'I think I know who can play Jassi—would be dying to in fact. Forgive the pun.'

Rahul looked at him in hope. He asked eagerly, 'Who?'

Aditya said, 'Charlie Angel.'

The four listeners gaped. 'I hope you're joking!' said Rahul finally.

Aditya said calmly, 'Not. Think of it. It adds another dimension to the story.'

Charlie Angel—the transvestite. The man-woman who was always willing to be a freak show on display. All of that supposedly to fund his sex change operation. But the truth was that Charlie Angel would probably never opt for the operation because that would cut off his income flow besides the other vital organ.

Aditya continued, 'We know his family wants nothing to do with him. We can say that his boyfriend dumped him, and this poor lonely chap, diagnosed with an incurable disease, had no one to turn to except the show. So he faked being Jassi because he knew a transvestite wouldn't get any sympathy.'

Even as he spoke, Aditya knew how patently ridiculous his story was. Any logical person with an average IQ would turn it down immediately. He waited for Rahul to react. He wasn't disappointed.

'Bro, there is an idea there. It is a plan. A good plan!' said an excited Rahul.

Tania held her breath. Just what was Aditya up to? Harish and Mohawk looked put out—Aditya had beaten them to aiding Rahul's salvation.

Aditya was having the time of his life now. He said sombrely, 'Also once the nation realizes that "Jassi" is a publicity hungry freak show, I bet the candlelight marches will stop. That Rajneesh will look like an idiot. It is one thing imagining some poor young child and another thing seeing a real-life drag queen. Viewers will be put off.'

Rahul shook his head eagerly. Harish and Mohawk looked at Aditya with a mix of resentment and awe. Tania made a strange, choking noise which she hastily suppressed, but no one seemed to notice.

Aditya went in for the final blow. 'Also, we get the moral high ground—we say we wanted to save this poor thing from social ridicule but unfortunately now we've been pushed into a corner.'

Rahul said hoarsely, 'Genius—lets go for it!'

——

In an hour's time, Charlie Angel walked into the office dressed in a red halter mini and black stockings. He had a blonde wig on and wore perilously high heels. He headed straight for Rahul. He tapped his cheek and said bashfully, 'Hi hot stuff!'

Rahul tried not to wince. Harish looked revolted—he was completely homophobic. Tania had finally dispatched a grumpy Mohawk to the edit bay. She made sure to be in Rahul's cabin—she didn't want to miss this for the world.

Nair walked in with Charlie Angel. Aditya wondered

idly what Nair would call his client of ambiguous gender. If Vrushali was 'Madamji', what would Charlie be? 'Sirji' was unlikely.

Nair said to Rahul briskly, 'Bhai, Angelji was really busy but at short notice, because you have asked, we have come now.'

Rahul, thrown by the two pronged attack, missed the flash of amusement on Aditya's face. Harish didn't but, since he lacked any powers of perception, couldn't make too much of it.

Aditya quickly reverted to a straight face. He wondered how Rahul could want to go ahead with such a daft scheme; clearly he had underestimated the man. He was a bonafide nutcase. He glanced quickly at Tania. Besides a slight twitch of her lower lip, her face was perfectly composed.

Charlie looked at Rahul coyly from under his lashes. 'So, cutie, you want me to be Jassi? For you I will be anything. Don't blush honey, I am just joking.'

Aditya intervened as Rahul looked distinctly uncomfortable. 'Charlie, will you be able to pull off the dying part? Though, of course, in some time we'll come up with a miracle cure.'

Nair interrupted, 'Angelji is ready to do any part. If you want attempted suicide, we can try with limited number of sleeping pills or surface cuts on wrists too.'

Angelji threw back his head and tittered, 'It's nothing. It'll be my fourth or fifth attempt, I think.'

'Sixth,' Nair said proudly.

Rahul looked queasy.

'We don't think the situation will come to that,' Nair continued, 'but only slashes and pills. Hanging, bhai, is a bit risky, no.'

Charlie held his neck and winked broadly at Rahul. 'For this cutie, maybe I will put my neck on the line also.'

Nair beamed. Rahul trembled. Harish felt ill. Tania averted her face quickly. Only Aditya continued calmly, 'What about the parents? Jassi's parents are dead. Are your parents up to attempting suicide as well?'

Charlie said darkly, 'They don't want anything to do with me. So if I kill them off in an accident, they are not going to deny it.'

Nair took charge, 'So then it's all settled. We can sign the contract today itself.'

Aditya waited for Rahul to call things off but Rahul nodded in rapturous agreement.

'You'll need to sign a non-disclosure agreement with us. We'll tell you what to say. You can't interact with the press without our approval,' Rahul said to Charlie.

Charlie beamed, 'Of course, sweetie pie! I was thinking, since I am dying now, I should wear less make-up and maybe wear only white—I have beautiful white corsets and tube tops. Will also look so sexy.'

Nair beamed approvingly.

Harish cleared his throat and spoke his first words

of significance, 'Our stylist will decide your look. We have to make sure that you look YTV. That is the most important thing here.'

Tania thought of the blundering Garnet Patel who would need to come up with a dress code for a dying drag queen. Some things they don't teach at fashion school. This was getting even better.

Aditya said to Charlie, 'Fantastic, you are going to be the best dressed dead person around, sweetheart. Keep the eye make-up though—no one does smoky eyes as well as you do.'

Charlie giggled, 'Naughty boy!' and then slapped Rahul on his thigh.

Tania stored up the image of a squirming Rahul for posterity—it was so much more satisfying than him in front of the firing squad. She wondered when Aditya would finally pull the plug on this madcap scheme though because her amusement was giving way to concern. What if they handed Charlie to her to groom as 'Jassi'?

Aditya looked at Rahul—when would rational thought return to this man? He hadn't imagined his study of human desperation to throw up such radical results. He could sense Tania's eyes on him, she obviously expected him to call this off, but it was now out of his hands. He deliberately didn't look in her direction.

Rahul summoned Zahira. She came in looking wary; corporate communications at YTV in recent times was taking a dimension that she didn't quite approve of. She then spotted Charlie Angel and realized that her wariness was completely called for.

Rahul said shortly, 'Be on standby. Keep the agency alerted. In a day's time we could do a presser on who the real Jassi is.'

Zahira raised her eyebrows and said, 'Okay. Have we found a girl?'

Rahul pointed at Charlie who blew a kiss at Zahira.

Zahira was speechless. Rahul turned to Charlie and said, 'Remember you are dying of cancer. We need to get some terminology and facts right on that.'

Charlie said dreamily, 'It should have been a heart disease. I am dying of a broken heart. Would've been so romantic no?'

Zahira sat on a chair looking into space. Was this the right time to go on a sabbatical? If it weren't for that damned home loan, maybe she would have. She shuddered inwardly as she looked at Charlie perched on a chair. Tania looked at her in sympathy.

Nair flapped his hands and said, 'Bhai, let's talk money now. How much?'

Rahul's BlackBerry buzzed—Stetson.

Stetson was doing a rethink on his ambitious move to get a decoy Jassi. Not because a decoy for a decoy was an absurdity in itself but because the managing board had expansion plans. On the anvil were two new channels—a music channel and a lifestyle channel. The licenses to operate these two had not come through, and this was the wrong time to be inviting the ire of the I & B Ministry.

'Sure, it'll get us a lot of attention and eyeballs, but a short term spurt cannot take the place of long-term expansion plans. The more we get into this mess, the tougher it will be to get ourselves out,' he said eruditely explaining his change of heart. That though was just one of the reasons for the rethink. There was another equally compelling reason, in fact that was perhaps the clincher. It had everything to do with the glass panes at YTV.

The reception area of YTV was flanked by long French windows. The rest of it was like most centrally air-conditioned offices—dumpy, poorly ventilated, and lit up by ugly white tube lights. But those details are not important—the French windows are. These were in the rather inconvenient habit of getting shattered once in three months.

This didn't have much to do with the quality of the glass but rather with the quality of programming at YTV. As the channel floundered from format to format with no impact on the ratings, every conceivable social welfare group out there still managed to find something offensive in its programming.

This year, YTV had already been stormed on three different occasions. First by transgendered people, and then by animal activists. The first casualty in both these cases—the French windows—were blackened and broken by livid protestors. Fortunately, on the third occasion, when members of Anorexics Anonymous showed up, the panes were spared as the activists had just enough stamina for sloganeering.

But Stetson knew they couldn't be that fortunate each time. *Love Calls* was already on the radar of the Stree Sabhyata Samiti—The Women's Propriety Organization. This organization had first created a ruckus by targeting women who visited pubs, and now Vrushali's clothes had offended their code of propriety. 'Indian ladies are being shown in a negative light by this channel. It is misrepresenting our ladykind. She is wearing American chaddis and spoiling our youth,' said the convenor of the Stree Sabhyata Samiti in soundbytes to assorted news channels.

Of course, no journalist there actually asked them the rather pertinent question—whether it would be acceptable for Vrushali to spoil the youth if she wore Indian chaddis instead. But that was a minor detail.

They hollered into the many cameras, 'We are warning YTV—show our Indian culture or we will show them how to.'

Since shattering French windows and anything else that came in their way was an intrinsic part of the culture of any Indian agitation, Stetson was worried. So was the board. It was a lean year and they had firmly voted that no further money could be diverted to glass panes' repair. So he instructed Rahul, 'Dress up that Vrushali and let us not add any more angles to this Jassi drama. Don't find any girl—it will just get us in deeper. Do what it takes to shut up those YNN guys. I cannot go back to the Board with a requisition for more repair work.'

Rahul had no time to brief Stetson about the Charlie Angel angle, just as well since Aditya didn't want Rahul's loss of employment on his conscience.

Rahul put down the phone and told Nair, 'Give us a few days. We'll get back to you with a plan. Let me bounce this off internally with the core team. The minute we have something concrete, let's connect again.'

Tania heaved a sigh of relief and rolled her eyes as she looked across at Aditya. He shrugged his shoulders and quickly put an arm across Nair's suddenly drooping shoulders. 'Don't worry, Nair sir, we will do something big and mind blowing soon.'

Nair smiled weakly and Charlie's face crumbled for a split second—it looked hard, cold, and unfriendly. But the moment passed in a flash and he was back to seductively assuring Rahul that he would call him every day.

He said in a low, husky voice, 'I feel a connect with you. I think we can be…friends.' And then he left in a trail of strong, cheap perfume.

Zahira and Nair followed him out.

Rahul shuddered. Tania stood there, torn between relief and laughter. Rahul told her worriedly to get more clothes on Vrushali. 'Cover her up—Stetson wants it that way.'

Aditya walked away, laughing quietly about the near disaster he had orchestrated.

Tania caught up with him and said, 'This time you really pushed it. What if we had really got stuck with Charlie Angel?'

Aditya pondered, 'I wish we had. I think by the next meeting he would have been slapping Rahul's ass and at least attempting to kiss Harish.'

Tania burst out laughing and then said abruptly in a softer tone, 'Thank you!'

'For what? For nearly giving you Charlie as your latest "talent" to handle?'

Tania continued seriously, 'Till I walked into that room, I was feeling incompetent. Like nothing I did could get the bosses to trust me. And then, when I saw Rahul lap up the most stupid scheme in the world, I realized that it was totally okay if he doesn't think I am on the same wavelength as him. Who wants to be? Mohawk is most welcome to it.'

Aditya grinned. 'Ah Tania, you're giving me far too much credit. I just wanted to have a good laugh. And you know me, I'm not some hero running to your rescue like your darling Bose. You are perfectly capable of looking after yourself.'

Tania smiled and gave his arm a quick squeeze. Aditya mocked, 'One tiny squeeze is all I get for my efforts?'

Tania laughed, suddenly very self conscious. Aditya continued meaningfully, 'Charlie Angel would have given me a lot more, and by that, I mean *a lot more* if I had pulled off Jassi for him.'

Tania shuddered, laughing still, only stopping when Aditya suddenly looked uncharacteristically serious and said, 'Find a way of getting out of this circus. These men are fools but dangerous fools, Tani.'

Tania nodded and was worried all over again.

———————

She called and instructed Garnet to get more clothes on Vrushali in the next schedule. Garnet squeaked, 'So what do I make her wear?'

Too preoccupied to think, Tania murmured crankily, 'Oh just let her wear maxis or something,' before hanging up on Garnet.

Garnet Patel stood there shaking in triumph—she looked heavenwards convinced that there was a larger divine force that worked only to vindicate stylists.

YTV went firmly back into the wait and watch mode.

Love Calls displaced *The Comedy Challenge* and became YTV's number one show. The controversy that it had managed to attract had also attracted many curious viewers. But Rahul had no time to celebrate as the Jassi story was far from going cold. In a major victory for Rajneesh, competing English news channels had to abandon their stodginess and pick up the story. They didn't make it a headline story, but carried updates on almost every other bulletin. Meanwhile pretty Neha Chitre was packed off to Chandigarh to trace the elusive Jassi.

'Don't worry,' Rajneesh told her, 'you just have to be the face of the story. The bureau will do all the leg work.'

Rajneesh was running a promo campaign on 'Finding Jassi' and he had no intentions of splashing Geeta Khanna, who was back at the Chandigarh bureau, all over it. Her journalistic ability was not in doubt but something a lot more crucial was. He wrinkled his nose. 'She's a bit overweight to carry off this story.'

To Geeta he said glibly, on the phone, 'This is a frivolous story and I know a journalist of your credibility will not want to lend her face to it. I'm sending this chit of a girl—please help her. And make sure that the channel does not look stupid just because it is beneath you to be a visible part of this story. You owe that to the channel.'

Geeta, wise to Rajneesh's tactics, said nothing but was once again convinced that she should return to her newspaper job. A story byline there had very little to do with how much you weighed on the weighing scale.

But being a diligent journalist, she did her homework. She scoured hospital records and police station records. There were terminally ill girls, and there were road accidents. But the two never came together to give shape to Jassi. Pretty Neha, meanwhile, devoted herself to understanding retail in Chandigarh first hand. She shopped till she dropped.

On the sixth day after the story first broke, there was still no sign of Jassi. Rajneesh went on air and said in desperation, 'As we speak, Neha has been in Chandigarh for three days, working day and night to get to Jassi. And while there have been leads, most of them have proved to be false starts. Let us now go back to Delhi where there is a candlelight march in progress, for Jassi.'

The show cut across to an excessively emotional story where overwrought nameless people wrung their hands and cried their eyes out for the faceless Jassi. And of course, burnt many candles.

Rajneesh said, 'That sight will move the hardest of hearts—even a weather-beaten journalist like me is moved. In a last ditch effort we entreat YTV to part with the mobile number of the girl. At least through that we can trace her whereabouts. Our extensive investigation has shown that she is probably no longer in Chandigarh.'

Geeta Khanna called Rajneesh after the show. She said, 'Chief, it's clear that this girl does not exist. I think we either need to say that upfront or back down now from this story. Or we'll end up looking stupid.'

'You know, I think news channels should have only one editor because it gets a bit complicated if everyone starts imagining that they run the channel. I've always believed in democracy but it only works well if everyone sticks to their portfolios. Home sticks to Home, Finance sticks to Finance, reporters stick to reporting. You get me, my dear?' Rajneesh said in tones of exaggerated sweetness.

Geeta understood perfectly, and she was suddenly glad that none of her weight loss initiatives had ever been successful. At least there would be no egg on her face. She hung up on the boss, feeling rather light headed, and snacked on her chocolate bar without any guilt for once.

———

In Chandigarh, Neha Chitre had a surprise visitor. Biplab Mitra dropped in unexpectedly at the YNN office from Delhi, much to her extreme ecstasy. She cooed and pouted all in the space of a minute. Geeta looked curiously at the object of Neha's affections and affectations.

Biplab was a thickset, average looking chap. He looked owlish and there was a calculating gleam in his eyes. Geeta decided on sight that Biplab was a pompous idiot. She especially didn't like the way he drawled 'lady' or 'child' whenever he spoke to Neha, and his air of bored magnanimity, as he fended off Neha's admittedly idiotic advances, grated on her nerves. But as Neha had succeeded in driving her up the wall with her special brand of ditsy, Geeta didn't for a minute think it was an ill suited match. Both scored pretty high on the irritation index. One was plain stupid and the other was hiding his stupidity with bombast—made for each other, she thought.

But Geeta was wrong—Biplab was not stupid. Sneaky perhaps, but not stupid.

'So how is it going, ladies? Is the ephemeral, elusive Jassi in sight?' drawled Biplab.

Neha pouted mournfully, 'No, I hate her. I am tired of this city, plus we are not going to find her because Geeta says she doesn't exist. She has looked at police records and hospital records, but there is no trace of her.'

Biplab yawned. 'It's a non story anyway but have you ladies done your due diligence? Checked everything? Some details may have escaped you.'

'I've been a reporter for ten years, I'm an expert on doing my homework. If this girl was in the city, I'd have found her,' Geeta bristled.

Biplab played with a pen distractedly, 'Doesn't the great man, Lord Tiwari, know this? He seems to be having a catharsis every night on that show of his, thanks to this girl.'

'He does. But I guess he has his reasons to keep the story going. It's been a dull news week,' said Geeta.

'I am so bored, Bips, and you are blabbing on about that Jassi. I swear, I am going to be jealous now of some strange, dying girl who may not be living in any case. Let's go for lunch.'

That unwitting statement was perhaps the most succinct summary of the entire Jassi saga—dying girl who was not living in any case.

'Yes, but let's order in. I will not let you bunk work, child. The lady here will have my skin for that. Geeta, you must join us,' said Biplab.

Neha pouted sulkily but settled for takeaway pizza in the office. The lunch lasted an hour and Neha was happier than she had been in some time. Biplab, usually an undemonstrative guy, seemed to have finally let his love for her overwhelm his inhibitions. He stroked her hair, her knee and thigh, tweaked her ear, tucked a tendril behind her ear, and held her hand throughout the lunch break. In all of that, he maintained a polite token conversation with Geeta on the only common topic of interest—Jassi. Neha revelled in Biplab's attentions and didn't pay too much heed to the conversation.

Geeta wished she could have backed out of this strange lunch. This young man was clearly more interested in petting his girlfriend. Geeta wasn't old fashioned but such heavy duty PDA disconcerted her slightly. However, she answered his disinterested questions about the Jassi affair in the interests of sociability.

And then as abruptly as Biplab had come, he departed. Neha was annoyed because she had already planned her evening with him. Geeta, too, was surprised for he had barely acknowledged Neha's entreaties to stay back. Clearly, she had overestimated his raging hormones.

Neha was soon raging. She stamped her feet and had three mini fits of hysteria. She complained about the lines for her PTC being too long, she whined about her make-up making her look sallow and finally took ten takes to get one simple PTC right. She ended it by wishing Jassi dead.

Geeta closed her eyes and wished Jassi, Neha, and the whole world dead.

Back in Mumbai, Rahul was attempting to fight fire. A crisis brings out the best in some men. They discover hidden reserves of strength that pull them through impossible situations. Rahul was not one of those men. He was a quaking, scowling, stubbly mess. Exactly the kind of guy you would pick to bungle, and he did just that.

It was decided that YTV would finally be heard on *The Mood of the Nation*. Zahira set up a studio appearance for Rahul. She hissed at him, 'You had better shave. You must look warm and concerned—the kind of person that parents would trust their children with.'

As luck would have it, what finally went on air was a furiously perspiring Harish Swamy in his live television debut. Rahul had contracted a sudden throat infection and had croaked to Harish, 'Brother, this is your trial by fire—your coming of age. It is very simple. Just stick to the version we have ready. Not a word more or less.'

It didn't do Harish's confidence any good that Zahira, who accompanied him, took one look at him and said, 'Don't take it personally but you are looking too oily. Just what we don't need.'

The make-up man at YNN helpfully slathered talcum powder over Harish's facial pores, but didn't extend his largesse to his neck. With the result that Rajneesh encountered an exceptionally ashen faced man with an exceptionally dark neck sitting across him in his studio. He noticed that this odd looking mass also seemed to sweat for all of humanity. He wondered fleetingly if the man was set to have a cardiac arrest and thought of the headlines that would make. 'YTV man dead on live TV. Was it a conscience attack? Was it guilt?' He looked at Harish hopefully, but concluded to himself that excessive sweat would not bring about his demise. At least not in the course of his show.

Harish was surprised that Rajneesh Tiwari looked much smaller in the flesh and blood and not half as menacing as he did on live television. He was suddenly hopeful—maybe YNN was tired of the story and they would accept their version and let the matter rest.

The opening packaging played out, and thirty-seven-year-old Harish Swamy found himself on live television for the first time. Beside him, Rajneesh thundered at the nation, 'YTV finally breaks its silence. After days of concerted pleas from all of us, the country will have the whole truth and nothing but that alone from YTV's man-in-charge, Harish Swamy.'

Harish's wildest dream was coming true. He had just been proclaimed the man in charge of YTV on national television. In any other set of circumstances, Harish would have been an extremely happy man. But he knew instinctively that this wasn't a moment to bask in.

Rajneesh turned to him. 'Sir, we are worried and you are the only ray of hope for us. Swear to me today that you will tell us the truth.'

Harish gulped and managed to nod his head. His head was pounding and his throat was blocked. He dabbed his face gratefully with a tissue. In the cubicle outside the studio, Zahira felt her stomach knot up in panic.

Rajneesh suddenly thundered, making her jump out of her seat, 'Look into the camera, hold your heart, and tell us where Jassi is!'

'Hopefully the idiot won't fall for this drama,' Zahira said to herself.

But Harish was a man hypnotized. So he put out one perspiring palm and then suspended it in mid air. Even though his heart was making its presence felt by beating violently, Harish couldn't remember where it was. So he covered his mouth with his palm instead, in a gesture of confusion, which was sort of okay because his heart was actually in his mouth. But that would have been too evolved an interpretation for viewers of news television so Rajneesh decided to bail him out. 'It is on the left of your chest. No, not extreme left...more left of centre,' said Rajneesh almost kindly.

After a brief fumble, Harish held his heart, and Zahira her breath.

Rajneesh goaded, 'So, now, Harish, tell us with a clear conscience and heart where she is.'

Harish stared blankly into the viewfinder and then, still clutching his heart, stuttered, 'W-who?'

Rajneesh said impatiently, 'This is not the time to be testing the patience of a nation. The time for games is over. The nation demands to know where Jassi is.'

Harish had blanked out. He couldn't remember the carefully worded statement Zahira had given him. He couldn't remember who Jassi was. His brief was to say firmly—'Jassi is a fully grown adult and if she wishes to reach out to the media, she will do so independently of YTV. On the channel, however, we have a privacy policy which we will adhere to, and we do not appreciate being made a part of this media circus. Our stance is clear—Jassi cannot have escaped this media blitz. So if she had wanted her identity to be disclosed, she would have been here today. The channel does not owe any explanation to self-appointed custodians, about the programming decisions it takes.'

Instead, Harish Swamy, making his debut on national television, said, 'J-Jassi is not there.'

Rajneesh said gravely, 'Has she passed away already?'

'Yes. No…actually we don't know,' said Harish.

'Please, sir, you are beating around the bush. I beg you not to take this lightly.'

Harish Swamy came out of his stupor and realized that he had managed to place himself in a rather sticky situation. So he did the unthinkable—he started thinking. He thought of a quick solution to extricate himself from the mess. It goes without saying that his solution only made things worse.

He said firmly, 'After the first call that Jassi made, we tried getting back in touch with her. The phone was disconnected and after a few more attempts, we had to give up because it was clear she wished to remain untraceable.'

Zahira covered her face with her hands.

Rajneesh spluttered, 'You mean no one spoke to her after that call? Your anchor had promised to call her back with professional help. No one did?'

Harish wiped his brow and said, 'We spared no effort. However, if the individual in question does not want to be contacted, we have to respect her wishes.'

'Please spell out how you spared no effort. You made three calls and that was the end of the effort?' said Rajneesh.

'We did the best possible.'

'Three calls? That is your "best possible"? You could have traced her through her phone. You could have passed on the case to a social welfare organization. Instead you let a girl die because her phone was not reachable in the first fifteen minutes that you called her. How do you live with yourself?'

Harish, by then, had remembered part of Zahira's prepared text. So he said coldly, 'The channel does not owe any explanation to self appointed custodians about the programming decisions it takes.'

Rajneesh appeared to restrain himself from saying something and then turned sadly to the camera and said, 'It is a sad day in the history of television. I feel old and weary and cannot bring myself to labour this point further. A young girl's life and death is the programming decision of a channel. Call me old fashioned, but I cannot bear what we have become. I cannot bring myself to be so cynical. That was YTV's stand on the issue—the suffering of our fellow human beings is not part of their programming philosophy— and as an objective journalist, I bring it to you. Before my personal convictions colour your view, I wish you a good evening.'

The last visual was of a visibly broken Rajneesh and a defiantly sweating Harish. Zahira sat speechless, wondering if she had a job to return to.

Just at that point, Rahul's BlackBerry buzzed and Stetson barked, 'Get rid of that triple-chinned sweat factory. Now!'

Rahul put the BlackBerry down and noticed his own palm was wet with sweat.

The Wrath of the Nation

Biplab Mitra got his first cover story on the thinking man's weekly—*Conscience Call*. The weekly catered to opinions of leaders and intellectuals—high on perception and low on circulation. Naturally then it was rather low on the advertising revenue as well.

That had a lot to do with the choice of its stories— women sarpanches, whistle blowers in the hinterland, and the forced cultural homogenization of the North East. There was no discernible sensation value or headline value in any of these stories, but for all of that, it was a magazine taken rather seriously by the journalistic community. And that included Rajneesh, whose resumé, strangely enough, still listed him as a journalist.

Biplab's cover story, though, was slightly different from the usual crop of cover stories that the magazine carried. The magazine had decided to widen its base and was looking for appropriately 'massy' stories. Biplab's story suggestion had met with whole hearted support. So much so that the magazine had held off going to press till the very last minute to accommodate it.

The cover story was called 'The Jassi Conspiracy: How fact was obfuscated in fiction'.

September 20,
Mumbai

For the last ten days, a reality circus has played out unwaveringly on our television screens. The honours have been divided between two channels—YNN & YTV— channels which, to the unencumbered eye, will seem as different as the proverbial chalk and cheese but which, as our story unfolds, we will discover, operate on the same underlying principles of obfuscation and fabrication.

At the centre of this spectacle watched with unalloyed and vicarious glee by all of us, is Jassi—a young girl abandoned by every conceivable relative. She is dying of cancer, her parents are dead, and her fiancé is set to marry her cousin. Indeed, her life reads better than the most fervid imagination of a B-grade soap writer. She is, in fact, the perfect candidate to call on a relationship show on a youth channel. The show, as well as the channel, being in an urgent need of resuscitating its ratings. You will forgive the insensitivity, but the dying girl will breathe new life into a show helmed by the latest addition to the brigade of supremely untalented bimbos on television.

Isn't it rather expedient that she should call at a time like this? A little too expedient, you ask? If you are not asking, you should be. That is because we have reason to believe that Jassi exists, but only in the imagination of a few overzealous, ratings-obsessed channel executives.

That Jassi is entirely a work of fiction, though, is not the shocker of our story. That is incidental. The shocker is the complicity of the other player in the scheme of things. YNN—the news channel which is spearheading the campaign to win 'Justice for Jassi'.

Every night when the demi god of the channel, Rajneesh Tiwari, exhorts us to demand justice for the hapless girl, all he has on his mind is the ratings curve of his channel. He knows, just like YTV did, that there is no Jassi, and he cares not if there were a Jassi. An entire network of bureaus across the country has thrown up nothing; a fact that YNN knew very early in the story, but never reported back to the viewer. After all, if that disclosure had been made so prematurely, there would have been no scope for the excessive emotionalism and hysterical breast-beating on primetime news. A display which has taken YNN to the top of the ratings table this week.

Sources at YNN told CC that, '...it was a dull news week and Jassi has saved us,' which is why dear reader, you have been subjected to unprecedented emotional pyrotechnics and many pointless candle light marches. This report is not grounded in mere speculation and conjecture for we have conducted our own independent investigation. CC was in Chandigarh, the nerve centre of the search for Jassi. We scoured hospital records and police station records and found nothing to even remotely suggest that she exists. But YNN continues with its campaign. The prettiest face on the channel is in Chandigarh and continues to try and convince us every evening that they are making headway in the Jassi case, while it is plain as the finest Evian water that they are not.

In the meanwhile, the heat is on YTV, which has maintained a studied silence on the subject. But the ratings of YTV's show, 'Love Calls', speak volumes. The 6 pm slot, where Jassi first called in, has grown by fifty percent. Informed sources say that underneath the hostility between the two channels is a larger, potentially symbiotic relationship, which does not stop at propping each other's ratings. The rumour factory says that YTV is looking for a strategic investor and the conglomerate that controls YNN is looking to buy. Market watchers are, therefore, quite attuned to the eminent sense it makes for both channels to prolong the Jassi affair.

Some conspiracy theorists even suggest that the entire Jassi affair—from start to finish—was a collaborative effort between the two channels. What you have witnessed then is a carefully-scripted reality show with simultaneous telecast on both channels—an unprecedented first in television. However, this theory, we must hasten to add, is speculative and in the nature of speculation in the media market grapevine.

YNN and YTV were both unavailable for comment at the time of going to press but we have just one last thought for you—if you are riveted by the Jassi spectacle, the back story is perhaps even more spectacular.

Welcome to the world of television, where nothing is ever what it appears. So next time, save those candles for a time when you might really need them. Like a power cut.

Biplab Mitra

Biplab Mitra had done a Rajneesh Tiwari on Rajneesh Tiwari. And Rajneesh was hopping mad. He paced up and down his cabin and lamented the lack of integrity in modern journalism. Shalini Sharma thought calmly of the occasional mudslinging between pots and kettles and took Rajneesh's fury in her stride.

'Complete fabrication! We are looking to be a strategic investor in YTV?' expostulated Rajneesh.

Shalini said thoughtfully, 'The good thing is no one will really understand what he has written—unalloyed, pyrotechnics, and the ob...ob word.'

'Obfuscate—it means to darken, to make unclear. I will obfuscate this Biplab's ass if I get my hands on him,' Rajneesh said darkly.

'He is Neha's boyfriend. Do you think she had anything to do with this?' asked Shalini.

'No. She is a complete fool,' said Rajneesh.

'Boss, the problem is that while *Conscience Call* in itself is not very widely read, the story has been picked up by others. So we need to get out of this Jassi story now. We are losing credibility,' said Shalini.

'We were going to anyway but here our hand has been forced. We have to find closure ourselves otherwise it will look like we chickened out.'

———

While Rajneesh looked for closure, Geeta Khanna couldn't believe she had been outdone so easily by an obnoxious fresher, right out of journalism college. She marched up to Neha, angrily put the paper in her hand,

and said, 'Not only does your boyfriend not have any ethics, he is also a lazy journalist. He's passed off all my research as his own and not even bothered to cross check a single thing. I thought TV was bad but even print has dropped its standards.'

She slammed the magazine hard on Neha's desk and walked away in a huff. Neha quickly skimmed through the article and smiled. Biplab had called her the prettiest face on the channel.

'So,' quipped Aditya as he handed Tania a cup of coffee at her desk, 'how does it feel to be producing a show which makes headlines every day?'

Tania was surfing between news channels. The Hindi news channels had lapped up the fake Jassi story and all fifty of them were running specials on the scam. Tania was particularly riveted by one called *Tauba Tera Dhoka*. The garishly dressed anchor was strident in her denunciation of the underhand programming tactics of channels. The show then cut across to an old couple at Mount Mary church in Bandra. The Rozarios came in every evening to offer mass for Jassi and were now giving teary-eyed soundbytes on their acute betrayal.

Tania shook her head in amazement. 'Is there nothing else happening in this country?'

Aditya smiled. 'Change the channel to Bharat TV—they have a show going on called *Idiot Box ne Banaya Idiot*.'

Tania laughed, 'Speaking of idiots…that idiot Rajneesh Tiwari has been completely silenced. Not a squeak out of him the whole day.'

'I wouldn't underestimate him if I were you. He'll find a way of getting back. But you please lie low. Don't get pulled into any of Rahul's daft bail-out schemes. Don't come into work, take sick leave if need be.'

Tania gasped, 'I can't take leave with so much happening. Plus I have a schedule coming up in two days.'

Aditya sighed. 'There is a time and place for everything. There is a time and place to be conscientious. This isn't it.'

Tania didn't look convinced. Aditya put a hand on her shoulder and said urgently, 'Okay you drudge. Come shoot your blasted show but steer clear of Harish. He is bad news right now.'

Tania frowned. Aditya turned her around to face him, 'He's a sinking ship, Tani. Just be a good rat and abandon the shipwreck.' He tapped her cheek lightly and left.

Tania was thoughtful. As usual, Aditya made sense. The only good thing to have come out of this mess, she admitted gratefully, was him. Just having Aditya around calmed her.

——•——

The sinking ship, meanwhile, was having nightmares. Rahul was avoiding him; conversation with him was rushed and stilted. Text messages and emails were ignored. In his head, Harish could feel the countdown timer to his doom ticking away frantically.

A day after the cover story in CC appeared, Stetson made an appearance at the YTV office. He walked into Rahul's room and lounged on the chair. Rahul sat at the edge of his table and dangled his legs like a school boy. He always did that when he wanted to feel in control of a situation. He felt it projected cool and casual control— after all correct body language was the hallmark of great leadership. Stetson felt it made Rahul look like a rather daft overgrown school boy, but kept his thoughts to himself.

He said instead, 'I think YNN has come out worse because of this story. But now, we need to get out of this. Do whatever it takes for the channel to come out looking clean.'

Rahul nodded slowly and, much to Stetson's irritation, swung his foot jauntily. Stetson decided that the time had come for him to tackle the sorry situation hands on. So for the next two hours, he spelt out the fire fighting plan. Rahul heard him out obediently, unflinchingly swinging his feet each time he felt the need for a confidence boost.

Completely aware of Rahul's legendary feet of clay, Harish, who was outside, lost all appetite and went to the loo and cried his eyes out.

The Beginning
of the End

News of Harish Swamy's imminent ouster spread with the speed of a high end broadband connection. All of YTV was abuzz with speculation—would Rahul amputate a body part that had served him so well? The general consensus was that Rahul had very little to do with the decision, and given a choice between two posteriors he would naturally pick his own to save.

Tania tried to carry on with the shoot schedules of *Love Calls*, but was too distracted. Rahul was always in meetings and Harish looked like he hadn't slept in days. She tried to ferret out information from Aditya who finally told her, 'Tani, if I knew, I would tell you.'

So when Bose stopped by and asked her to join him for coffee at the cafeteria, she was more than willing to accept. He would know what was happening.

As they sat facing each other at the café, Bose looked intently at Tania.

Tania's heart suddenly lurched in panic, 'What if this

chap falls at my feet and declares his undying love?' She cursed Aditya silently for putting all these overly melodramatic visions in her head.

Of course, Tania was being overly melodramatic. Bose had no such cheesy intentions. His plan was for *Tania* to fall at *his* feet and declare her undying love. Not immediately, but eventually and inevitably. This was step one.

After a protracted silence, in which Tania could hear her heart pound away, he said quietly, 'If you were to move to my team, I would raise no objections.'

Tania felt an overwhelming rush of relief mixed with excitement. Bose was asking her to be part of the temperamental talented.

She reined in the excitement and asked calmly, 'You want me to work on a show with you? Which one? Won't I need to check with Rahul?'

Bose narrowed his eyes. 'The question is not what I want. The question is what you want. Do you want to work with me? I'm in the middle of production for the life swap show. You know it is one of our most high profile launches.'

Tania chose her words carefully, trying to mask her growing excitement 'Anyone at YTV would want to work with you. There is so much to learn.'

Bose smiled. This was not going to be an easy conquest. 'Not everyone can just ask to work with me. You can,' he said.

Comprehension slowly dawned on Tania. She said slowly, 'Bose, you are not asking me to work with you. You are asking me to ask you to work with you.'

Bose looked at her impassively. Tania burst out laughing. This had to be the most ridiculous proposition ever. She wished Aditya were here to have witnessed it. Bose didn't look amused. Tania tried to convert the spontaneous laughter into a coughing fit, but failed miserably.

He snapped, 'I don't ask anyone anything, but if this is so funny, then let's end the conversation here. I will have you know that most people at YTV would give an arm and a leg to do this new show.'

Tania said hastily, 'No, don't get me wrong. Of course, I want to work with you. The last few days have been a bit stressful. I haven't had much sleep and am feeling and behaving a bit oddly. That is why the strange reaction... it's just my nerves.' She then invested all the reserves of charm she had in a dazzling smile.

Bose softened and said intensely, 'I can change your life. I can mould you...Make you what you have dreamed of being but never thought possible. I can change the way you think and see things. When I am done with you, you will barely recognize yourself. I will awaken the real woman...I mean the real professional in you.'

Tania suddenly felt like a charitable cause that had unwittingly stumbled upon a celebrity advocate. Nobody really asks charitable causes to pick and choose their celebrities—it is just assumed that they would be happy to get any benefactor. And nobody is going to ask me if I want Bose, least of all Bose, thought Tania uncharitably.

Then she quickly rationalized. Maybe all men of genius spoke in such lofty, exalted terms. She wouldn't know—she worked with Rahul and Harish, men of zilch genius. A whimsical maverick such as Bose could hardly be talking about mundane things like designations, career growth, bonus, and incentives while selling a job. This must be how he talked to all his team members, thought Tania. She had a sudden vision of Bose as the YTV evangelist, clothed in flowing robes, his braid swishing violently, changing lives though his rousing rhetoric. She suppressed a nervous giggle and thought, instead, of her admission into his hallowed ranks.

She could no longer pretend ignorance of his infatuation but if she played it smart, she could keep him at arm's length and still have him eating out of her hands. She smiled as she merrily mixed up idioms in her head. She wondered what Aditya would have to say about this, and then told herself firmly that he had nothing to do with any of her decisions and this one, he would probably approve of. She continued smiling at Bose.

Bose was encouraged by her smile. He said in a higher tone, 'You may think you are average. But anyone who is in my team is not average. They can't be. I won't let them be. I look after them.'

Tania's tummy reacted to this declaration oddly. It

lurched, somersaulted, and pole vaulted all at once in panic. Suddenly, she wasn't too sure about her ability to handle Bose. After all, she wasn't a qualified shrink. She smiled shakily, as Bose continued softly now, 'I'll look after you. I'll protect you, Tania.'

And then he reached out and patted her hand gently. It was the gentlest of touches, and lasted for a mere fraction of a second but Tania felt violated, like she'd been groped. She stood up abruptly and said, 'I can't do this. Rahul has some stuff lined up for me...I need to meet those deadlines. So this will have to wait. I can't move to your team right now. I am not going to ask Rahul to move me.'

Bose was visibly taken aback. He bit out the words, 'This is suicidal. You want to keep making shows that no one cares about. You're turning your back on the opportunity of a lifetime. And this is the first and last time you get it because when it comes to me, there are no second chances.'

It was an impressive speech and had an impact on Tania. She suddenly felt unsure all over again. Was she making a mistake? Should she play for more time? 'Bose- I-would you give me some...' she stuttered.

Bose cut in angrily. 'It's that over-smart fool Aditya who you hang out with. He's turned your head!'

Tania suddenly didn't need to think any more. It was clear what she had to do. 'This has nothing to do with Aditya. I'm happy to work with anybody if the organization wants it, and if you think there's something that I'm suitable for it would be best if you spoke to Rahul and asked for me,' she said firmly as she looked at him challengingly. Bose suppressed his rising temper.

'I repeat, I don't ask for anyone,' he said biting out each word.

Tania smiled, 'What a coincidence. Nor do I...Bibo.' She got up and left.

It was a body blow. Bose felt achingly like Bibo—unsure and unwanted. The canteen boy cleared his cup and Bibo desperately seeking to be Bose said weakly, 'This is the biggest mistake of your life.'

The boy paid him no attention and nor did Tania as she continued to march out.

———

'You called him Bibo?!' said Aditya. Tania said incredulously. 'Thanks. I tell you this full-on dramatic story and that is all you pick on! The most irrelevant detail.'

Aditya observed drily, 'For Bose that would be the point of heartbreak. You think of him as Bibo the prize ass, and not Bose, the dude. You cruel thing; your words will haunt him for the rest of his life.' Tania said a touch remorsefully, 'He is a deluded idiot but I didn't mean to call him Bibo. It just slipped out— he got me so annoyed. You know, I'd rather work with Harish...honestly. At least what you see is what you get…I can't handle this I-am-a-genius-and-I-will-change-your-life nonsense.' Aditya said quietly, 'If Harish lasts. There are very strong rumours that Rahul will have to get rid of him because Stetson wants it that way. After the prize ass he made of himself on national news.'

Tania was perhaps the only person in YTV who felt slightly sorry for Harish. 'What job is he going to find now? His entire career was about being Rahul's loyalist. He knows nothing about television or marketing.'

Aditya scoffed, 'There are always job openings for yes men. He'll find something. And you have to stop pretending like you care what happens to him. Are you still stuck with *Love Calls*?'

Tania said, breathing a visible sigh of relief, 'No, we are finally taking a season break which is good. Thanks to all the attention the show got, Nair has been able to get Vrushali some celebrity reality show. She'll be out of town for three months. Also, we may not continue with her, so we'll need to find a replacement which will take time.'

Aditya laughed. 'Wherever she is going to be locked up, hopefully they'll lose the key! So what are you moving to?'

'I need to discuss that with Rahul. The show rated so I think now, I should be able to choose what I want to do next,' said Tania.

Aditya asked, 'And you are sure that the credit for the ratings will go to you?'

'I didn't see anyone else there, at the shoot and the edits,' said Tania with an edginess taking over her voice.

'It doesn't matter who you see, what matters is what the boss sees, and I think right now a Mohawk is blurring his line of vision…'

Tania took a deep breath. 'He's just a motor mouth. I'm sure Rahul would have sussed him out by now.'

Aditya snorted and said, 'I don't know, Tania, that filmy exit with Bose was great but move to his team. This Harish situation is too volatile… You have a better chance with Bose.'

Tania suddenly felt a flash of irritation. She snapped, 'I don't want to have a chance with Bose. Why the heck do I bother with you? Here I am pissed off with Bose because he called you an over-smart fool, and here you're pushing his cause.' She turned away annoyed and missed the smile that suddenly lit up Aditya's face.

Aditya said calmly, 'Over-smart fool? That's nice. He is much too kind in overestimating my abilities. Remind me to thank him. But why were you talking about me?'

Tania said reluctantly, 'He was under the impression that you were influencing me to stay away from him,' and then she laughed and said, 'if only he knew that you are his biggest advocate.'

Aditya drawled, 'Correction. I am his biggest fan and he is right, you've chosen the wrong man.'

Tania turned sharply to look at him and was struck by the unusually serious expression on his face.

'Instead of Lord Bose who looks after his subjects, you're stuck with me. I'm no romantic hero like him who'll run to your rescue or think you're some wonderful creature who just needs to be given a push to find out how perfect she is,' he said softly.

Tania smiled and looked positively radiant.

Aditya paused to look at her and his eyes lit up. He continued, 'You see, dear Tani, I happen to know that you're a complete twit. And I would really have it no other way.'

Tania felt light headed. She managed to say breathlessly, 'Thank you. That is the kind of ego boost that every girl really needs.'

Aditya laughed. Tania asked almost shyly, 'So then, is that a done deal? Am I stuck with you?'

Aditya's eyes twinkled, 'It is beginning to look like that unfortunately. We may as well seal the deal with coffee right away.'

Tania's stomach was lurching in the most pleasant fashion ever. 'Coffee we drink all the time. This better be special, Aditya Menon.'

Aditya looked thoughtful. 'You're right. I think you should buy me dinner tonight.'

Tania tried to punch Aditya on his arm but he quickly caught her hand in mid air and gripped it tightly, laughing the whole time. He drew her a little closer.

'Aditya, a friend once told me there is a time and place for everything.'

Aditya let go of her hand and said softly, 'Okay tonight then.'

Tania smiled wanting to say more, but was summoned to Rahul's cabin. Aditya grinned, 'Rahul always has great timing doesn't he?'

Tania grimaced.

'It's okay, Tani, get it over with. I'm off to the suburbs. Catch you in the evening.'

Tania smiled as she walked into Rahul's cabin. She was free of *Love Calls* and now…there was Aditya. She was feeling unusually optimistic.

She walked in with the residue of a smile on her face, but quickly sobered down at the unusually sombre atmosphere in the room.

The Axe Effect

Rahul looked uneasy and his 'Wassup, Tania' was a bit too hearty. In a corner sat Harish Swamy with his eyes suspiciously red. Tania looked at him in sympathy. He looked away and stared at his feet. Tania wondered if this was the hand over—Harish didn't have too many people reporting to him and she was the senior most resource in his team. She felt acutely uncomfortable.

Rahul asked her to sit and said with a strained pleasantness, 'I guess you have heard the rumours.'

Tania said carefully, 'There is talk—yes.'

He screwed up his face in distaste. 'Terrible things being said about key people?'

Tania nodded silently.

'Unfortunately, they are true. We are going to have to let go of a few people. This has nothing to do with the Jassi fiasco. Organizationally, we are looking at realignment and a leaner structure. We need to cut the flab,' said Rahul.

At that point, a shuddering sob emanated from Harish's flabby frame.

Tania felt that Rahul's choice of words was unfortunate and rather insensitive. She felt that an entirely new phraseology should be devised for the sacking of overweight people. To say 'cutting the flab' was a blow distinctly below the belt. So she said in an undertone, 'Please don't make weight references, I get what you mean. You have to be sensitive.'

Rahul looked taken aback. Harish in the meanwhile was sobbing openly and violating the contents of a tissue box violently.

Rahul said genially, 'Women are just so touchy about weight, it's amazing. Even at a time like this…Coming back to the point—Tania, it's nothing personal—a business decision. We're looking at a lean and mean structure and that is it. It is not an indicator of performance.'

Harish started blubbering then. He had clearly lost his bearings. Tania said calmly, 'But it does not stop people from taking it personally,' and went over to Harish to place a comforting hand on his shoulder. Harish looked at her gratefully and kept sobbing.

Rahul thought Tania a remarkably composed woman. He said, 'Losing a job is not easy but it's not just your job that is being affected, Tania. We are letting go of key personnel in other departments also.'

Tania stopped handing tissue to Harish. Her stomach lurched in panic and her throat was constricted. She looked at Rahul and croaked out a strangled, 'Oh.'

Rahul said, 'Think of it as a paid vacation. We'll give

you three months salary and your annual bonus. It is unfortunate but we can't retain you.'

Harish said between sobs, 'I am sorry, T-Tania. I c-can't look you in the eye. I couldn't be there for you—I've let you down.'

Tania said nothing. A part of her realized that what was unfolding currently would be a hurtful and unpleasant memory one day. But at that moment, shock had completely numbed her. Harish's constant snivelling and sniffling were distracting her, so she told him kindly, 'Get a grip. It's okay.'

Rahul looked at her uneasily—her coolness fazed him. Harish had started pounding his chest by now and was loudly lamenting his sensitive nature that made him prone to easy and effusive tears. It was a brand of theatrics that would fit in well with an over-the-top Bhojpuri film. Rahul looked at him in disapproval—the YTV brand custodian was not being very YTV.

Tania asked abruptly, 'Who are the other key personnel being asked to go?'

Rahul looked uncomfortable. 'For reasons of confidentiality, I can't disclose that.'

Tania stared at him hard and said, 'Oh come on now, you owe me that.'

'Tania, we have had very adverse media attention in the last few days. We really don't want to call attention to ourselves, so we are doing what we call the phased lay-off plan. We're not going for en masse removal.

265

Every month, about two or three positions will go,' said Rahul.

Tania said bitterly, 'And I am the chosen one this month—who else?'

Rahul mumbled, 'It is really not important.'

Tania said firmly, 'Tell me...'

Rahul said sheepishly, 'Subbu.'

Tania stared at him, speechless. Subbu—the most inefficient production person in Bhosle's army. His special skill was that he had no skill whatsoever. Not only was the man a complete idiot, his rather unfortunate need to take power naps through the day had also contributed to the underdevelopment of any skill set.

Tania said in wonder, 'Subbu is key personnel? This is the sum total of your realignment of key personnel—me and a production moron?'

'A production moron and I, Tania...I told you that we want to keep it low key,' Rahul said firmly.

Days of spending time with Aditya had rubbed off on Tania. So she laughed darkly and said, 'Low key? I guess that would be correct. He is low and I am key.'

'I understand how you are feeling,' said Rahul.

Tania snapped, 'No, I understand. This is because of the Jassi episode. I didn't even want to put that call on air. You forced me. But I am being made the fall guy here.'

Rahul said nothing. Harish cleared his throat and said in a choked voice, 'You don't understand. The channel is losing money. Times are bad—nothing is rating. You have to take a few surgical decisions. If it is a choice between you and the channel, we have to go with the channel.'

Tania said quietly, 'How much notice do I have to give?'

'You can leave now. We don't expect you to stay on for your notice period... It will be uncomfortable.'

Tania said sweetly, 'That is very kind of you,' and turned on her heel and walked out. Her firing squad made no appearance—like her, they had been given the pink slip.

She returned to her desk to find that the usually lumbering administrative staff of YTV had suddenly acquired speed. A sheepish HR representative stood by her desk as she cleared it out. The IT department had blocked her official email id in the half hour she was in Rahul's cabin. Tania asked acidly, 'I can't even write a hand over or farewell mail, is it?'

The HR representative shuffled uncomfortably on his feet but didn't answer. Tania fought back tears and thought it was just as well that YTV was in the middle of simultaneous shoot schedules, with the result that only a few interns were around to witness the ignominy of her exit. The interns being self-occupied teens showed no interest in the proceedings. If only Aditya were here she thought. There was no sign of Bose too which was a relief—she couldn't bear to see him gloat.

But the other person that Tania could have done

without, skulked nearby, not looking as cocksure as he usually did. Tania wondered if that had anything to do with his hair being tamed by copious amounts of gel. It made Mohawk look like a particularly ugly, wet chicken.

Mohawk cleared his throat. Tania ignored him as she tore up some waste paper lying on her desk with far more intensity and concentration than it required. Mohawk stepped closer, put a hand on Tania's arm, and said in a slightly choked voice, 'I'm sorry.'

Tania looked up prepared to brush him off but was surprised to see him looking pale and worried. So she said in a kinder voice than she had initially planned, 'You don't need to apologize. None of this is your fault.'

Mohawk stared at Tania anxiously and said, 'It is. It is…you don't know but it is my fault…' He trailed off mid sentence and walked off hurriedly.

Tania continued to look at his retreating back in surprise. Maybe, she thought with grim humour, I am his dream woman as well. The thought of being an unwilling muse to a legion of wannabe mavericks with hairstyling disorders made her laugh. And then Tania picked up two years of her life, neatly packed in a cardboard box, and walked out of the YTV office. She was living out her part as the martyr in this real life drama.

———•———

Harish's sobs had subsided. Rahul was jabbing at his keyboard. He said, 'That didn't go too badly. That girl is a cool customer. Do you think she'll make trouble though?'

Harish said, 'No, sir. I don't think so. Plus she must know it's her fault. She should have never shot that Jassi call in the first place. If she had not shot it, how could we have put it on air?'

It was irrefutable and solid logic like this that made Harish indispensable to Rahul and made choosing between him and Tania a no contest. Rahul was glad he had made Stetson come around to his decision. He smiled at Harish with affection and abruptly said, 'Brother, you have to sweat less. It nearly cost you your job.'

Harish felt beads of perspiration break out on his forehead, but there was no time for Rahul to elaborate. The select press briefing was in fifteen minutes. The first journalist to be briefed would be Biplab Mitra from *Conscience Call*.

Tania wept her eyes out on the tissue that Aditya had handed her. He sat next to her, holding a large cup of strong black coffee, which he got her to sip each time she took a break from sobbing.

'I-I'm sorry. I know it's stupid to cry like this but I'm just so angry. I must look a mess,' said Tania.

'I gather this is what you meant by the "something special" we needed to do to seal our deal,' Aditya observed.

Tania gave him a watery smile and then promptly dissolved into tears again. Aditya said nothing but held her close, gently patting her head. He didn't ask her to stop crying or offer any token platitudes, with the result that she eventually stopped crying.

She said shakily, 'Bear with me, I just need to get it out of my system…'

'The way you've been sobbing, anyone would think Harish impregnated you and promptly abandoned you. I have to admit, though, that the prospect of any child of Harish running around is a national tragedy,' said Aditya.

Tania's shoulders shook with laughter. Aditya held her tighter and said, 'Get the crying over with and out of your system and then let's plan the next move.'

Tania said in misery, 'What next move? I'll take some time off, go to Baroda and spend time with my parents. You know, I'm not even sure I want to do television anymore. Maybe I should teach or something.'

Aditya said, with a slight rise in his usually even tone, 'One jerk is all it took to scare you off. Seven years of building a career and you are prepared to just let it all go. You will always be the victim, Tania, if you let yourself be one. This is television—it isn't about dignified exits. It is about going down screaming and fighting and it isn't about going alone, or going at all. Stay in the game, Tani, and play it better than anyone else.'

'I don't know if I can. I just want to go away and not

have to deal with this negativity. Just do something else.'

Aditya let go of her and said in exasperation, 'Go away? Do something else? How long can you be on holiday? Why should you let go of something that you are trained for? No one is asking you to take the moral high ground. Get what Rahul has—his position, his bank balance, his club memberships—he didn't get all of that by running away at the first hint of trouble. Don't do it for ideology, do it for something far more important. Survival.'

Tania said slowly, 'So now...what do I do and how do I do it?' She laughed darkly, 'All I have is a firing squad and that too, in my head. And I am such a loser—even there I can't get them to fire at Rahul and Harish. They are this close to pulling the trigger and I back out.'

Aditya didn't look alarmed in the least that sedate Tania was a potential murderess. In fact, he looked distinctly appreciative as he sat down next to her. He said, 'Don't worry, my dear Miss "So now?". The squad will come good. Right now, you are drowning the poor things in this deluge of emotion. Use that brain of yours. Being a silent martyr never helped anyone—martyrdom is a big cop out.'

Tania sniffled gratefully and clasped Aditya's hand. His hold on her hand tightened briefly and then a smile lit up his boyish face.

'You know, Tani, it's just as well we don't work in the same office anymore. Office romances seem a little

271

desperate, no? Like you ran out of options or were just plain lazy?'

Tania said drily, 'If you put it that way, I suppose I should be glad I got sacked! I can be unemployed but desperate? Never!'

'You're not being very clear sighted. You've just had the most exciting two months anyone could have asked for. You directed a television show that no one is going to forget in a hurry. You made national news every day. You damaged Bose's ego forever. Powerful television barons conspired to oust you and you found Prince Charming right under your nose without even having to try too hard. It is a fairy tale.'

Tania said, her sense of irony fully restored, 'I suppose it is befitting then that in this completely warped fairy tale you make it as the dysfunctional Prince Charming.'

Aditya's eyes twinkled as he said approvingly, 'There… that's more like the Tania I like.'

Tania smiled, still teary eyed, and put her head on Aditya's shoulder not wanting to think or talk any more. She would defer dealing with life to later.

The Emperor on the Back Foot

The next morning, the world and Rajneesh Tiwari woke up to screaming headlines. The *Bombay Mirror* said, 'When Love Didn't Call'. *Mumbai Times* said, 'Jassi Jaisi Koi Nahin—the Great Indian TV Sham.' And *Conscience Call* simply said, 'Conscience Calls—Channel Capitulates, Coughs up Con.'

The news quickly converted Rajneesh's plush cabin into a stuffy sauna. His blood boiled and vapourized into gusts of angry steam which scalded anyone who dared to step into his room that day. One article in particular inflamed him completely.

JASSI JAISI KOI NAHIN— THE GREAT INDIAN TV SHAM

Mumbai: It is confirmed. After days of intense speculation and suspicion, YTV finally came clean. Jassi, the young girl whose anguished call on a love helpline tore our hearts, does not exist. The writing is on your television screens—JASSI

JAISI KOI NAHIN. The caller in question was an actor and the contents of the call were completely fake.

The channel now says the sham call was the individual decision of the producer of the show. Rahul Singh, the MD of YTV says, 'We did not know at first that it was a sham. It was an individual call taken by the producer who got carried away by the zeal to push up ratings.'

Rahul Singh, the charming and well spoken man in charge of YTV, tells us that it was only after the Jassi call became a national issue, did the producer come clean on the hoax. He says, 'Initially, the producer was very evasive about details on Jassi. Finally when the producer confessed to the whole scam, we had to protect the individual. Everyone makes mistakes, and at YTV we value our employees. Plus, it is not our policy to find scapegoats and wash our hands off a crisis.'

Singh says firmly that the gaffe will go down in YTV's record books as a blot. 'Even though one person took the decision, we are taking responsibility for this collective mistake. And YTV apologizes to all its viewers—we have let you down.'

In fact such is the channel's employee protectiveness that it is not even revealing whether the producer is a man or a woman, even though the producer, whose name remains undisclosed, is no longer with YTV. Singh says, 'It was a decision yet again taken by the individual. The individual felt the need to take time off from television and we respect that decision. Hopefully the person in question will return— after introspection—a better and a more responsible television professional. On our part we are going to become very vigilant and not trust our employees as blindly as we have done before.'

Media watchers say lessons in better and more responsible television will also sorely be needed by the news channel brigade in the wake of the Jassi fiasco. Their hysterical breast beating over a non issue should cause them some embarrassment. Particularly Rajneesh Tiwari, Executive Editor of the news channel YNN, who spearheaded the 'Justice for Jassi' campaign. It is a severe loss of credibility for the channel, as it emerges that Tiwari may have known very early in the story that Jassi Jaisi Koi Nahin. YNN could have redeemed itself had it exposed the scam but YTV seems to have hijacked the moral high ground by coming clean, even as the news channel organizes candle night marches for the fictional Jassi.

It seems, then for the charismatic Rajneesh Tiwari, April Fools' Day may have come six months too early! In conclusion, we have just one burning, and rather heartfelt query, for the much respected Mr Tiwari—'Mr Tiwari, hold your heart. Put your hand on your heart and look into the camera. And tell us, is that egg on your face that we see?'

The charismatic Rajneesh Tiwari had turned a mottled purple at the end of reading the article. Tiwari was used to being vilified—he had been called a sensationalist, a rumour monger and a rabble rouser at various points in his career. He could bear attacks on his integrity and journalistic reputation but this article was a full frontal assault on a vital organ—his monumental ego. It was no surprise then that he gasped for breath as he paced up and down his cabin. He made matters worse by kicking the table leg and stubbing his toe. He sat down in pain and spluttered, 'April Fools' Day has come early? I am going to sue *Mumbai Times*.'

Shalini said firmly, 'We can't sue. I suggest we just forget about this story. Save face and get out.'

Rajneesh stood up and hollered, 'I don't save face…I make others hide their faces! I will close this story in my own way.'

Shalini wrung her hands and said impatiently, 'How?'

Rajneesh wasn't listening—he was re-reading the offending article. After five minutes when Rajneesh looked up again, he was back to feeling in control. He would get the last word in—he always did.

———•———

Meanwhile, in the YTV office, Rahul sat back feeling quite pleased with the turn of events. In spite of being caught out, YTV had come out looking good. It was not the corporate image they had aspired for but at least it wouldn't do them any harm—a protective employer that had tried to make the best of a bad situation.

Harish hovered around, commending Rahul on his masterly management of the crisis.

Rahul shrugged his shoulders casually and tried not to look too pleased. He said, 'Harry my boy, 6 pm is fucking rocking. No slot has shown this kind of growth in the last five years. It'll be good to launch the life swap show on this slot now.'

Harish looked equally pleased. He then asked tentatively, 'What about *Love Calls*?'

'That reminds me—let's get Mohit in here,' said Rahul.

Harish looked blank. 'Who's Mohit? Oh you mean Mohawk? I had forgotten he had a real name.'

Rahul said thoughtfully, 'That boy is a bright young spark. I have huge hopes from him.'

Since the only other 'bright spark', commended by Rahul, and known to Harish, was Harish himself, he had no choice but to be in total agreement with Rahul, despite his vague dislike of Mohawk. The bright young spark walked in looking fairly extinguished. Mohawk had taken to combing back his hair and holding it in place with a hair band. This exposed him as the rather nondescript person that he really was. He had a face that could easily become a blur in your memory even if you had met him an hour back. It was a remarkably forgettable face with no differentiating feature.

Rahul beamed at him and said, 'I like the variation on the hair. It's good to keep changing things around.'

Mohawk gave him a half hearted smile.

Rahul said gently, 'I know you are upset about Tania. She was your supervising producer but she has taken it very well and professionally. You must too.'

Mohawk gulped and said, 'I am a bit shocked, sir, but I'll be fine.'

Harish glared at the boy. No one apart from Harish

had ever called Rahul 'sir' in the quasi-bohemian climes of YTV. Rahul had tried to dissuade Harish from the practice, but Harish intuitively knew that he secretly quite liked it so persisted. This was the intuition of a natural born sycophant and the same instinct also told Harish that Mohawk and he were two of a kind. His vague dislike rapidly converted into proactive hostility.

In the meanwhile, Rahul had taken to cooing at the boy, 'Oh you creative people, you guys are so sensitive. We just have to clamp down on the sentiment. We need to move on, and we have great plans for you, my boy.'

Mohawk's ambition flickered back to life and so did he. He looked eagerly at Rahul.

'Season 2 of *Love Calls* is yours. We get bigger and better, and come back in three months. We are starting things with a clean slate, and brother, the fucking slate is officially yours,' said Rahul.

'Does that mean I get the credit of producer?'

Rahul laughed. 'Fucking hell you do! We are a young organisation and not into serving time. You've been here only three months but we like what we see and you get your own show.'

'I won't let you down, sir. Thank you so much for this.' Mohawk's head was spinning with the possibilities. His own show! He could create on air opportunities for himself. Rahul was sold on him and he had only just displayed his wares. He bounced out of the cabin in a happy haze.

He paused for a minute at Tania's empty desk and felt, tiresomely, the inconvenience of a half developed conscience. It wasn't his fault he repeated to himself for the nth time.

It wasn't his fault that Tania had rushed things on the shoot, and instead of his friend Sonia, someone else had called in. His brief to Sonia had been for her to come up with anything but to cry a lot. He had genuinely thought Jassi was Sonia, and had only discovered the mistake when he had called Sonia a week later to thank her. Sonia confessed that she had tried calling at the allotted time but had not gotten through, and since Mohawk hadn't called her back, she had thought they had found someone else to call in instead.

Mohawk had not followed Tania's instructions and screened genuine callers or made a list of their contact numbers, and when 'Jassi' blew up in their faces, the only face he wanted to save was his own. And so he had said nothing. With some effort, he could probably have tracked the number down but he had decided it was best not to.

He wondered then, as he always did, if 'Jassi' actually existed and then quickly rationalized that if she had, all the publicity would have got her out from wherever she was hiding. It was probably someone who had done it for a lark—there were enough people out there who'd do anything to be on TV. He should know.

He shrugged his shoulders and shrugged off his

conscience, discarding it most appropriately at Tania's empty desk. It sat at Tania's desk feeling a lot like its former occupant—clueless and abandoned.

———

Bose watched the young Mohawk stop by Tania's empty desk, and he felt the usual pangs of deep regret and longing. Tania was the woman he would never have. What he didn't know then was that this was exactly how it should be for him. Exalted creative beings like him could not have a mundane romance—coffee and movies were for regulation couples.

This unrealized love and longing would realize his immense potential as the brooding genius. Added to it, his anger at being spurned and misunderstood by her would finally give him that core of angst which had so far eluded him, and which was so essential for the sustenance of genius, so in a way he had got what he wanted—except he didn't know that yet.

All's Well that
Doesn't End

Tania peered into the mirror. She didn't like what she saw there. Without eyeliner or kohl, she looked pallid and washed out. Grey was an awful colour and did nothing for her complexion. Her hair was pinned back like a school girl's, and there were signs of strain around her eyes. She beamed—this would work.

Aditya was slightly taken aback when she had told him what she was considering doing. This was not the cautious Tania he knew. But he had approved, and that was the only encouragement she needed.

She smiled as she thought of Aditya. If there had been no *Love Calls* all she would have ever done was exchange notes on absconding pets with him and that would have been a tragedy. She didn't know the future but it felt good to have him in the present.

The knot of tension at the pit of her stomach was rapidly taking over her entire abdomen. She wished she had taken Aditya's advice earlier—none of her exchanges on show formats and key decisions of *Love Calls* with Rahul and Harish were on record. Usually Tania put everything on email and excelled at the excel sheet but in all the chaos of *Love Calls* she hadn't, and it was an important lesson. Always stay true to your convictions even if the convictions begin and end with maintaining excel sheets.

But Tania didn't have too much time to think further. There was a knock on the door of the make-up room followed by Rajneesh Tiwari striding in. He beamed, 'You look wonderful.'

Tania smiled back. Rajneesh had taken an instant shine to her—it was such a relief for him to interact with a young person without any ideological pretensions. Tania didn't labour under the pointless notion that news television was about information. Television of any kind needed to entertain. Period.

The first time he had met her, she had looked much too pretty and poised to be a victim. He had told her that—she had understood instantly and perfectly. 'Yes,' she said wisely. 'The look is key. I will fix that.'

That had spurred him on to ask, 'Tania, can I ask you honestly—there's this interesting dynamic of male bosses and vulnerable female employees in this entire situation. Did that play a part?'

Tania said without missing a beat, 'You mean you want to hint at sexual harassment? I think you can hint at it, but I will have to leave it ambiguous and open ended.

But, yes, we could get that dynamic in because it will make better television and add empathy.'

Rajneesh had wished fervently that his producers could be more like Tania. She would put close shots of blood splattered carcasses on primetime without a single qualm.

He cleared his throat and said, 'Once all this blows over, maybe you should look at news television.'

Tania said thoughtfully, 'Maybe. But let's get this over with.'

It was seven minutes to 10 pm, and a brand new story was going to break on *The Mood of the Nation*—Rajneesh had anointed the series, 'Tania's Truth & Trauma'.

As they walked to the studio, Rajneesh said, 'We are also going to play out clips of that sweaty chap from YTV. It will be a good contrast…total sympathy for you.'

Tania thought that was an extremely good idea. Rajneesh, basking in the warmth of her admiration, walked into the studio with a spring in his step and a potential acolyte at his side. It seemed Tania's lot was to be conjoined with assorted men of genius, and this new coupling could prove to be the most fruitful.

The Mood of the Nation outdid itself. Tania was the picture of dignity as she spoke in her low, clear voice about being made the scapegoat. 'Think about it logically, can one individual carry out such a big sham without the knowledge of the management? I took no decisions, only executed decisions,' she said.

Rajneesh said sadly, 'It is old fashioned for bosses to stand-up for their employees—Corporate India has a bank balance but no heart or conscience'. Rajneesh's employees at that point tried to remember the last time their boss had displayed the old fashioned values he was extolling. But all such memories seemed strangely to be wiped out from their collective consciousness.

Nair had also convinced Vrushali to be a part of this interview. 'Madamji, very good publicity for the show,' he had said to her.

Vrushali was her usual incoherent self on a satellite link but managed to shed a lot of tears, which always works on primetime news television.

She cried piteously about being put through the wringer with a fake phone call and said she hadn't slept for a month because of the trauma. She said one of the main reasons for taking up her new reality show, where she would be locked away for three months, was because she needed time to heal and forget. Vrushali blamed the channel, and said that its producer Tania was a 'helpless woman' just like her.

There was breaking news even as 'Tania's Truth & Trauma', played out live. Charlie Angel had attempted suicide for the seventh time. He had miraculously escaped and was now a wan, weeping wraith on a hospital bed. He confessed shamefacedly that his conscience had driven him to it. After a great show of reluctance, he finally let on why he had chosen to rid the world of his presence. He said brokenly, 'YTV had approached me to play Jassi. They said if a freak show like me turned up as Jassi, all the news channels would lose interest. I said yes, but then Jesus stopped me. But I still felt so guilty that I couldn't bear it.'

Charlie Angel wept as he continued, 'Look at me—people make fun of me. If I had the money, I could become the woman I am, have a husband, and a family.'

Aditya, watching the proceedings on television, resolved to watch more news—it was more entertaining than any soap could hope to be.

Rajneesh made a mental note of appreciation for Shalini Sharma. It was smart of her to have cut across to the Charlie story in the middle of the bulletin. It was the icing on one hell of a cake.

Rajneesh turned to Tania, 'Were you part of this shameful sham as well? Getting this…erm…person Angel whatever to play Jassi?'

Tania said shakily, 'I was part of nothing, sir. I was just doing my job,' and then made sure to look suitably stricken. She had a recurring vision—Harish and Rahul in front of her firing squad and this time round she had finally said 'Fire'. The bullets had ricocheted from Harish's pot belly and finished off Rahul before her platoon could get to him.

'Is there no limit to how much TV will exploit people for ratings?' Rajneesh looked heavenwards and shook his head grimly.

Rajneesh's heart was bursting with joy—this was a blockbuster of a show. He turned to his camera and said, 'We have no shame in telling you that, yes, we got taken in by the 'Jassi' sham. We got taken in because we still believe in the goodness of the human spirit and the transparency of human motives. And we will hold on to these beliefs in the face of opportunistic, callous, and heartless people who unfortunately are also in the television business. They are the ones who should be ashamed and not us. Don't judge us by them. We are prepared to be taken in again and again, but our commitment to human goodness stays. Thank you for understanding, dear viewer. This is a proud and gullible Rajneesh Tiwari signing off from *The Mood of the Nation*.

———

But Harish and Rahul were far from ashamed, and not just due to their gift of thick hides. They managed to miss out on the first telecast of *The Mood of the Nation*. Both men were engrossed in intense and intensive art appreciation. In fact when Harish had first seen it, he had taken in his breath in a sharp intake—a first for a connoisseur like him.

He said in tones of heartfelt admiration, 'This has set such a new benchmark of quality that I'm worried that nothing in the future will match up.'

Rahul beamed. He knew he had outdone himself on the new PPT. It was magnificent as it lay open on his laptop. The slides, splayed out in a deep purple, looked like luscious brinjals to Harish's feverish foodcentric imagination.

There were fifty two slides—each painstakingly crafted and formatted. Rahul had labelled the presentation 'The 6 pm Slot—Now Running Successfully'. The entire presentation was fashioned as the making of a mega Bollywood hit, and this gave Rahul leeway to liberally borrow imagery and catch phrases from popular Hindi films. So before the slide on the future plans for 6 pm, an image of Shahrukh Khan popped up with a graphic which said, 'Picture abhi baaki hai mere dost'. The slide on the rationale for a show like *Love Calls* was accompanied by an image of a pretty Katrina Kaif with a thought bubble which said, 'Maine Pyar Kyun Kiya?' And the slide announcing season 2 of *Love Calls* had Shahrukh Khan again, in an image from *Don 2* captioned 'The Chase Begins Again'. Mass culture and corporate culture had fused into an epochal PPT.

Rahul couldn't wait to present this work of art to the Board. He had everything in place—the anticipatory pitch of his voice, the measured pauses, the space to accommodate a few witticisms, one or two carefully thrown in expletives all building up to an action packed finale. The Board was going to have the corporate equivalent of an orgasm—a PPT shouting out success from each slide. This, as some would testify, was even better than the real thing.

Rahul then was in a happy place save for one niggling doubt. He cleared his throat and looked at Harish hesitantly, 'Buddy, I need to ask you one little thing. It's very important that you be completely honest.'

Harish felt his chest swell with self importance. A supreme artisan who had crafted a flawless masterpiece still needed his advice. He said effusively, 'I am always honest, sir. Speaking my mind has always got me into trouble but I can't stop myself.'

Rahul looked at him eagerly and asked then like an excited schoolboy, 'Should I do my Shahrukh voice at the presentation? You know for the parts where we have Hindi film dialogues or will it be too much?'

Harish's heart sank. Rahul's Shahrukh voice was awful—he sounded wheezy and comical. Unfortunately, he had mistaken the polite embarrassed titters that followed his weak imitation at office parties each time as thunderous applause. Bosses, as that age old truth goes, hear only what they want to hear. Harish didn't speak immediately, and Rahul's face fell. He said quickly and a little too heartily, 'I was kidding, buddy. Of course I would not do something as dumb as that. Imagine Stetson's face.'

The incurably honest Harish spoke up, 'It's a great idea and you'd do such a good job of it. I think we should go for it. The only thing, Sir, is let's practise a bit.'

And that was how Rahul and his faithful deputy came to miss the first telecast of *The Mood of the Nation*. Rahul was practicing his Shahrukh voice and Harish was making notes on delivery, pitch, and inflection.

———

Tania buzzed the pantry for her morning cup of coffee and spread out the morning newspapers on her desk. In the last three months this had become an important morning routine; there was still one hour to the daily meeting at noon so enough time for her to make notes. She picked up her BlackBerry and re-read the text message which had put her in a good mood from early morning itself. It said, 'Super job on the Rakshanda story. Great new spin.' She had replied making sure to be suitably effusive, 'Thanks, boss. Really appreciate your guidance and encouragement.'

Tania had outdone herself on her last half hour special feature. It was a great piece of investigative television. It had questioned whether a Persian cat could possibly have given the starlet Rakshanda those bites on her neck. Rakshanda had angered the moral police by turning up at an awards ceremony with what suspiciously looked like love bites. Rakshanda clarified finally that those marks were thanks to her pesky Persian Googly. The reason they were so prominent was because she'd been foolish enough to scratch them.

Tania had spoken up firmly in the edit meeting, 'That Googly is a lazy thing, and there's no chance that he'll lift a paw to do anything. She's clearly lying, Boss.'

Tania had figured out very early in her YNN career that Rajneesh liked being called 'Boss', so she liberally used the term in all communication with him.

A much impressed Rajneesh had asked her to craft a special show on the duplicity and hypocrisy in Bollywood. She did it promptly, packing in all her insight on the workings of Googly's feline mind. The rest of the edit team was suitably awestruck—ever since Tania had joined YNN as senior producer, Special Features, she had been touted as Rajneesh's new blue-eyed girl. Her YTV history worked in her favour, and she was quickly dubbed 'the creative type' in a stodgy live news environment.

Tania enjoyed the position she had at YNN. She told Aditya once, 'I'm like the Bose of YNN. There's this huge myth about my talent and temperament. No one speaks when I do. All I need to do is streak my hair and pierce my belly—they'll probably not even breathe in the same air as I do.'

Aditya had laughed. 'Don't break the illusion, but don't start believing it. Have a sense of humour about it because you don't want to turn into that prick.'

Tania liked how the mention of Bose always got a slight, almost imperceptible, rise from the normally unflappable Aditya. He hadn't stayed on much longer at YTV after her exit—Stetson had put him in charge of the new music channel. The channel had topped the ratings almost immediately on launch because of a programming master stroke. Instead of investing in content creation and expensive anchors, Aditya had used his funds in acquiring complete film songs and music videos. The channel played one and a half minute versions of songs as opposed to the thirty second versions on the competition. The songs were played back to back, taking only the occasional commercial break. 'You know me, Tani,' quipped Aditya, 'I'll do anything to avoid too much work. And this way I now leave work at 5 pm.'

Right on cue, her phone buzzed. It was Aditya. She picked up her phone with a smile and said, 'Was just thinking of you.'

Aditya laughed, 'How romantic, Tani. I have news for you. Guess who's making a movie?'

Tania said, 'No time for guessing games so you tell me and fast because I have that meeting to go to.'

'Your hero—Biswajeet Bose. He's apparently been working on a script for quite some time now.'

Tania laughed. 'No way. Really? I...'

Aditya interrupted, 'Wait, hear me out. You know what the film is about? It's another remake of *Devdas*, but this time, it's set in the world of television. He's been quoted as saying that it's a modern and edgy take on the story of the eternal lover.'

Tania paused significantly and then burst out laughing, 'Oh dear, this Devdas will have a braid till his waist then. Now that'll be fun!'

Aditya sighed exaggeratedly. 'My dear little twit, what should concern you is that Paro may well be called Tania.'

Tania gasped. 'No, no. I'm sure he is well over his silly crush. Imagine boring me in a film,' and then burst out laughing again.

'Like a wise man said once—you're living a fairy tale,' said Aditya.

'And Rajneesh will turn me into a pumpkin if I don't get to the meeting on time. Pick me up in the evening, ok?' Tania hung up on Aditya and rushed to the meeting with her notepad in hand. YTV and her bumbling bosses were in the distant past. Rajneesh and YNN were all that mattered, and this time she was going to get it right.

———

In the MD's cabin at YTV, two men were squinting at a PPT, going through each slide in excruciating detail. One of them finally spoke. 'You know what we need to do— let's take it slot by slot. 7 pm is our weakest fucking slot, we need to sex it up. I say we have a gimmick around it, get in the eyeballs and get the viewer by his balls.'

Mohawk nodded approvingly. He said, 'Yes, sir, great plan!' He deferentially handed out tissues to him and wondered why his boss perspired so much, even in the air conditioned environs of YTV.

In a tragic turn of events, Rahul was never able to present his best PPT ever to the Board. A week after 'Tania's Tumult & Trauma' made it to *The Mood of the Nation*, there was a formal announcement from the Board. It said that Rahul Singh would now head YTV's

New Ventures & Digital Innovation. It thanked him for his contribution to the television part of the business but said that it would now use his expertise in the fast growing digital space. In other words, Rahul would now head a website and online contests. The layman would call it a demotion—the Board called it role realignment. Harish had cried the longest and loudest on Rahul's last day in office. He had also consumed most of Rahul's farewell cake.

Two days after Rahul's departure, Harish had presented the 6 pm slot PPT to the Board, and in a touching little tribute to his former boss, he even did the Shahrukh voice. Some say that could have been the clincher for his elevation to Rahul's job. Other, less charitable people say that no one else was available. Aditya had moved to the music channel and a managerial post would have snuffed out Bose's creative soul. Harish was the default choice for managing director, and he was quite determined to make sure that soon he would be the only choice.

Harish hadn't met or called Rahul since the day he left but he did occasionally throw sheep at him on Facebook as a testament to his enduring affection for him. Rahul never threw anything back which Harish thought was rather poor spirited of him, but he didn't dwell on it too much. Most of his time and energy went in holding on to his job—three months were up and Harish knew it was time to impress the Board with some radical new programming.

Revamping the 7 pm slot was part of that master plan. Harish beamed, looking sweaty, self satisfied, and smug all at once. He looked at Mohawk, his most loyal aide, intently and said, 'We get a babe, a shit hot babe and put her in her chaddis. We'll have all the horny bastards wanking off at the sight of her. That's what we want. It's television's all-time score. Sex sells,' Mohawk nodded approvingly as he was expected to and said, 'It rocks, sir, what an idea!'

Harish smiled and swivelled in what used to be Rahul's chair. Soon Mohawk and he were fully immersed in the revamp of the 7 pm slot.

Nothing to do with television ever has a logical end. It just keeps coming back in circles.